THE RAKE'S RUIN

The Earl of Sinamor thought he knew all there was to know about handling women. Certainly his record of conquests proved he was a master at mastering the fair sex.

But that was before he had met so confusing a creature as Miss Phillipa Raithby, who preferred riding horseback in the early morning to dancing till dawn . . . who scorned the finery and frippery that other ladies longed for . . . and who refused to recognize the right of London's reigning rake to teach her *his* rules of respectability.

What could the earl do with Phillipa when she would not allow him to do what he did best—which was to make love . . . ?

AN UNLIKELY GUARDIAN

Carol Proctor

A SIGNET BOOK
NEW AMERICAN LIBRARY
A DIVISION OF PENGUIN BOOKS USA INC.

NAL BOOKS ARE AVAILABLE AT QUANTITY DISCOUNTS WHEN USED TO PROMOTE PRODUCTS OR SERVICES. FOR INFORMATION PLEASE WRITE TO PREMIUM MARKETING DIVISION, NEW AMERICAN LIBRARY, 1633 BROADWAY, NEW YORK, NEW YORK 10019.

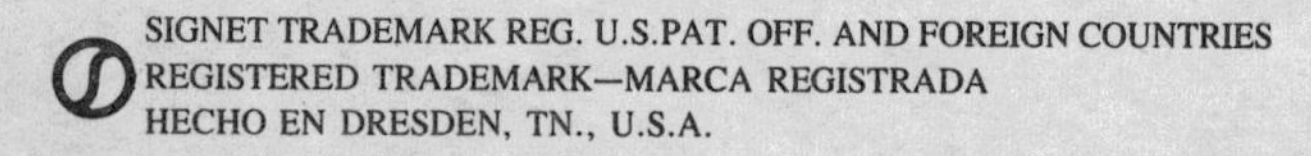

SIGNET, SIGNET CLASSIC, MENTOR, ONYX, PLUME, MERIDIAN and NAL BOOKS are published by New American Library, a division of Penguin Books USA Inc., 1633 Broadway, New York, New York 10019

First Printing, March, 1990

1 2 3 4 5 6 7 8 9

PRINTED IN THE UNITED STATES OF AMERICA

With love and thanks to Ed and Cris,
this book is dedicated to Marie A. Coons.

Deo optimo maximo

1

Evelyn Lovelace, eighth Earl of Sinamor, paused to survey the glittering throng below him. He did not appear to notice the hush that fell over the crowd as his name was announced, nor the rising buzz of conversation that followed. Supreme unconcern written across his face, he began to limp his way through the whispering multitude, ignoring the dagger glances shot at him by the matrons and acknowledging acquaintances with careless inclinations of the head.

"Oh, dear, where's my Hildegarde?" whimpered a sharp-featured lady in a florid gown. "I shouldn't like the Wicked Earl to cast his eyes upon her."

The august dowager beside her drew up her eyebrows in a skeptical manner. "You concern yourself unduly, my dear. I myself believe that the rumors about the earl are greatly exaggerated."

"Who is he?" murmured a fresh-faced young lady newly arrived from the country, her eyes fixed on the earl.

The first lady scowled at the admiration in the girl's voice. "He is a blackguard," she stated firmly, then added in a whisper, "He has destroyed the reputation of more than one young woman."

"I think you are being unjust to the earl," retorted the dowager, frowning.

"I think he's rather beautiful," exclaimed the young woman involuntarily; then, catching her companion's eyes, she blushed.

Indeed, the earl seemed to inspire both disgust and admiration equally. Even his harshest critic, however, could not but admit that he appeared to perfection in his exquisitely cut tailcoat and form-fitting pantaloons, both in somber black. The sobriety of this ensemble was alleviated only by the white satin waistcoat, which could be glimpsed beneath his cutaway, and the magnificent snowy stock above it, those precise well-stiffened folds caused many a young buck to regard it enviously. The crowning touch was the magnificent diamond pin nestled in the cravat, which was as recognizable as the earl himself.

"There's Sinamor," observed the hostess to the countess at her side. "Wish we hadn't had to invite him," she added, nodding graciously at the earl.

The countess smiled at her incredulously. "But why do you say this? He is one whose attendance may assure the success of any party."

"That's true enough," replied the first, still watching the earl keenly, "though I have no idea why. I only hope that some young girl doesn't make a fool of herself over him tonight."

The countess laughed softly. "Well, from what I have been told, that is not Sinamor's fault," she countered with a wicked gleam in her eye. "From what I have heard, his taste runs to, how shall I say, riper fruit."

"My dear countess!"

The earl himself was oblivious to the ripples of excitement engendered all about him. A friend who knew him well might have observed by the unusually grim line of his mouth, or the particular frostiness of those icy-blue eyes that the earl was not in an especially good temper tonight.

As a matter of fact, the earl was in an extremely disagreeable mood, and had been since the previous evening, when he had escorted the daughter of a widowed cousin to Almack's. The thought of attending an assembly in those hot, crowded rooms was enough to irritate him, without even considering that the only refreshments available were tepid lemonade, tea, and stale cake. It also meant he'd had to spend the evening defending himself against ambitious matchmaking mothers.

Despite whatever he might say, though, he felt a strong sense of family responsibility and so had nerved himself to the task, notwithstanding his personal dislike of Cousin Middleton. The daughter, Marianne, had proven to be equally detestable. Though not precisely an antidote, she apparently considered the earl a good catch and had spent the evening simpering at him in a most nauseating way.

The greatest blow had come in the form of an invitation. His current amour, the Baroness Serre, had organized an intimate dinner party for that same night. Since her invitations were tantamount to commands, he held out little hope that his hastily scribbled note of apology would have met with a gracious reception. Helene was sure to be furious, he thought moodily, and it would cost a pretty penny to put her back in a good humor.

He had attended the ball tonight only reluctantly, with the sole object of finding Helene and beginning the long task of making amends. His jaw tightened with irritation at the thought.

It did not take him long to locate her. Though the ballroom floor was crowded with dancers in silks and satins, she shone out among them like a diamond in its setting. Her fair head was cocked to one side as she listened to her partner's repartee, her blue eyes sparkled, and her lips were set in an irresistible pout. She shimmered in a silver gown, cut daringly low, which did little to conceal her charms. It had long been whispered by some that she damped her petticoats, though others maintained that she wore nothing at all beneath her fashionable dresses. Though she earned the matron's scorn in either case, it was evident that the gentlemen did not share these prejudices. The young officer with whom she was waltzing, for example, clearly found nothing distasteful about his lovely partner. Sinamor disliked the proprietal way in which the young man steered the baroness about the room. Since he did not dance himself, there was little he could do. He waited quietly until the dance was over and they left the floor, then made his way over to where they were standing.

The young captain looked nervous at his approach, for Sinamor's involvement with the baroness was well-known, as was the fact that the earl was an excellent shot. Sinamor's civil greeting to them both seemed to relieve his fears, though it had no such calming effect on Helene.

"How interesting to see you, my lord," she hissed. "I had the impression that you had given up social life."

It was going to be more difficult than he had thought. Sinamor steeled himself to smile pleasantly at her. "I came tonight in the hope that I might feast my eyes on your radiance. And," he added quickly, cutting off the retort that had risen to her lips, "exchange a word with you."

She lifted her chin defiantly. "Well, now that you have, I hope you will excuse us, as I wish to dance." A malicious smile curled her lips. "That is, unless you wish to take the captain's place?"

Sinamor paled with anger. The young captain beside her blushed. It was well-known that Sinamor's leg wound prevented his dancing, as he even walked with a pronounced limp. It was also common knowledge that he had received the wound in his country's service, in battle against the French. The officer looked at his companion with a new set of eyes, and excused himself rapidly, murmuring something about a glass of lemonade.

Sinamor had recovered himself and now he smiled frostily at Helene. "It looks as if you've cost yourself an admirer, my dear. Shall we retire to another room to continue our discussion?"

Helene was full of fury at the earl and at herself. She had been on the verge of causing a public scene, a scene that could have cost her Sinamor for good. She bit back an angry rejoinder and instead contrived to say carelessly, "Very well, my lord, the yellow salon in five minutes."

He bowed as he took his leave of her, heading off in an opposite direction from the salon. Although their relationship was generally known, the earl was a strict observer of decorum. It was perhaps this quality that made him everywhere received, despite the scandals swirling about him.

Helene began to make her way to the salon, though her progress was slowed somewhat by the attentions of her myriad admirers. The lapse of time should have served to cool her anger, but instead she felt her fury increase as she entered the salon and encountered the earl's dispassionate gaze. She closed the door behind her and glared at him, simmering with rage.

He was handsome, she had to concede that. The thick dark curls, which fell carelessly across the pale brow, formed a sharp contrast to those surprisingly blue eyes. The classical, rather delicate features belied that strong jaw underneath. Probably the most striking aspect of the face, though, were those remarkable winged brows—one of which sometimes, as at this moment, could fly upward with a mocking question in it.

She never was certain how to handle him in this mood, but today she threw caution to the winds.

"May I ask, sir, by what right you forced me to leave this gathering?" she accused angrily.

Sinamor's patience was wearing thin, and for some reason his leg had chosen to pain him particularly this evening.

"I didn't force you to do anything, Helene, so let's drop this ridiculous dramatic nonsense."

She sputtered with rage, "So you think I am ridiculous—"

He cut her off with a look. "I didn't say that, as you very well know." He sighed wearily. "Now, will you hear me out, or no?"

The sigh should have clued her that something was amiss, but she ignored it. She crossed her arms, her foot tapping angrily. "I should be very glad to hear anything you might have to say in your own defense."

He shook his head. "Helene, it was only a dinner party, I had a previous engagement, as I explained in my note."

"Your note!" Her head swam as she recalled this final affront. What good did it do to be the one who had captured the attentions of the elusive Earl of Sinamor if she couldn't even produce him at her own dinner party? To send her a note as if she were some mere acquaintance!

"Very kind of you, I'm sure," she said, unwisely attempting sarcasm. "Do you realize whom I had to invite to make up the numbers?"

"Whoever it was, I'm sure that—" he began in a weary tone when she cut him off.

"You're completely indifferent to all this, aren't you?" she asked, in rising hysteria. "And you're indifferent to me as well. What is it, Sinamor? Are you so bored with me that you make excuses to avoid my company?"

He made no reply, but merely stood there in silence. A moment passed. She realized she had asked one question too many. He inclined his head slightly toward her.

"I would never venture to contradict a lady," he said icily.

Her fury rose within her and she slapped him with all the

force she could muster. She would have hit him again, but he caught her arm and held it cruelly tight.

"I think, my dear, that you perhaps are forgetting I have been known to be generous in the matter of farewell gifts?" He loosened his hold on her arm, which now was unresisting. "You may select whatever you wish, the emerald necklace you admired so much the other day, possibly?"

Her mouth had fallen slackly open. She gazed at him in shock. "Sinamor . . ." she began.

He cut her off. "I will inform my secretary, Mr. Bates, to expect to hear from you. You need only contact him." He bowed coldly to her and left.

She watched him go, dumbfounded. As the door closed behind him, she realized what she had done. She had thrown away one of the handsomest, wealthiest, and most desirable social prizes in the kingdom, and all because of a silly dinner party. She threw herself down on the sofa with the intention of sobbing, but then remembered where she was. No, she needed to convey the impression that all was well between her and Sinamor as long as she could. Then it might be possible to find another interest of equal rank and wealth, if not of equal attractiveness.

In order to preserve decorum, the earl put in his usual appearance at White's in St. James's Street. After a halfhearted hour at play, he gave up and retired to an armchair with a bottle of port. He was discovered in this position by his friend, Aristophanes St. Clair.

"Hullo, Sinamor," said his friend, seating himself beside the earl and filling his own glass with the port.

"How are you, St. Clair?" asked the earl in a disinterested way.

"Rather better than you, I should imagine," St. Clair replied easily. He took a swallow of the port and drew in his lips appreciatively, then drained the glass.

"I was losing tonight," Sinamor admitted.

"That's what I heard. Abstracted, they said. It's a bad habit, this losing business," commented St. Clair, pouring himself another glass. "I should know." He shot a keen glance at his companion, but the earl seemed lost in thought. He leaned back in the chair. "So, what do you think of my new rig?" he asked.

The earl turned to look at him for the first time and winced. St. Clair was known for his extremes in dress. Tonight he had on a coat that was heavily padded in the shoulders and drawn in so tightly at the waist that Sinamor suspected he must be corseted underneath.

"Don't tell me. Nugee," he said. "And the portrait will be by Cruickshank."

St. Clair looked at him alertly. "What's this? An attempt at witticism from the stoic Earl of Sinamor?"

A grim smile hovered about the earl's face. "That's your forte, my literary friend, not mine."

"Yes, my fortes are to produce sayings that are so good that everyone must steal them, and also to lose at cards. Your fortes are to make beautiful women fall in love with you, and to win at cards." He paused. This sally met no rejoinder. "I take it that you do not approve of my new ensemble, my lord."

"Sometimes I wonder why you want to be such a fool."

"Sometimes I wonder why I want to be such a friend to one."

As Sinamor looked up, stricken, he met an unusually grave expression on St. Clair's face beneath the curled and pomaded hair. His friend smiled, though his eyes remained serious.

"No, I have no more wish to rattle your skeletons than you have to rattle mine, my friend."

St. Clair rose and extended an arm to the earl. "You've had too much wine this evening, or that's what I shall say. I shall help you to your carriage, and you will invite me to dinner this week for the pleasure of my company."

Sinamor had risen and now pressed his friend's hand. "Thank you, St. Clair."

The little smile danced about his friend's face. "Now you must lean on my arm, or you'll scarce give credence to my story."

As Sinamor rode home in his carriage, he reproached himself. It was not like him to inflict his misery on others. Not that he regretted ridding himself of Helene. When she had accused him of being tired of her, he had with a sudden clarity seen that he was, as he was of all the beautiful and heartless women who had pursued him since his return from the Peninsula. He sighed. They at least had seemed more suited to him than the giggling, simpering misses who were always being thrust at him as matrimonial prospects. With them, he hadn't needed to profess undying affection or to relinquish any of the sporting pastimes that were left to him.

He winced suddenly as the carriage hit a particularly rough portion of road. His leg was throbbing painfully, despite the wine. He was pale when the carriage arrived at his house in Berkeley Square, and he leaned heavily on the liveried footman as he left the carriage. He was eager to get in bed, for it was the only thing that could relieve his agony.

He was unpleasantly surprised, then, to be confronted by the butler, wearing an uneasy expression and bearing a letter on a silver salver.

"I beg your pardon, my lord," he said, proffering the salver, "but there are two . . . persons here."

In spite of himself, the earl's famous eyebrow shot up. "*Persons*, Chelvey?"

The butler swallowed. "Yes, my lord. Female persons. They arrived rather late . . . and they have baggage with them."

The mention of baggage dispelled an idea that had risen to the earl's mind. "How did they arrive?" he asked.

"I was informed that they had arrived in a hackney, my lord," said Chelvey loftily, to show that he was not one to originate such gossip. "They said they had to see you. They were most insistent. I told them you were out and that they should send you a note, but . . ."

The earl frowned. It was hard to imagine Chelvey being bested. "What sorts of persons are they?" he asked.

Chelvey cleared his throat in confusion. "Well, I would say that one is youngish, and the other older. They are dressed in mourning." He dropped his head to look at the earl apologetically. "I am afraid they are . . . rural people, my lord." He again extended the salver. "They seemed most insistent that you should read this note, my lord."

The earl took it from him automatically. "Where did you put them?"

"I, uh, under the circumstances, I thought it best to . . ." stammered Chelvey.

The earl looked at him in some surprise. He had never seen the usually imperturbable Chelvey uncertain before.

"In the study, my lord."

The earl sighed. These were undoubtedly more indigents, claiming to be long-lost relatives. It was one of the headaches associated with the title. It was odd that Chelvey hadn't driven them off as he normally would. Perhaps these were more persistent than the rest. He'd give them a purse and send them on their way.

He straightened himself. The leg would have to wait. With a cool smile to show that he was now in control of this situation, he nodded to the butler. "Very well, I'll take care of this. I'll ring if I should need you for anything, Chelvey."

"Very good, my lord." The butler bowed, once again his impassive self.

The earl examined the envelope as he made his way to the study. It bore only his name, and the bold handwriting was unfamiliar.

He stepped into the study and saw that the two persons had fallen asleep sitting upright on the red-striped satin sofa. What he judged to be the younger one had her head on the older one's shoulder. They both wore stiff black dresses of a fashion twenty years old, and both were spattered with dirt from their travels. There was little sign of beauty in either of the two faces. The elder's was plump and careworn beneath her gray hair. The younger's was similarly unremarkable. They were both clearly members of the servant class, and the earl wondered how they had imposed upon Chelvey to let them stay. They probably had spun him some Banbury yarn. Chelvey was nothing if not discreet.

Sinamor sighed again and turned to his desk for the silver letter opener. He slit it open and drew his brows together at the sight of the salutation.

My Dear Lovelace,

You must forgive me for addressing you so, but that is how I always knew you in our days together. Little did any of us dream that Lt.

Lovelace of the 14th Light Dragoons was soon to be the Right Honorable Earl of Sinamor. But then you always were full of surprises.

I know that you didn't expect to get a letter from old Harry Raithby after all these years. I myself didn't expect to see you again after you caught the ball in your leg at Fuentes d'Onoro. I caught a ball myself at Salamanca and that ended the war for me. Rogers has been kind enough to keep me apprised of things, and it was from him that I learned of your succeeding to the title.

You may wonder, dear Lovelace, why I am writing you; and as I write, I wonder myself. I am going to ask you for a favor, something I've never done before. I would not ask such a great thing of you except for the memory of one who was dearer than life to me. It is for her sake that I ask.

I know that I acquainted you somewhat with my history: that I was a younger son, whose family managed to scrape together enough money to buy me a commission; that I had married young; and that my wife had died, leaving me with a daughter. I think that I even mentioned to you that my wife's family disapproved of the match. I must now tell you the reason.

My wife, a living angel if there ever were one, was the eldest daughter of Lord Wakehurst. They naturally expected her to make a match with the highest in the land rather than a penniless soldier like myself. When they saw the choice she'd made, they lavished abuse on my poor dear angel for two long years, until she came of age and married me of her own free will. They promptly cut her off, but we cared little for their money. My angel and I were happy as long as we had each other.

As you know, the life of a soldier's wife is a hard one, and my Phillipa was frail. I thought it best to leave her on my little farm in Yorkshire while I was abroad. When I learned we were to have a child, you can't imagine my joy. Alas, the birth was a difficult one, and my wife died a few days later. I named my daughter Phillipa in her memory.

I couldn't stay at home to raise the babe, so I brought my great-aunt to live with her. I suppose it was my own mistake not to bring in someone younger, for when I'd return home, Phillipa would be as wild as an unbroken filly and as headstrong as ever I was. I was at fault, too, for encouraging her in the boyish pursuits she liked, which I'd never be able to share with a son. In my latter years, we had begun breeding horses and achieved some moderate success. Phillipa is a born horsewoman. The animals trust her unquestioningly and she can outride any lad in the county. In any case, her upbringing is not what I suppose a young lady's should be.

It didn't worry me until I came home from the war. I knew that I had only a few months left and I fretted to see her so unsettled. She had changed from a child to a young woman during my absence, but I also saw another change in her. I saw her mother in her, and I knew that Phillipa could never be happy among the country gentlefolk, as I had hoped. Sh was a Wakehurst to the core, and she belonged in a higher sphere than the one to which I could introduce her. You have known me as a proud man, Lovelace, but in my dying desperation I wrote Lord Wakehurst, hoping that the sins of the mother might not be visited upon the child. It was useless, I need not say. The letter was returned unopened.

As I say, I was a dying man and a desperate one. I thought as hard as I could. I would have used any connection that came to mind. And then I thought of you.

You remember how, after Duoro, you said that you owed me your life and that you would gladly give or do for me anything I asked of you? You repeated it more than once while we were together, so I saw that you were serious about this obligation. I never thought to call upon a debt of honor, but I am doing so now. I have met with my lawyer and made you Phillipa's legal guardian.

The earl could not help a slight exclamation as he read the words. He looked over at the two visitors. They were still sleeping. He turned back to the letter.

You alone can offer Phillipa the introduction to society that she merits. Since you have lived among people of a humbler station as well as the world you live in now, I know that you can help Phillipa overcome the fears she naturally will have about assuming her rightful place in society. I think it is where she is born to be, though I did promise her that, if after a year she had received no suitable offers and if you agreed, she should be able to return to Yorkshire to raise horses on her own. I made her promise me that she would cooperate with you all that she could, and that she would try her best at any task you set before her.

She is a headstrong girl, but she has her mother's tender heart. She is as true and as loving as any daughter could be, and I hope that for my sake you will be fond of her. She is high-spirted, but never malicious, and I think that she will try hard to please you.

You need not worry about finances. Phillipa has a small inheritance through her mother's mother. I also have come into a fortune through an uncle of mine. Also a younger son, he'd always had a fondness for me. He died a nabob, which means that Phillipa is now a considerable heiress. With that, her background, the traits nature has bestowed upon her, and the training you give her, I have no doubt that she will find some gentleman whom she can make a good and loving wife.

I have asked her to remain in Yorkshire for one year after my death, so that she need not attend these social gatherings in mourning. Do not grieve for me, my friend, as I was happy to be spared long enough to provide for her future. I will be happy, reunited to my angel. I send this letter with Phillipa, and with my love, dear Lovelace. Thank you for being a true friend.

The earl stared at the signature, still bold despite the man's illness. His head was whirling. It was true that Harry Raithby had saved his life. "He can't have known my reputation," said the earl softly to himself.

He put the letter down and sighed. He had no choice. Harry Raithby was dead and he had been left with an obligation to fulfill, no matter that it seemed impossible. To convert that insignificant-looking rustic into a society belle! He shook his head at the thought.

"She probably speaks broad Yorkshire, too." He spoke aloud without thinking.

"My lord."

Sinamor turned his head in puzzlement. The smaller of the two figures was standing stiffly erect, seeming to have added inches and years by the dignity of her posture.

"My lord," repeated the voice. "You must forgive my ignorance of London customs, but in Yorkshire it is considered rude to discuss someone to their face without addressing them."

The voice held not a trace of a Yorkshire accent and it was beautifully modulated. In response to it, the earl automatically rose to his feet. "I beg your pardon," he said, "but I imagined that you were still asleep. Allow me to present myself. I am Evelyn Lovelace, Lord Sinamor, and apparently your new guardian." He bowed to her.

She curtsied in return. "I am Phillipa Raithby, and this is our housekeeper, Mrs. Abbot. We are pleased to make your acquaintance," she added formally.

The serving woman bobbed a quick curtsy, though she was obviously more uncomfortable than her mistress.

"Might I ask your age, Phillipa?" said the earl.

"Certainly. I am seventeen," she replied composedly.

"Your father . . ." said the earl, suddenly ill-at-ease.

"He passed away just over a year ago," Phillipa said. "He had taken a ball through the lung, so it was rather a miracle that he survived that long." She seemed to see an unspoken question in the earl's face. "He thought very highly of you," she said quietly. "He said I was to obey you in everything."

She waited respectfully for him to reply. The Sevres clock on the mantelpiece chimed half-past ten. It seemed to awaken the earl.

"What the deuce am I to do with you?"

2

Some thirty to forty minutes later, Phillipa sat in the earl's crested carriage outside a handsome house in Hamilton Place, her temper rising every minute. Without a word of explanation, she and Mrs. Abbot and the portmanteaus had been whisked from the earl's mansion as if they might contaminate it. She had tried to protest feebly that she was tired, but this had met with a shocked look from the earl and an exclamation: "Good Lord, girl, you can't stay here." She had no idea where they had been taken or why. Upon their arrival, the earl simply had ordered her to remain where she was, and disappeared into the house. She would have vented her spleen on her companion, but that insensitive woman once again had fallen asleep.

The earl meanwhile was addressing the butler.

"I need to speak with Lady Dearborne on an urgent matter."

"Very good, my lord. I will tell her that you are here. Would you care to wait in the green salon?" Bickerstaffe betrayed no emotion. One did not turn away the Earl of Sinamor, even when he called at eleven o'clock in the evening.

The earl nodded in response to his question and limped wretchedly into the salon, whose walls were lined in damask in a delicate shade of green. The room was furnished in a modern, airy style that reflected Lady Dearborne's elegance and good taste. She was not one to clutter her house with the latest Egyptian or Gothic fancies.

He settled himself into a gracefully curved armchair and waited for her. Within a few minutes, she appeared, still attired in the red silk evening gown that she had worn to this evening's entertainment.

Not even her husband would call Lady Winifred Dearborne a beauty. She was of the medium height, which put her almost on an even footing with the earl, who was a small man, for all his irresistibility. She also had a decided tendency toward plumpness, which somewhat softened the rather harsh features of her face. As a first cousin, she bore little resemblance to the earl, except for the thick dark curling locks that surrounded her face. Her eyes, though a more predictable brown, were her greatest asset, for they shone with the gentleness and kindness that won for her many friends. At this moment, they were filled with anxiety at the earl's unexpected call. As an only child, he had spent a great deal of time playing with his nearby cousins, and as the eldest in her family, she had taken a sister's proprietary interest in him. Though the height of respectability herself, she never shunned her scapegrace younger cousin, for she was only too familiar with the demons that drove him.

"Evelyn," she said, holding out her hands to him.

"Hello, Win," he said, taking hers, but not attempting to rise.

His leg is troubling him, she thought as she sat down.

"I'm glad I did not awaken you," he said apologetically.

"No, I just arrived from the Duchess of Marshton's ball. My son was kind enough to escort me."

"Ah, yes, I was there briefly myself."

"So I was told," she said, trying to keep any expression from her voice. She had heard that the Baroness Serre had spent a great deal of time flirting with a young captain that evening. If Sinamor was free of her, so much the better.

He leaned forward suddenly and shook her hand. "Win, I have the devil of a problem."

"What is it?" She sat upright, suddenly concerned for him.

"It's an awkward thing, really. I have a young girl I need you to house for me."

She looked at him, her eyes full of questions.

"She's only seventeen and has no proper chaperon. I can't send her to a hotel and obviously she can't stay at Berkeley Square."

The question burst from her, "But, Sinamor, who is she?"

Wordlessly, he handed her the letter.

She took it from him and perused it thoroughly. When she looked up, her worry was apparent. "Oh, Evelyn, is this true?"

He nodded. "So far as I know, yes. He enclosed the legal document."

"But you were under an . . ."

"He saved my life, yes. I am under the greatest debt to him that I could owe any man."

"But surely you . . ."

He leaned forward and took her hand. "Don't you see, Win? He was dying when he wrote it. The girl has no one else to whom she can turn. She's my responsibility."

A thought occurred to her. She was reluctant to voice it. "Sinamor, he can't . . . he can't have known of your . . ."

"Of my somewhat blemished reputation?" He gave a bitter smile. "Believe me, that was my premiere objection to this scheme. I can't imagine a more unlikely guardian than myself."

Embarrassed, she blushed and began to stammer out an apology, but he silenced her.

"No, the problem is that I can think of no way out of this predicament. I suppose I could try the Wakehursts, but it doesn't sound hopeful, does it? In any case, something has to be done with the girl until then. That's why I came to you, Win. Do you think you could keep her here, for tonight, anyway?"

He could see the doubts gathering in her eyes, but she hesitated only an instant. "Why, certainly, I'd be glad to keep her as long as you need. I'll help with the coming-out, too, however I may."

He shook his head. "I'm afraid that's hopeless. She's an insignificant-looking girl and appears a complete rustic. Besides which, the Season is already half over." He rose, wincing slightly as he did so. "Dear Win, what would I do without you?"

She shooed him away. "Well, go and bring her in."

An instant later, Phillipa stood before her, the earl having effected the necessary introductions. Winifred smiled brightly at her as she studied the little figure. It was true that the girl was no diamond, but Winifred judged that, with the proper clothes, she would be a well-looking young lady. Even though the fashion was not for petite women, she at least carried herself well. She unfortunately had the strongly Roman Wakehurst nose, but somehow, combined with the sensitivity in the little face, it contrived to lend her an air of distinction.

Something out of the common, Winifred thought to herself, then added aloud, "I can see why your father did not think you should be hidden away in Yorkshire. You have maligned the girl, Sinamor. Look at that lovely hair and those beautiful blue eyes. She will make a charming protégée."

The earl turned to regard Phillipa more closely. For the first time, he saw that her hair was a luxuriant fiery chestnut and that her eyes were sapphire blue. He had thought there was nothing of bluff Harry Raithby in this undistinguished girl. He said aloud, gruffly, "She has her father's coloring."

Phillipa's foot stamped once in anger. It stamped once again, louder, for emphasis. Her eyes flashed at the earl.

"When you are through discussing me, I would like to have a turn to speak."

The earl frowned. It was a look known to quell even roisterous tipplers at his club. Phillipa refused to be deterred.

"Because when you are, I should like to have a say regarding the plans for my future, if that's not asking too much of you."

The earl's face slowly darkened with anger. "Miss Raithby, you are very fortunate that this lady not only has taken you in at this unreasonable hour, but also kindly has offered to assist with your introduction to society."

Phillipa charged up to him. "But I didn't ask her to take me in, did I? You did."

"Winifred, I apologize."

"And I didn't ask her for help with my coming-out, did I? And what's more, I never did want an introduction to society, and I don't want one now, and if you're an example of what I may expect, then I will be much happier without it."

"Phillipa!"

"And I don't intend to stay here any longer and I will see if the lawyer can make someone else my guardian and—"

"*Phillipa*!"

The earl looked ready to throttle his new ward, but Winifred hastily intervened.

"Sinamor, I think it's better if you leave us."

He scowled at her. "What?"

Winifred smiled at him. "We'll be better on our own. Go home. Your leg needs rest."

He hesitated.

Lady Dearborne drew herself up. "I'm entirely serious. You may call on us tomorrow."

He opened his mouth to utter a final word.

She issued him from the room like a schoolboy. "I mean it. Now go."

As soon as he had left, she turned to Phillipa. Winifred had noticed that the girl's bottom lip was trembling suspiciously.

"Now, then," she said, taking her hand and patting it comfortingly, "I imagine you're tired and hungry after your long trip. Evelyn probably didn't offer you anything, did he?"

Confronted by this unexpected sympathy, Phillipa uttered a sob and fell into Lady Dearborne's arms, weeping violently.

When the storm of tears finally had abated, Phillipa sat up and began to dry her eyes with a black-edged handkerchief.

Winifred rang for a servant. "I'll just have them send you a cold collation, then. Would you like that?"

"Yes," Phillipa sniffed, "and something for Mrs. Abbot, too, please. She's as tired and as hungry as I."

Winifred lifted her eyebrows slightly, but continued to smile. "Yes, I'll make sure that Mrs. Abbot is made comfortable also."

When the problem of food had been attended to, Winifred settled herself comfortably beside Phillipa. "Sinamor told me so little," she said. "Did you just arrive this evening?"

"Yes," replied Phillipa in a tremulous voice, "much earlier this evening. We rode on the mail and it took us three days from York. Our coach met with an accident and was delayed."

Winifred clucked her tongue sympathetically, "You poor dear," she said, "you must tell me all about it."

In twenty minutes of conversation, Winifred was able to extract most of the details of her new charge's life. After saying what she could to make the girl feel at home, Winifred trundled her off to bed, then retired to her own chamber to reflect.

The child was high-spirited, that much was obvious. Evelyn had handled her the wrong way from the start. Gentle encouragement would produce better results than severity. In all, Phillipa seemed to be a sweet child, in need of affection and guidance. With a little polish, she might be a very taking young woman. Winifred felt pleased with her impetuous decision to aid her cousin. A tap sounded on her door. She looked around inquiringly and saw her husband. She gave a rather unladylike squeal of delight. "Robert!"

Lord Robert Dearborne was a tall, well-built man with a craggy, good-humored face and rather unkempt dark-brown hair. The keen brown eyes, which shone with intelligence, were at the moment bloodshot and ringed with gray circles of weariness.

"Hello, my dear," he said.

She flew to him and threw her arms around him. "I am so glad to see you."

He smiled tiredly and removed his hat. "I've just finished now, though doubtless there was more I should have done."

She took a step back to look at him in dismay. "But you left at six this morning. You are only human, after all, my love. You must have some rest."

He shook off his coat and sat down to remove his boots. "Unfortunately, it seems as if the business of peace takes as much effort as the business of war." He looked up at her dismayed face and smiled. "I myself will be glad when their majesties have departed from England."

She sighed and shook her head. "I am glad to have an end to that dreadful war, and I know how important the peace negotations are, but I don't see how you can continue with so little sleep."

He yawned, his eyelids heavy. "I admit that sleep sounds a wonderful idea right now."

Winifred froze in place. "Heavens, Robert, I forgot!"

"Forgot what?" he asked incuriously.

"Sinamor's ward is staying here with us."

"What?" The word echoed sharply about her bedchamber.

She raised her chin a little. "Phillipa Raithby, his ward, is here."

"His ward?"

Winifred did not like the way her husband emphasized the word "ward."

"She is his ward, Robert," she said a trifle huffily. "I've seen the papers myself. It was a companion of his in the Fourteenth who—"

He cut her off, disbelief in his voice. "Who on this earth would be foolish enough to entrust his daughter to Sinamor? I can't imagine a more unlikely guardian."

"That's just what Sinamor said himself, but this gentleman had saved his life and—"

Lord Robert had little use for his wife's cousin. "I would never entrust a child of mine—"

"She's not a child, she's seventeen."

"That's even worse." He glowered at her for a moment, then his face became grave. "How could you do this, Win?"

She spread her hands pleadingly. "He had nowhere else to turn."

"He is a grown man and not your responsibility."

"But the girl, Robert, where was she to go if I did not take her in? She's fresh from the country and as innocent as a lamb."

He shook his head. "Do you imagine that you are doing her a favor by letting her associate with a name renowned for scandals that—"

She flushed angrily. "Sinamor never caused any of those scandals. It is not his fault if foolish girls throw themselves at his head. I have never heard anyone suggest that he encouraged even one."

Robert waved a hand dismissively. "Well, what about what he said to Lord Beaton?"

She shook her head. "Now, you know, Robert, that if there's anyone that Sinamor can't stand, it's a busybody. Even worse is a bore. And he hates a prig most of all. Lord Beaton is a combination of all three."

"Well, I admit it was officious of the old fellow to ask Sinamor about the state of his soul, especially since they are hardly acquainted, but that didn't justify Sinamor's saying he hadn't one."

"I would be tempted to, myself. Particularly if I had a leg that pained me and I had been standing for four hours at a reception."

Robert gazed at her implacably and she saw that this line of argument was not aiding her cause. Her voice took on a pleading tone. "Really, Robert, I think you would like the child if you met her. She is so desperately in need of guidance. And she would be a good influence on the boys, too. I have noticed that Edmond is awkward around young ladies. She would help him to become accustomed to their society."

Robert heard the suppliant note in her voice and weakened slightly. He knew Winifred's unspoken entreaty. Although they had five promising boys, it was the great sorrow of her life that she had never produced a girl.

"I think it would be good for Sinamor, too. I think that this responsibility could—"

He held up a weary hand. "I surrender. I am vanquished."

She threw her arms about him.

"As far as I am concerned, Napoleon himself might stay here tonight, as long as I am allowed to have some rest. It's one o'clock in the morning, my love."

"Oh, yes, of course." She realized with a guilty start that she herself had risen at the fashionable hour of half-past seven that morning. "I'm sorry, my dear, please go right to sleep."

She turned and saw that he had already done so. She smiled to herself, for she knew the point that had won the argument. He is so good to me, she thought happily. And what a pleasure it will be to have a young lady to shop with and introduce and dress.

Her anticipatory pleasure might have shattered into fragments had she entered the stables at the unlikely hour of eight o'clock the next morning. The head groom, Harris, found himself in a rare quandary. The diminutive young gentleman who had marched into the stables demanding a mount hardly resembled anyone of the Quality. The old-fashioned frock coat, knee breeches, and brown-topped boots proclaimed him a rustic, at best. Yet there was something imperious in the youth's manner. The haughty expression on that face had frozen the rude retort in Harris's mouth and instead he had dispatched a lad to see if the tale about being a guest could really be true. The lad had returned with the incredible news that Lady Dearborne indeed had taken in a young houseguest last night and had given orders that they were to spare no pains for his comfort and convenience.

Whether or not this command included letting the youth exercise one of Lord Robert's favorite hunters was more than Harris could say.

"He's a proper high-spirited 'un," he was saying discouragingly when the young gentleman interrupted.

"Yes, he should do nicely," said the youth. Catching the uncertainty in the groom's eye, he lifted the Roman nose another inch. "Well, are you going to saddle him for me or shall I do it myself?"

The perspiration began to bead upon Harris's forehead. "Sir—" he began hesitantly.

The youth gave his booted leg a slap with his riding crop. "Well," he said in exasperation, "I suppose I shall have to go to Lady Dearborne and ask that she—"

Knowing full well that his mistress, who habitually slept until eleven, had the greatest dislike of being roused early, Harris surrendered.

"You needn't go to that trouble sir," Harris interposed hastily. "One of the lads will make him ready for you right now."

"Thank you," said the youth frostily as the grooms sprang into action. It wasn't until he had mounted the restive animal that he flashed a quick smile at Harris. "I'm well up to him. You needn't worry."

Uncertain whether or not his decision had been correct, Harris was unable to comply with this request. With an anxious expression, he watched the young gentleman ride off.

"He's got a good seat," he admitted grudgingly.

"Why did they say it was a young lady that was staying at the house, d'ye suppose?" asked one of the other grooms.

Harris turned and glowered at the stable lad that had been unfortunate enough to act as messenger. "What can you expect with such want-wits as we have about?"

Unconcerned with the furor she had caused, Phillipa turned her horse off the street and walked it into the park. The groom had explained that Hyde Park would provide ample room for her to exercise the horse. What a lucky chance that it was so convenient.

Phillipa felt a sense of freedom which she had lost since

leaving Yorkshire. It had been odd to rise at her usual hour and see no one about; the streets were fairly quiet, too. It might not have been necessary for her to don her disguise or tuck her hair into the antique tricorne hat. Well, it was never unwise to take precautions. Even with her limited upbringing, she knew full well that ladies were not supposed to ride without a groom and never astride.

She dismissed these petty matters from her mind. It was a glorious morning and she meant to make good use of it. What better way to forget her troubles than by going for a run?

The idea proved more than acceptable to her mount. The big chestnut had been given far too little exercise lately. Phillipa lifted the reins and gave him a bit of encouragement with her heels, and soon they were flying effortlessly across the park. All else was forgotten but the delight of the wind whistling past her ears and the steady rhythm of the big horse beneath her. A fallen tree loomed before them. Phillipa could feel her mount hesitate, but she recklessly urged him forward with her heels. In response to her unspoken command, he gathered herself and sailed over it like a bird. She was laughing aloud in delight when a horse and rider abruptly entered her view, seemingly intent upon a collision. She began to pull up the chestnut as the other rider leaned forward in the saddle, grabbing her reins. The two horses in unison slowed to a stop. Phillipa was gathering her breath to ask the other rider what all this was about when she suddenly heard a familiar voice.

"Are you all right, then, my lad?" He gasped for breath himself and continued, "I wonder at your parents letting a young fellow like you out on a powerful horse like this. It's no wonder it got away with you."

Phillipa would have exclaimed in anger, but she realized that she must do everything she could to keep her identity secret. She dropped her head and mumbled by way of reply. She could almost feel her companion's eyes boring into her.

"That is, of course, provided that your parents knew about it."

She held her tongue, realizing that now he was taking note of her well-worn and antiquated clothes. Suspicion sounded in his voice.

"You haven't borrowed this horse from someone, have you, lad?"

She shook her head desperately and gathered the reins, ready for flight.

"It's a handsome animal," he continued accusingly, then hastily exclaimed, "I know this horse, it's Lord Dearborne's."

At this, she tried to urge the horse forward, but his hand shot forward and took her wrist in a grip of steel. She couldn't help crying out in pain as he pulled her to him.

"What's this?" Sinamor asked, startled by the feminine tone. She looked up at him and his jaw fell open. "Phillipa," he said in shock.

She tried to tug away from him again, but he unconsciously held her fast.

"What does this mean?" he asked.

"You're hurting me," she replied, still struggling. He released her abruptly. She rubbed her wrist.

"Well?" he said.

"I always ride in the mornings," she said plaintively, all at once aware of the depth of her transgression. He remained frigidly silent. "Lady Dearborne said I was to look on her home as my own," she added helpfully, "I asked her about the stables last night."

"But naturally you omitted to mention that you always took your ride in a pair of . . . leather breeches." He almost choked on the words.

She blushed with shame.

"Do you realize that it was by the sheerest coincidence that I came across you this morning? The consequences might very well be disastrous."

"I can manage this horse," she retorted hotly.

"I was speaking of your making Lady Dearborne, myself, and yourself the laughingstocks of London, a danger which, I might add, still exists."

He looked at her sternly. "I do not pretend to understand why you have conceived such a dislike for me, Phillipa, but I think you will agree that Lady Dearborne, at least, is not deserving of such enmity."

The beginning of a sob escaped her, but she managed to suppress it.

He looked about them. "You therefore will follow my commands exactly. You will ride slightly behind me at a slow pace, so as not to attract any attention to ourselves. You will keep your head lowered, and if we are approached by anyone, you will under any circumstance remain quiet. We will proceed in this manner back to my cousin's house. Do you understand me?"

"Yes," she whispered huskily, hardly daring to trust her voice.

"Very well," said the earl. He clucked to his horse and they set off sedately together.

The minutes seemed like hours to Phillipa as they rode along in chilly silence. She scarcely drew an audible breath, so fearful was she of incurring further displeasure.

As they drew near Hyde Park Corner, Phillipa let out a little sigh of relief. They would emerge unscathed from her escapade, after all.

A stifled expletive escaped the earl's lips. Phillipa realized that she had been premature in her hopes.

"Of all the blasted ill-luck! It's Lord Malling, the most notorious gossip in London," he hissed at her under his breath. "Keep your head down, and whatever you do, don't say a word."

Phillipa scarcely needed any urging. She peeped up at the approaching figure, then sank her chin down on her chest.

"Hullo, Sinamor," called Lord Malling familiarly as he rode up on a showy bay.

"Good day, my lord," replied Sinamor coolly.

Although she kept her head lowered, Phillipa managed another peep at his lordship. He was a gaudy sight. In contrast to Sinamor's understated attire of top boots and buckskin breeches, accompanied by a somber black coat, this individual was attired in a coat of an unsubtle shade of green, accompanied by a brilliantly striped waistcoat and shockingly bright yellow pantaloons.

"I must say, Sinamor, I'm surprised to see you up and about so early," he said inquisitively.

"I might say the same of your lordship."

"Well, my physician told me that I needed to begin early-morning exercise, but I will tell you that I find it deuced flat."

The earl merely raised his famous eyebrow by way of a reply.

Lord Malling refused to be quelled. His quick eyes had been studying Phillipa's antiquated costume, and now he added in an undertone, "I say, Sinamor, that's surely not one of your lads."

The earl glanced behind him as if unsure to whom Lord Malling might be referring. He turned back and said in a tone of masterful indifference, "Oh, no, my agent had the horse sent to me, hoping that I might purchase it."

"What would you want with a hunter?" said Lord Malling puzzledly. "I've never known you to spend time in the country."

"My feelings exactly." The earl delicately smothered a yawn of boredom behind one gloved hand. "Charity case, though. You know how it is."

Lord Malling seemed about to make another observation, but something in the earl's face seemed to make him change his mind. "I wish I knew how you achieve that shine on your boots, Sinamor," he said instead.

"My valet has never confided his secrets to me," replied the earl.

"If only I knew what proportion of champagne to use . . ."

"Champagne . . . Good Lord!" retorted the earl unpleasantly. "You must excuse me, Malling, but I am meeting with my man of business this morning. Good day."

He nodded his head to Malling, who could do little but respond in like manner and wonder how Lord Sinamor managed to achieve such popularity with such abrupt manners.

As soon as they were out of earshot, Phillipa couldn't help leaning forward in her saddle to ask, "Does he really use champagne on his boots?"

Something like a snort escaped the earl. "Undoubtedly he does, for what little good it does him. You will find that society is only too eager to follow Brummell's dictates, however whimsical they may be."

Phillipa wondered to herself who this Brummell person was.

London was certainly a strange place. She looked at her guardian's back with new appreciation. It was not that she liked him any better, but at least he knew how to sit a horse—and how to choose one, too, she mused to herself. And at least he didn't wear yellow pantaloons. She sighed. She could tell she wasn't going to like London much.

3

If Phillipa had entertained any hopes that her transgression had been driven from the earl's mind by Lord Malling's interference, they were shortly to be dashed. When they reached Hamilton Place, he dragged her into the green salon and proceeded to give such a dressing-down as she'd never received before in her life. She was close to weeping with a combination of frustrated anger and shame, but she resolved not to give him that satisfaction.

He elucidated for her the precise number of ways in which she had transgressed, and he expressed the doubt that Lady Dearborne would wish her to remain under her roof.

"For you see, Phillipa, her husband holds a position in government. This one rash act would not only bar us from society; the resulting scandal could cost him his post."

Phillipa pressed her lips together firmly in order to maintain some semblance of self-control. She expected to hear next that he washed his hands of her. Instead, he paused, and when he spoke again, it was in even, measured tones.

"I will admit that I am strongly tempted to resign my position as your guardian. One thing prevents me, and that is the memory of your father."

He sighed, catching Phillipa off her guard.

"He was both a good man and a brave man. Did he ever tell you how he saved my life?"

She shook her head wordlessly.

"I expected not."

She saw a faraway look come into his eyes as he remembered the incident.

"I was a green youth, your father a seasoned veteran of many campaigns. For some unknown reason, he took a fancy to me. He showed me many of the tricks that could make a soldier's life more bearable, as well as the skills that would enable me to acquit myself well in battle."

He paused for a moment, then continued. "It was at Oporto, toward the end of the day. We had been ordered to attack the French's rearguard column. As we cleared our infantry, we saw that the French had formed in front of us and were ready with their bayonets. The road we charged up was walled, and we were certain the enemy had been posted behind it on our left, to provide a running fire at us. My horse caught a ball and fell, unfortunately pinning me under him. Although we had broken their line, the French continued to oppose us with hand-to-hand combat. I had lost my sword when I fell. One of the French, seeing me trapped, thought to make short work of me with his bayonet, but I forestalled him by drawing my pistol and shooting him through the heart. I dispatched another in like manner, but had no means to reload. My carbine had been pinned under the horse also and I tugged desperately to free it, with little success. Another of the enemy, seeing me helpless, made ready to run me through, but your father, fighting nearby, dropped him with a shot."

A little gasp escaped the intent Phillipa.

"He took up a position near me, literally standing between me and death. He somehow managed to signal a trooper and together they were able to free me, though at risk to their own lives."

The earl fell silent. He walked over to the mantelpiece and leaned heavily on it. When he spoke again, his voice was weary. "I thought it might help you to know what kind of a man your father was, and what kind of obligation I owe him."

He sighed. "I am no more anxious to be your guardian than you are to have me for one, Phillipa, but your father, if sometimes headstrong, was not a man to do things lightly. He spoke of his affection for you in his letter. I cannot help believing he had considered this step carefully and rightly or wrongly, thought it would be to your benefit."

He looked up at her and she saw with a shock that the normally icy-blue eyes now held a look of pain.

"He also said you had promised to do your best to cooperate with me. Are you not under an obligation to his memory, Phillipa, even as I am?"

She could no longer meet those accusing blue eyes. Overwhelmed by a sense of shame, she burst into tears and fled the room.

The earl gazed moodily into the fire. His reverie was interrupted by an exclamation from the door.

"Sinamor!"

He looked up to see his cousin Winifred.

"What on earth is going on? Phillipa ran past me on the stairs, sobbing as if her heart were going to break."

The earl smiled grimly. "I presume that you took note of her garments."

"Yes, what in the world—" sputtered Winifred, but he cut her off.

"My ward has seen fit to take her morning ride in the park in a pair of . . . in male attire."

Winifred sank into a chair. "Sinamor, no." She hesitated for a moment before voicing her question. "Was anyone there?"

"Malling, but fortunately we fobbed him off."

"Evelyn, what were *you* doing there so early in the morning?"

He gave her a look.

Her face creased in sympathy. "Does your leg still keep you awake, then?"

"It's nothing. I thought I would go for a ride this morning, then come check on Phillipa. Obviously, I was too late." He drummed his fingers on the mantelpiece. "If you would ask your maid to pack her things and see that she is decently dressed, I will relieve you of her presence." He smiled at his cousin apologetically. "I hope that your servants are discreet."

She tilted her chin upward. "I have never placed any stock in servants' gossip." A cloud settled upon her brow. "Are you sending her back to Yorkshire, then, Evelyn?"

He shook his head. "Foolhardy as it may seem, I am not renouncing my guardianship. I may take her to my Aunt Ondine's if nothing else occurs to me."

"Leave her here."

The impulsive words startled Winifred almost as much as the earl. His eyes narrowed.

"You can't mean it, Win."

"But I do," she said, gaining conviction as she spoke. "You said that no harm had been done. It was an ignorant mistake, not a malicious one."

He shook his head. "You cannot persuade me that even in Yorkshire young ladies have abandoned riding habits in favor of—"

"Don't be facetious," scolded Winifred. "You know just as well as I do that the child had no idea of the harm she could have caused."

The earl walked over to her and took her hand. His blue eyes were serious now as they gazed at her.

"Whether she acted deliberately or out of ignorance, the harm would have been the same. I can't allow you to take that risk, my dear." A hint of a smile curled his lips. "Besides, Dearborne would have my hide, and deservedly so."

Winifred shook her head. "But she realized her mistake now. She'll be on her best behavior. And besides, I'll keep her in my sight at all times."

Sinamor frowned. "The chit is my problem, not yours."

"I know." She lowered her head. "Evelyn, that girl is at a critical age. She desperately needs a woman's guidance." Winifred looked into her cousin's eyes searchingly. "Haven't you ever seen someone and thought to yourself that you could make a great deal of difference to his or her life?"

The sudden flash of pain in his eyes caught her unawares. It was quickly replaced by his usual icy remoteness. He dropped her hand gently. "Never I'm afraid. However," he paused for a moment to marshal his thoughts, "if you're determined to keep this girl, you may do so, provided your husband approves, of course. That is, you may keep her until I secure a chaperon."

"Thank you," said Winifred, composed now. "Please join us for dinner this evening."

"I'm afraid that I can't. I've invited St. Clair."

"Bring him along, by all means. It will be just the family."

He bowed.

"Another thing," said Winifred peremptorily. "I should think that Phillipa requires a new wardrobe without delay."

"I'll trust your judgment in these matters." He smiled icily at her. "My credit should be good."

They made their farewells, and Winifred, oddly pleased by her victory, went upstairs to see what could be done with Phillipa.

Lady Dearborne spent half an hour patting the girl on the back and speaking to her comfortingly before Phillipa was able to regain control of herself. She had thoughtfully ordered chocolate for each of them, and this seemed to pick up Phillipa's spirits somewhat.

"Well, the first order of business, my dear, is for you to have a bath."

"A bath?" Phillipa scowled. "It's only Friday."

"We are in the habit of bathing daily," said Winifred with only a mild hint of reproof.

Phillipa wiped her nose with a handkerchief and decided at this point she must humor their excesses. "Very well," she said.

The bath, drawn by an obliging maidservant, proved to be an agreeable surprise. In sharp contrast to what she was used to, the tub was large, the water deliciously warm and scented with rose petals. She enjoyed this pleasing new sensation so much that she might have remained in the bath for hours, if she hadn't recollected that Lady Dearborne was waiting for her. She wrapped herself in the silk dressing gown the maid held out for her, luxuriating in its feel.

She floated into her bedroom to see that her portmanteaus were emptied and the contents strewn about the room. Winifred was shaking her head and clucking her tongue in disgust.

"This will never do. Child, where do you get these gowns?"

"Most of them were my mother's," Phillipa said. "My great-aunt said it was a shame to waste them."

I think it was a shame to make you wear them, Winifred mused to herself, but aloud she said, "They're twenty years old at least. My dear, fashions have changed since then."

A mulish expression came into Phillipa's face. "I have no interest in fashion."

Preoccupied, Winifred did not notice. "Well, we must hasten to the dressmaker without further delay. Davies, come see which of these gowns is the closest to being presentable." She glanced at Phillipa. "It's a pity we're not of a size."

Phillipa frowned. "But why are we going to a dressmaker? I have no wish for more gowns."

Winifred sighed and put down the dress she was examining, which was spotted with age. "My dear, you must trust me when I say that you need them."

Phillipa set her jaw. "But I do not like dresses. They are uncomfortable."

Winifred picked up the heavy, ugly corset from the bed. "I daresay these are, but you will find, my dear, that times have changed."

"I do not wish to go," Phillipa said flatly.

Winifred drew herself up to her full height. "Lord Sinamor told me specifically that you were to have some new dresses."

The unspoken threat registered with Phillipa. "Very well," she said with the ungraciousness of youth, "but don't expect me to help choose them."

Winifred sighed to herself. So much for the pleasurable shopping expedition. "Help Miss Raithby on with her things, Davies. Then I shall need you."

As she went to her room, an idea occurred to her. There is one way to make Phillipa take an interest in her clothes, she thought wickedly.

Approximately an hour and a half later, a bored Phillipa sat beside Lady Dearborne in the fashionable dressmaker's salon on Oxford Street. The dressmaker had covered her surprise well upon learning that the small, drab figure was the ward of the Earl of Sinamor. Her delight was genuine, however, when she learned that Phillipa would require an entire wardrobe.

"I will tell you now," Lady Dearborne was saying in a nonchalant tone, "that Miss Raithby has kindly consented to leave the selection of her wardrobe to me, as she has little interest in fashion." Here Winifred quite startled the dressmaker by winking at her while Phillipa gazed out the window.

"Very good, Madame."

"Now, then," said Winifred, her eyes twinkling with mischief, "why don't we begin with evening dresses. Let's see, I believe pink is always appropriate for young ladies."

"But surely, Madame, with the young lady's hair—" the dressmaker was saying urgently.

"Pink," exclaimed Phillipa in a tone of disgust.

"Why, yes, dear," replied Winifred innocently, shooting a warning look at the dressmaker. "You did say you wished me to chose your dresses, didn't you?"

Phillipa turned back to the window. Winifred winked surreptitiously at the dressmaker again. "And perhaps you have something in a yellow, a buttercup possibly, something bright and cheerful."

The dressmaker, who had experience herself with sulky young ladies, now saw Winifred's object. "Ah, yes, Madame, something bright you say. I will see what we have available."

Phillipa let out a noise that could have been a snort, but vouchsafed nothing more.

The dressmaker returned with a pink muslin sprigged with little flowers and a yellow that might have been seen in the dark.

Winifred clapped her hands in delight. "Precisely the sort of thing I had in mind. Phillipa, my dear, would you let her hold those up to you so that we might see the effect?"

Phillipa's face registered horror, but the dressmaker held the materials up to her as if she didn't notice.

"Perfect," applauded Winifred. "They suit her exactly."

"Lady Dearborne," began Phillipa protestingly, but Winifred affected not to hear her.

"Do you know, I think that five, no, six layers of ruffles would give the dress . . ."

"Of course and if I could suggest, Madame, bows on the . . ."

"No," Phillipa shrieked despairingly.

The two women looked at her in surprise.

"Is something the matter, my dear?" asked Winifred blandly.

"I don't like that pink, and I don't like that yellow, and I don't want to be covered in ruffles or bows or anything else of the kind."

"Well, I certainly don't wish to make you unhappy," Winifred said reasonably. "Why don't you tell Madame Couteaux your ideas."

Interrupted in her outburst, Phillipa lapsed into startled silence. She glanced at her companion's face suspiciously, but Winifred had managed to assume an appropriately inane expression.

Somewhat mollified, Phillipa began. "First of all, I think that lavender suits me, and so does blue."

Winifred smiled to herself. There is a young woman underneath, after all, she thought.

There was at least one advantage to being the Earl of Sinamor's ward, Phillipa decided as they climbed into the fashionable landau a few hours later. Lady Dearborne had asked Madame Couteaux if there weren't any dresses that she had ready, which would be suitable. The woman had issued protestations and denials until Lady Dearborne nonchalantly mentioned how grateful the earl would be and how such a great favor might positively assure his future custom. Several dresses had been whisked out immediately, with strict promises of secrecy demanded. They had been made for a young lady in Brighton, who fortunately wouldn't be in town for another week or two. Phillipa frowned to herself. It was odd, surely, that a dressmaker should be so worried about losing a man's business. She shrugged to herself. He must have a great many female relatives.

"That's much better," Winifred pronounced, critically eyeing the white jaconet muslin gown Phillipa was wearing.

"It feels odd to me," admitted Phillipa. "This high waist, and this little blue jacket, what do you call it?"

"A spencer."

"I have not worn anything but black for so long," said Phillipa as if to herself.

Winifred smiled at her sympathetically.

They had hardly gone any distance when the carriage rumbled to a stop.

"Where are we?" asked Phillipa naively.

Winifred chuckled. "My dear, surely you didn't imagine we were finished. We've only begun. You'll need bonnets, gloves, stockings, petticoats, boots, ribbons, handkerchiefs, reticules . . ." She stopped to take a breath of air and nearly laughed aloud at the expression of dismay on Phillipa's face. "Take heart, my dear. We have to return in time for dinner."

By the time they returned to Hamilton Place that afternoon, Phillipa had used up all her reserves of energy and patience. Only a strong sense of duty had kept her acquiescently silent as she was being turned this way and that, measured from head to toe, and discussed as if she were a racehorse whose chances at Newmarket seemed uncertain. The most dismal blow fell when Lady Dearborne assured her that they would have at least as many shops to visit again on the morrow. Brooding on this injustice, she was idly examining her hand when they alighted.

"I never knew that so many measurements were necessary for everything; gloves, for example, I thought one simply bought."

Lady Dearborne smiled at her simplicity as they ascended the stairs. "I am afraid that is not the way it is done here. Why, Brummell has been known to go to two different glovemakers—one to cut the thumb and the other the fingers."

Phillipa stared at her, bemused. "Why would he do that?"

"Well, I am not advocating that you follow his example, child. He does tend to carry things to excess."

Phillipa frowned as they entered the inner hall. "Who is this Brummell person anyway, and why does everyone care what he does? Is he some relation to the Prince?"

She was unprepared for the sudden chuckle that escaped Lady Dearborne's lips. She stared at her uncomprehendingly as the impassive Bickerstaffe took their things.

Winifred searched in her reticule for a handkerchief and, finding one, dabbed at her eyes with it. "I am sorry, child," she choked apologetically. "Please have tea for both of us sent to my room, Bickerstaffe," she added, dismissing the waiting butler. She linked her arm with Phillipa as they started up the stairs. "My dear, you and I really must have a talk."

Their ascent was interrupted by the headlong dash of a tall dark-haired young man. Nearly colliding with the ladies, he halted to murmur a quick apology.

"Edmond," Winifred said with some severity, "this is Miss

Phillipa Raithby, who will be staying with us for some time. She is Sinamor's ward. Phillipa, this is my eldest son, Edmond."

Edmond, whose quick eyes had spotted the small breeches-clad figure on the stairs that morning, regarded Phillipa with some curiosity. Clearly, this girl was out of the ordinary. A small "Hmph" from his mother recalled him to himself and he made a hasty bow. "Your servant, Miss Raithby." He turned to his mother pleadingly. "I told Roger that I'd meet him and I'm already late."

"And where are you going?" she asked, noting the sparkle in his dark eyes. He hesitated. She shook her head. "Never mind, I suppose you're going to Jackson's or somewhere equally objectionable, so I'd rather not know. Be off with you, then."

He flashed them a brilliant smile, relieved at escaping so easily, and resumed his run down the stairs.

"Will you be joining us for dinner?" his mother called after him.

"I think not," he yelled as he was disappearing through the doorway.

Winifred heaved a little sigh, then they turned and made their way to her room. The tea tray arrived shortly, loaded with hot buns and cakes. It was wonderful how Phillipa's sense of grievance diminished with each bite. She was beginning to feel quite cheerful when her companion put down her teacup and said, "If you are through, Phillipa, I shall ring for Davies. We need to decide what's to be done with your hair."

"My hair!"

"Yes, my dear," Winifred said somewhat absently. "Sinamor and his friend Mr. St. Clair are coming to dinner this evening, so you will wish to look your best."

Phillipa just managed to stifle the protest that was rising to her lips. She drew in a deep breath and let it out angrily. "Lady Dearborne," she said, "I appreciate what you have done for me, whether or not it is all necessary. I will make every effort to try to be what you wish, but if you imagine that I am doing all this in order to make a good impression on the earl, you are sadly mistaken. I could not have a lower opinion of . . ."

She halted in the midst of her speech, stricken by the look

on Winifred's face. "I am sorry," she choked. "I had forgotten that he is your relative."

There was a moment of silence. Winifred then nodded her head slightly. "It is all right," she said wearily. "Your opinion unfortunately is shared by more than one person."

She looked at Phillipa with sadness in her eyes. "I know that there is much that is objectionable in his character. I believe it to be the fault of a disastrous upbringing. If you could have known him, as I did, when he was a boy, a loving, sensitive, proud and lonely boy."

She shook her head, as if to dismiss the remembrances. She gazed at Phillipa earnestly. "My dear, please do not judge him on such short acquaintance. His life has not been a happy one." She hesitated, but something in Phillipa's face made her continue. "It is not for me to give you the particulars now, but I do know that he is making every effort to do his best for you. He feels a sincere obligation to your father's memory."

The words reminded Phillipa of her interview with the earl that morning. She dropped her head. Blushing with shame, she said, "I know. Thank you. I apologize."

Winifred flew to her and put her arms around her. "There's no need for that, child." She lifted Phillipa's chin and gazed into the rapidly filling eyes. "Just be kind to him, and then he can't help but be kind to you."

Phillipa nodded, sniffing.

Winifred smiled at her. "I'll ring for Davies now, then."

Unbeknownst to Phillipa, just a few short blocks away in Berkeley Square the subject of her recent conversation was busy discussing her.

"And that's the entire story," the earl was concluding as he took the glass from St. Clair's hand and proceeded to replenish it from a crystal decanter. "I am in the devil of a fix."

St. Clair curled his lips slightly, but it would have been difficult to say whether it was out of sympathy or amusement. "I will admit that it sounds a bit ticklish, but surely things could be worse, after all? With your *savoir-faire*, you should be able to contrive some way to carry this thing off creditably."

The earl shook his head. "But I have not told you about the chief obstacle, which is the girl herself. Putting aside the difficulties, the unsuitability of my guardianship for a moment, I really have not the slightest idea how the creature could be launched successfully. She is insignificant-looking, possesses a foul temper, and on top of that is as contrary as a mule."

"My dear Sinamor, she can't be as bad as all that."

"Wait, I haven't even informed you of the worst. Would you believe that the chit had the effrontery to tell me that she did not wish me for a guardian?"

"No!"

"What's more, she said she didn't wish an introduction to society if I were an example of what she might expect to meet!"

The earl stared at him, nonplussed.

St. Clair was obliged to cough into his handkerchief for a moment in order to disguise a chuckle. "Really, my dear fellow, that was too bad of her. It must have been quite a shock to you."

"To find a female that did not find the Sinamor charm irresisitible, I mean," added St. Clair. "It must be an unnerving experience."

The earl sipped from his own glass moodily. "Ah, well you may laugh at me if you wish, but I doubt you'll be laughing after spending your dinner hour with this termagant."

St. Clair contrived to keep a straight face. "Well, if she's truly as contrary as you say, she may find my charm irresistible."

The earl snorted in an unkindly way. "Not very likely . . . unless you wish to discuss the finer points of horse-breeding with her."

"Certainly not!" St. Clair's shocked tone was not mirrored by his thoughtful expression.

The earl was due for a surprise that evening, thought Lady Dearborne as she observed her work with satisfaction. "I think perhaps, just a touch of powder on the nose. There." She turned to her handmaiden. "You have worked wonders, Davies."

"Thank you, my lady."

"Come, Phillipa." Winifred drew her charge toward a mirror. "See how pretty you are."

Phillipa looked into the mirror and started in surprise. Her long, often unruly hair had been brushed to a satin smoothness and was caught up artfully on the top of her head. A great wave on either side of her face served to lessen the severity of the coiffure while subtly emphasizing the delicate bone structure of the face. The sapphire-blue evening dress she wore brought out the luminous color of her eyes. The gown had an extremely high waist and revealed more décolletage than the old-fashioned dresses Phillipa had always worn. The skill of the designer was evident in the deceptive simplicity with which it suggested her youthful curves. A fashionable, artistocratic, and decidedly striking young lady gazed back at Phillipa from the mirror. She put a hand to her face as if to ascertain that the dazzling creature in the mirror was really herself.

Winifred fussed about her, adjusting the gown. "Of course, I really did not expect Davies to crop your hair; everyone seems to be wearing theirs long now. I must confess I was shocked, though, when she insisted that you must not wear ringlets. She was absolutely right, though, as always, weren't you, Davies?"

"I am grateful that my lady condescends to say so."

"Nonsense. You are a genius, Davies. Simplicity. That is the key to Phillipa's appearance. And this gown, it might have been made for her."

Davies surveyed Phillipa with a critical eye. "I think it is very well, my lady. The young lady will do you credit."

"Thank you, Davies," Winifred said, dismissing her. Unexpectedly, she winked at Phillipa. "That's high praise indeed, coming from Davies."

Her altered appearance gave Phillipa new confidence,but it did not keep her from feelings of trepidation when the earl's name was announced. She was only too aware of what she had been wearing the last time they met. She took a deep breath, straightened herself, and began to descend the stairs regally.

St. Clair's eyes widened in surprise. His lips curled slightly and he whispered to his friend, "You have wronged the girl shamefully, Sinamor."

If Phillipa noticed his presence, she gave no sign of it. Her eyes were on the earl. He maintained his silence but betrayed his surprise by the quick ascent of the famous eyebrow. Phillipa read his astonishment in his face and it gave her an extra measure of self-assurance. She reached the two gentlemen, wished them good evening in dulcet tones, then gazed at the earl with a hint of reproof.

Recalled from his stupefaction, the earl hastily performed introductions. "Miss Phillipa Raithby, my friend, Mr. Aristophanes St. Clair. St. Clair, my ward, Miss Raithby."

Phillipa coolly extended a gloved hand to St. Clair. "How do you do?"

He bent over it and kissed it. "Your devoted servant, Miss Raithby."

She looked inquiringly at him. "Such an unusual name."

He smiled at her. "My father was bookish, a vice that fortunately I lack."

She let out a low, silvery laugh that further surprised the earl. He frowned suddenly to himself.

"And if you will permit me, I must say that I am delighted to be dining with such an exceptionally lovely young lady," added St. Clair.

She was thanking him demurely when Lady Winifred joined them. Winifred had deliberately delayed her arrival, so that she might observe the earl's reactions without interruption. She had been well-pleased with his look of surprise, and was even more delighted with his frown. She greeted them all cheerfully, then turned to St. Clair with twinkling eyes. "I see that you and Phillipa already have become acquainted. I am so glad. I hope that Sinamor warned you that this was just to be a small family party."

His lips quirked into a smile, which he rapidly repressed. He met her eyes with understanding in his. "Nothing could be more delightful than to have two such charming ladies entirely to ourselves."

She laughed, shaking her head as she did so. "Oh, you are a shameless flatterer, St. Clair." She turned to the earl, noting with satisfaction that his frown had not diminished. "Therefore, I will ask you to escort me into dinner, Sinamor."

He took her arm with less than his accustomed grace, leaving St. Clair to follow with Phillipa.

The earl's conversation also lacked its usual sparkle that evening, for he kept being distracted by Phillipa's musical laugh. He could not imagine what she and St. Clair could find to discuss, and particularly with such animation. He did think it was ill-bred of St. Clair not to turn his attention to Lady Winifred halfway through dinner. His gaze kept reeturning to Phillipa again and again. Could this be the same hoyden whom he had caught riding in the park this morning in a pair of breeches? And St. Clair, why, he seemed to be positively enjoying himself.

Winifred intercepted his gaze and smiled at him. "Phillipa is looking well tonight, isn't she?"

He managed to contrive one of his cool smiles. "You have worked a miracle, Win. I would never have believed it."

She smiled again to herself. "Most of the credit must go to Phillipa. I must admit that I was surprised myself by the taste she exhibited when choosing her gowns. She seems to have an instinctive understanding of what best suits her own personal—how shall I say it?—style."

Involuntarily, he glanced again at Phillipa. "St. Clair certainly seems taken with her."

"She does seem to amuse him, and he her," said Winifred with a straight face. "It is marvelous that you brought him. She needs experience in dealing with a man of the world. And St. Clair is friend enough that he would not expose her little gaucheries to public ridicule."

The earl did not seem to have heard the last part of her statement. "I do not wish her to have too much experience in dealing with a man of the world."

A little chuckle escaped Winifred. He glanced at her. "I am afraid, my dear, that you are beginning to sound like a guardian. Which reminds me, Phillipa has something to discuss with you after dinner."

When dinner was concluded, therefore, St. Clair made his graceful farewells, praising his hostess's hospitality as well as the company. Pressing Winifred's hand privately, he told her, "I think that Miss Raithby will prove to be an unqualified success. She is an original."

Winifred's face lit up. "How kind of you to say so."

"You know that I always do my best to make my predictions come true."

After his departure, Winifred retired discreetly. The earl then followed Phillipa into the green salon. At the sight of that icy countenance, she felt her courage dissipating. There was a moment of awkward silence. The earl was the first to break it.

"You seem to have had a fruitful day."

"Yes, my lord."

"Apparently you liked St. Clair."

"Yes, my lord." Phillipa felt like a stupid schoolgirl, but she could not think of anything to add.

"You found a great deal to talk about."

Phillipa kept silent for variety's sake.

He strolled over to the mantelpiece and drummed his fingers upon it in an elaborately casual way. "Did you discuss anything in particular?"

Phillipa's forehead furrowed with thought. "Only . . . horses, my lord. And he told me about Tattersall's and Newmarket and . . ." She shook her head and began to laugh. "And then he told me some very silly stories about people that . . ." Her laugh died in her throat as she met the earl's cold eyes. "That was all, my lord."

He drummed his fingers more rapidly this time, then stopped suddenly. "I understand there is a matter you wish to discuss with me."

She dropped her eyes. "Lady Dearborne said that I should."

"Well?"

She summoned her courage. "I am in the habit of riding out every morning, and Lady Dearborne said that as long as I went early, so as not to encounter anyone, and took a groom, that it would do no harm." She glanced up at his forbidding expression and turned scarlet with embarrassment. "I have a proper riding habit now," she said. There was a moment or two of silence. "Lady Dearborne said that I must have your permission." The word almost choked her. "Please, my lord, please may I go?" She looked up at him anxiously.

He tilted his chin up, consideringly, then dropped it. His words startled her. "Very well, but I will accompany you, to make sure that you meet with no mischief." He looked at her. "Is that acceptable?"

A wave of relief swept over Phillipa. "Yes, my lord. Thank you."

He nodded curtly. "If that is all, then, I will see you at half-past seven. If you will excuse me, I must make my farewells to Lady Dearborne." He left the room abruptly.

Phillipa was left to marvel at her good fortune. She had expected to be forbidden all such pleasures for months at the very least. Could it be that the earl was not such a monster as she had decided? Certainly Winifred was correct in how to handle him. Phillipa thought of those cold eyes and shivered to herself. I still cannot like him, she thought.

4

"Pshaw!" The word exploded from Phillipa's mouth. Her eyes glittered dangerously as she surveyed the docile gray mare that stood saddled before her.

The earl's eyebrow ascended. "Did you say something, Phillipa?" he asked in an icily polite manner.

She swallowed hard. "No, my lord," she murmured. She was the epitome of an elegant lady of fashion this morning in an amber-colored riding habit, which would have become few women and yet made the luster of her hair and her creamy complexion seem even richer. The bodice of the habit was braided in the military style, which had become popular with the czar's arrival. That influence was also apparent in the dashing hat that completed the ensemble. The earl had little time to admire this picture, though, for a small hand in amber-colored Limerick gloves was twirling a whip angrily.

"My dear," said the earl unexpectedly. "You had only to tell me that you had never ridden a sidesaddle before. Naturally, it is disconcerting."

"What?" said Phillipa incredulously.

"I could arrange for lessons for you. My groom is rather good at—"

"What!" exclaimed Phillipa, outraged.

"Well, of course it would be difficult for you on your first attempt. I don't blame you a bit for being frightened."

A swirl of amber-colored cloth settled itself on the mare's back. "I have ridden since I was born," said Phillipa, her face white with anger. "I have ridden without a saddle or a bridle, just a halter, nothing more. How dare you say that I would be frightened?"

The earl gave her his quelling look. "Obviously I was mistaken. Shall we go?"

Still seething with inner fury, Phillipa nodded curtly and wheeled her horse toward the street. Her indignation at being given such a placid mount was exacerbated by the fact that she'd been given no opportunity to object to it. She glanced enviously at her companion, who was astride the same magnificent black that he'd ridden the day before. If she had Ripon here, she could show him that she knew a thing or two about horses.

Ripon. She felt a stab of pain as she thought of him. It hadn't been quite a week, and yet she missed him dreadfully. She had tried every argument she knew to be allowed to bring him, but reluctantly she had been convinced that it was impossible. When she had bid a tearful farewell to Mrs. Abbot this morning, she had charged her with the task of reporting how Ripon was doing.

That good woman had been a little indignant. "Now, Miss Phillipa, you know that there is no one better with horses than Mr. McPherson. He looks after them as if they were his children, especially that devil of yours. So let's have no more of that nonsense, if you please."

Phillipa sighed to herself. It had been hard to let go of that last tie with home, particularly since Mrs. Abbot had been almost a mother to her.

"Phillipa." She was startled out of her reverie by the earl's voice. She looked up to see that they had reached the park. He indicated to her that they might quicken their pace. She nodded, gathered her reins, and with a suggestion from her heels, the mare broke into a gentle canter. There was not a possibility of taking this horse over a fallen tree, thought Phillipa regretfully.

Unbeknownst to Phillipa, the earl was studying her covertly. He had to admit that she had surpassed his expectations for her. If he did not believe, as did his friend St. Clair, that she would be a sensation, he did at least accept that she would meet with some success. If only he could make that hoydenish interior conform to the ladylike exterior. The earl was not deceived by her silence. He knew she inwardly was cursing him for saddling her with such a spiritless animal. He had to admit that his ruse with the sidesaddle had worked rather well. She definitely was undermounted. Well, he'd see that she had a proper horse when she could be trusted not to set it into a run whenever she felt like it.

The ride passed with little incident and less conversation. They returned to Hamilton Place quietly. An eager groom seized the reins of Phillipa's horse as she prepared to dismount. At that same moment, a door opened and a small, naked figure burst from the house, running as fast as his short legs would carry him. Without a moment's hesitation, Phillipa ran over to scoop the escapee up in her arms. She found herself being regarded reproachfully by a pair of brown eyes.

The earl materialized at her side. "Ah, I believe that is the youngest scion of the house," he breathed.

The child began to struggle in her arms, and without ceremony the earl took him from her. He had begun to carry his writhing burden limpingly to the house when two more boys exploded from the door. Seeing Sinamor, they began to cavort about, pointing and yelling.

"Here he is! Here he is! See, Rose, he's over here. They caught him."

A harassed-looking nursemaid then charged from the door, head down. "Now, Master William and Master Anthony, I see him. Please be more quiet, you'll wake up the neighbors." Her eyes widened when she saw Sinamor bearing her charge. "My lord!"

A pair of brown eyes now turned reproachfully to the earl's. "But I don't want a bath," said a small, plaintive voice.

The nursemaid swept Sinamor a hasty curtsy and took Arthur from his arms. "I apologize, my lord."

Phillipa swept forward delightedly. "Are you all Lady Dearborne's boys?"

"I don't want a bath," repeated Arthur stubbornly.

The oldest boy, who looked about eight, took charge. "I am William," he said, bowing hastily, "and that is Anthony, he's six, and Arthur is the baby, he's only three."

A voice came from behind Phillipa. "And this is Miss Phillipa Raithby, my new ward," said Sinamor.

The boys began to mutter their how-do-you-dos when Arthur

interrupted the proceedings. *"I don't want a bath,"* he exclaimed in piercing accents.

Phillipa walked over to him. "Do you like to play spillikins?" she asked him seriously.

Arthur put a finger in his mouth thoughtfully. "Yes?" he replied questioningly.

"Well, if you take your bath like a big boy, you and I shall have a game today," Phillipa said solemnly.

His eyes widened and he stopped struggling in his nursemaid's arms. She bore him off unresisting to his bath.

Phillipa turned to the other brothers. They both had the dark eyes and dark curls, which were apparently characteristic of the family, and both promised to have their older brother's height.

"I met Edmond yesterday. Do you have any other brothers?"

"There's Francis, but he's at Eton," said William.

"Do you play battledore too?" asked Anthony speculatively.

She laughed an affirmative, then turned to the earl, as if she had forgotten his presence. "You will excuse us, my lord. We have important matters to which we must attend." Sinamor was amazed once again at how a smile could transform that face. "Thank you for our ride today," she added, and with the boys in tow, she disappeared through the door.

The earl only rarely had been dismissed so efficiently. He stood like stone for a moment, before a quick grin quirked one side of his mouth. He strode back to his horse and took the reins from the respectful groom. He swung himself into the saddle, clucked to his horse, and headed toward home. St. Clair was right, he thought. She is an original.

Phillipa was not to enjoy the pleasure of her new companions for long, however. A maid curtsied to her as soon as she stepped inside, and told her that her bath had been drawn, in accordance with Lady Winifred's order. "She also told me to ask which derss you wished to wear today for your shopping, the dotted muslin or the green sprigged?"

Phillipa made her choice, promised the boys that she would join them after the shopping expedition, and turned wearily to ascend the stairs. There is much more work to being a lady of fashion than I realized, she thought.

The shopping proved every bit as tiring as the day before, though, if Phillipa had analyzed her feelings, she might have realized that it was a trifle less boring. In any case, by the time that she and Lady Dearborne returned in the afternoon, both were exhausted. Winifred rang for tea immediately and the two settled themselves comfortably in the green salon.

Their *tête-à-tête* was interrupted when Edmond entered, greeted them casually, and lifted a cake from the tea tray. He threw himself down on the sofa and munched on the cake.

"Please, Edmond," said his mother. "I was hoping to deceive Phillipa into thinking that we were a well-bred family."

"Sorry." He straightened up and continued to nibble on the cake.

"Where have you been today?" asked his mother, pouring him a cup of tea.

"Over to Fitzroy's. He has a horse he wants me to buy."

Winifred sighed. "I wish you could wait until your father can help you."

"He doesn't have much time to spare," Edmond said without bitterness. "Besides, you needn't worry about my buying Fitzroy's nag. I wouldn't have that spavined brute if he gave it to me."

The conversation was interrupted by a footman. "Miss Marianne Middleton to see Miss Phillipa Raithby."

Phillipa was completely puzzled.

Lady Dearborne let out an unladylike snort of disgust. "She's a distant cousin of Sinamor's," Winifred said, "and doubtless is hoping to catch him here, or at least see what competition you are."

Phillipa found these words similarly enigmatic.

"Well, I suppose we have no choice. She'll undoubtedly hound us otherwise. Encroaching creature. Show her in, Frederick."

"Very good, my lady."

In a moment, in fluttered a vision in pink muslin, ornamented in ribbons, bows, and ruffles. Beneath the chip-straw bonnet clustered dark curls, framing a pretty dark-eyed face. The skin was spotless, the nose retroussé, the mouth a pouting rosebud. Phillipa detested her on sight.

"I'm sorry for interrupting your tea," whispered Marianne in a voice that was pitched artificially high. "I was out shopping when I heard that Sinamor had a new ward, and I just couldn't wait to greet her."

Winifred frowned. She didn't wish to invite the girl to stay, but she had little choice. "Won't you join us for tea, Miss Middleton?"

"I am sorry, but I can't take the time." Marianne smiled suddenly, revealing pearly-white teeth. "But this must be Miss Raithby." She flew to Phillipa and bestowed an unwelcoming hug on her. "I know we'll be the closest of friends," she said. "You must call me Marianne and I will call you Phillipa."

Phillipa, taken aback by this unexpected intimacy, could think of nothing to say.

Marianne released her and stood, staring brightly down at her. "How attractive you are! What attention we shall draw when we walk down the street together."

"Please have a seat, Miss Middleton," said Winifred dryly.

"Well, just for a moment, thank you, Lady Dearborne," said Marianne. She settled herself into a chair and looked at Edmond in an arch way. "It's so nice to see your handsome son here, too."

Edmond turned beet-red and murmured something awkward by way of a reply.

Marianne turned her attention back to Phillipa. "You're so fortunate to have a young man of fashion to escort you places. I would say that I wish I could say the same, but then Sinamor has been very good about escorting me." She looked at Phillipa smugly.

Despite Marianne's initial disclaimer, it was well over an hour before she finally took her leave. Edmond discourteously had disappeared and even Winifred's patience was beginning to wear thin. Phillipa had remained ominously mute, for the most part.

As soon as Marianne had left, Winifred rebuked Phillipa gently. "It would have been well-mannered of you to have spoken up a bit more, Phillipa, to have indicated more of an interest in Miss Middleton's conversation."

Phillipa scowled. "She didn't seem to notice, besides, I couldn't think of anything *polite* to say to her."

"Phillipa!"

"Well, young ladies never like me. When I went to parties at home, they used to laugh at me."

Winifred frowned. "Phillipa, when you learn what we are trying to teach you, there will be no one who will laugh at you," she said with great seriousness.

"But you saw how she did her best to put me in my place—"

"That does not excuse your behavior," Winifred said gently. "A great part of getting along in polite society consists of learning to be agreeable to people of whom you're not overly fond."

Phillipa sighed resignedly. "Yes, Lady Dearborne." A sudden thought occurred to her, bringing an expression of alarm to her face. "That doesn't mean I actually have to go out walking with her, does it?"

Winifred hid a smile. "No, I would not expect so great a sacrifice of you."

Their conversation was interrupted when Winifred's youngest child materialized in the doorway.

"Phillipa," he said accusingly, "you promised."

Phillipa's eyes widened. "The spillikins—I forgot! Pray excuse me, Lady Dearborne. Arthur and I have an important engagement."

She took Arthur's hand and they marched together from the room, leaving a bemused Lady Dearborne to wonder when Arthur and Phillipa had become acquainted.

If Phillipa imagined that all her pleasures already had been curtailed, a further blow awaited her the next morning. She awakened to a steady downpour of rain which eliminated the possibility for her morning ride. Chafing at the thought of spending the day indoors, her spirits sank as the morning progressed with no sign of the rain's ceasing.

Winifred did her best to comfort her. "You mustn't let this weather cast your spirits down," she told Phillipa. "Why the sun may be shining beautifully tomorrow morning.''

Phillipa responded only with a hopeless little sigh.

''You told me that you play the pianoforte,'' Winifred reminded her. ''Today might be an excellent opportunity for you to begin practicing again.''

Abruptly, Phillipa's eyes lit up as a notion of how to escape this confinement came to her.

''Lady Dearborne,'' she said ingratiatingly, ''that is an excellent suggestion, but I will need to purchase some music. Perhaps we could go out and buy some.''

Winifred thought that Phillipa must be desperate indeed to ask to go shopping; but she supposed that to her protégée buying music might seem more entertaining than buying clothes. ''I'm sorry, my dear,'' she said, ''but I am expecting a visit this morning from one of my friends, and I need to ask some important advice of her.''

''Oh.'' Phillipa sank her chin onto one hand and gazed unhappily at the rain driving against the window.

Her reverie was interrupted by the arrival of Edmond, clearly dressed for an outing, despite the inclement weather. ''Mama,'' he said, ''if it will not inconvenience you, I would like to use the carriage as I must take care of some errands today.''

Phillipa turned to him, a gleam of hope in her eyes. ''Edmond,'' she said, ''where are you going?''

Surprised by this unprecedented interest, he replied, ''Why to Bond Street. I have to stop in at the hatter's and—''

Phillipa fairly beamed at him. ''May I go with you? Please?''

Startled, Edmond did not know what to reply.

''Please?'' Phillipa asked. ''I won't be any trouble.'' Her sapphire eyes were wide and imploring.

''Phillipa—'' began Winifred warningly but the eager girl cut her off.

''I could stay in the carriage,'' she said imploringly, ''and perhaps if we have time, we might be able to stop and buy my music.'' The pleading eyes had not wavered from Edmond's face.

''Phillipa, I don't think it would be—'' began Winifred again, but this time it was Edmond who interrupted her.

"She can go if she wants to so badly," he said, uncomfortably aware of Phillipa's gaze. "I daresay it will be a bore for her, but she's welcome for all that."

Winifred frowned. "Edmond, are you sure?"

He saw the unspoken worry in his mother's eyes but shrugged it off. "It's only a carriage ride, after all."

Phillipa had spun about to look eagerly at Winifred, who found those eyes as difficult to resist as Edmond did. "Chappell and Company, the music publishers are located in Bond Street," she admitted reluctantly.

Phillipa beamed at her.

"But you will need some sort of companion," said Winifred, pointing out an obstacle. Phillipa's face fell. Winifred sighed. "Well, I suppose I can spare Davies," she said.

"It will take me just a minute to get my bonnet and pelisse," said Phillipa eagerly, leaping up from the sofa.

It was two hours later that a bored Phillipa found herself sitting in the Dearborne's landau in Bond Street. They had stopped at Edmond's tailor's establishment. Edmond had explained that all he needed was a final fitting on his new tailcoat. Phillipa could not imagine why such a simple operation should take well over an hour. The rain having lessened somewhat, she suggested to Davies that they take a stroll down the street. The lady's maid had rejected this suggestion with something approaching horror. Thus rebuffed, Phillipa's only option was to gaze dully out at the empty, wet streets.

Unexpectedly, a girl's shriek caught her attention and she turned her gaze to see a fracas erupting down the street. A young girl had issued from a milliner's shop and was having her ears soundly boxed by a man twice her size. He was berating her as he beat her and Phillipa could hear his words clearly.

"You're lucky I don't have you thrown into Brideswell, a young thieving wench," he was yelling. He staggered her with another punch for emphasis.

Aghast, Phillipa had half-risen out of her seat.

"Please sir," the girl was sobbing. "I don't know what happened to the lace. I left it on the table last night."

"A likely story. You probably slipped out and sold it instead."

Phillipa was out of the carriage and running down the street before Davies had time to realize what was happening.

The girl had fallen to her knees. "I swear I didn't, sir. I'm an honest girl. Please, you must believe me."

His next blow, delivered with a vicious sort of pleasure, sent her sprawling in the mud and filth of the street. He was standing over her with a self-satisfied smile on his face when a small fury materialized in front of him.

"How could you be so cruel?" Phillipa knelt beside the girl in the street, who now was bleeding profusely from a split lip.

The man took in her expensive attire and apparently unchaperoned state and drew his own conclusions. "Mind your own business, fancy-piece." He drew menacingly near to the girl again.

Phillipa rose to her full if diminutive height. "How dare you!"

The man pushed her aside with one arm, as he made ready to go after his helpless victim once again.

"Miss Phillipa!" Davies was drawing near to her charge when a most remarkable thing happened. The big man, who had pushed Phillipa aside a moment earlier, now lay stretched out upon the ground. Phillipa herself was extending a hand to the weeping girl in the street.

"Miss Phillipa," Davies tugged urgently at her sleeve, "we must go."

Ignoring her, Phillipa was helping the pitiful victim to her feet. "Are you all right?" she asked.

The girl, shaking her head, could not stop crying. "He owes me three weeks' wages. Oh, what am I to do now? How will I ever find another position?"

"Phillipa." Edmond had appeared beside the group. His face shone with enthusiasm. "I was just coming out of the tailor's when—I say, what a scientific blow. You have a punishing right—"

"Mr. Edmond," Davies directed her appeal to him. "We must leave." She glanced about them significantly.

Edmond saw a curtain being opened in the window above them. He paled. "You're right!"

He took Phillipa's other arm. "We have to go *now*, Phillipa or there'll be the devil to pay!"

Phillipa's only concern was for the girl she had rescued.

"I don't even have enough money to return home," said the girl. "Where will I go? Who will ever hire me now?"

Phillipa looked at Edmond. "We cannot go and leave her here."

Edmond pulled at her. "We must—dash it, Phillipa—we must go now!"

Phillipa planted her feet and stared at him squarely. "I won't go without her."

"We've no time to argue."

"You heard her—she has nowhere to go."

He looked about him and saw a curious face peeping out the window. He decided upon the lesser of two evils. "Then take her, but we must go now!"

Fortunately, Winifred's company had departed by the time Edmond and Phillipa returned home. Edmond, since the outing had been under his aegis, decided that he must be the one to apprise Winifred of the mishap. It was to him, therefore, that Winifred was indebted for a highly colorful account of the proceedings. Though he did not attempt to minimize the gravity of the incident, in his admiration for Phillipa's pugilistic prowess, he so far forgot himself as to introduce several sporting expressions which earned him Winifred's reproof.

"I am surprised at you, Edmond," Winifred told him with some severity. "This is not Jackson's saloon."

"Yes, Mama." He hung his head shamefacedly.

"There is no telling what harm may have been caused," she told him seriously. "Phillipa involved in a public brawl, and in Bond Street, of all places. Why, if the whole world doesn't know by tomorrow, I shall be amazed."

"Yes, Mama." He lifted his eyes to venture a timid comment. "Fortunately, with the rain, there was hardly anyone about—"

"It would take only one."

"I did not see anyone that I knew, and Phillipa had on her bonnet, which covered most of her face."

Winifred shook her head. "None of this excuses you, Edmond. Phillipa was *your* responsibility."

"Yes, Mama." To his credit, Edmond made no attempt to shift the blame from himself.

Winifred sighed as she looked at the silent figure, standing with head bowed before her. "Very well, then, you may go. Have Phillipa sent in to me."

"Yes, Mama." He took a step, then halted at the door. "I am sorry, Mama, but if I had been there, I am not sure I would have wanted to stop Phillipa. The brute was twice the girl's size and he was thrashing her unmercifully."

Winifred froze him with a look. "It was none of our affair." She relaxed slightly. "There are more civilized ways to handle such matters," she reminded him gently.

"Yes, Mama." He exited the room and in a few moments Phillipa entered, a look of anxiety upon her face. Her eyes were moist but her chin was resolute.

"I apologize to you for creating a scene today, Lady Dearborne," Phillipa said. Her chin went up a fraction of an inch. "But I'm not sorry I did it!"

"It's your own reputation you will have injured by your actions, not mine," Winifred said in an unusually stern voice.

In spite of herself, a tear slipped down Phillipa's cheek. She wiped it away angrily. "I don't care for that!"

"And I don't suppose you care how it will reflect on your guardian, or how it will affect your late father's wishes for your future."

More tears were joining the first volunteer. Phillipa rummaged awkwardly in her reticule for a handkerchief. After a few moments, Winifred took pity on her and offered Phillipa her own. This act of kindness crumbled Phillipa's last defenses. She broke into sobs. Winifred brought her over to the sofa and sat her down. She patted the girl's back while Phillipa wept into her shoulder.

At length, Phillipa raised her head and gasped out her words. "I am so sorry," she said. "I did not wish to bring trouble upon any of you. It's just that . . . I never have been able to bear to see anything or anyone used so cruelly." She lifted tear-stained eyes to Winifred. "If you could have seen them. Why he was enjoying pummelling her. And she's smaller than I am even, and so thin."

"I can understand your feelings," said Winifred. "But ladies do not indulge in fisticuffs, and particularly not on public thoroughfares."

Phillipa's eyes fell. "I know," she said softly. "It's this horrible temper of mine." The tears began to slip down her cheeks again. "I know I have disgraced you and the earl. I suppose he will hate me for what I did today, too."

"No one hates you," Winifred said, "least of all Sinamor." She hesitated for a moment before continuing. "He is concerned about you, and he has reason to be. I have not told you before, but Sinamor's reputation—well, it is not all that it should be."

"I knew that," Phillipa said calmly, before blowing her nose soundly. "Father told me, and he also said that I was to pay no attention to that, for the earl was a fine person."

Winifred managed to conceal her surprise and continue. "You can understand Sinamor's position then. Because you are *his* ward, there will be talk. He knows that you must be doubly circumspect in order to avoid gossip."

She could see the light dawning in Phillipa's face. "Is that why he scolded me so after that first ride in the park?"

"Yes."

Phillipa blew her nose again, reflectively. "That makes it a good deal easier to bear. Thank you, Lady Dearborne."

Winifred took her hand and patted it lovingly. "Phillipa, I know you are capable of making us all proud of you. You made a great impression on St. Clair, who is not easy to please. He predicted you would be a sensation."

"He did?" asked Phillipa, puzzled. "I will try," she added seriously.

5

When the earl arrived for an unexpected visit, Winifred lost no time in acquainting him with the incident.

''Honestly, Evelyn, I do not know how she does it. One moment I was scolding her for being so wayward and the next I was agreeing to let the girl she rescued remain here.''

The earl's famous eyebrow shot upward. ''An accused thief? Really, Win!''

She tried to look as if she had been imposed upon and failed. ''Well, I must agree with Phillipa that it sounds like nonsense. If they really thought she had stolen from them, why wouldn't they call in the authorities? No, it seems likely that they were only trying to evade paying her for her labor.''

As Sinamor's face retained a disbelieving expression, she added heatedly, ''You should have seen her, Evelyn. So small and pinched-looking, and scared half out of her wits, with her lip bleeding and her dress muddied, and—''

She caught a suspicious twinkle in his eyes and continued defiantly. ''The child can't be more than fourteen. Fresh from the country, too, with a large family she was trying to help support. So when Phillipa asked if she might keep her as her maid—''

''Rather young for a maid, isn't she, then?'' interjected Sinamor provocatively.

Somewhat flustered, Winifred stammered. ''You're right, of course, but I thought that it could do no harm for a while. And Davies offered to help instruct her''—here she frowned at the thought—''which I must say, surprised me a great deal. I suppose Phillipa had been to work on her, too.''

Sinamor let out a little chuckle. ''Personally, I think that Phillipa is not the only soft-hearted one in this house.''

"Well, you needn't find it all so amusing," said Winifred crossly. "I don't know how we shall contrive to pass it all off."

"I don't imagine that there will be any trouble about that, as long as Edmond acted as quickly as he said he did," replied Sinamor. "Do you wish me to speak to Phillipa?"

"I . . . yes . . . no, that is, I suppose not," said Winifred. She let out a sigh. "I think she is truly repentant, though heaven knows what sort of mischief she'll land in next."

Tactfully, the earl changed the subject. "The reason for my visit, Win, is that I realized that we must engage tutors for Phillipa and I wished to have your recommendations."

"I've anticipated you, my dear. I spent much of the morning conferring with my friend Penelope Ashling, asking for her suggestions. The dancing master will be here tomorrow."

"You seem to have thought of it all."

"Yes, I've also engaged a drawing master, and a music-teacher. I thought that a French tutor also might be useful."

He strode over to her and kissed her hand. "I'm glad that one of us, at least, has some forethought."

Having concluded that his presence would do little to further his ward's progress, the earl chose to absent himself from Hamilton Place. Though he punctually kept his riding appointment with Phillipa, he had no other contact with her or the Dearbornes.

So, for the next few days, Sinamor returned to his former pursuits. He was to be found tooling his curricle expertly about town, practicing his marksmanship at Manton's, looking over a likely pair at Tattersall's, or ordering a new pair of boots from Hoby's. The more questionable of his activities he had curtailed for the period of his guardianship. Phillipa was not the only one who needed to be circumspect.

It was only to be expected, therefore, that he should be found at the Countess Dumonde's rout. It was perhaps unfortunate that he had only just arrived when the Baroness Serre was announced. He turned to see Helene being escorted into the room by a somewhat elderly but very wealthy peer. He made her a very cold, small bow and she inclined her head frostily in his direction. He turned to make his way down the marbled staircase, but had some difficulty limping through the jostling crowd. Somehow they were momentarily thrust together, and in such proximity that they could not avoid speaking. They greeted each other with cool good evenings. There was silence for a moment before they saw they were momentarily trapped. Helene spoke first.

"I understand that your lordship has a new ward. How I shall look forward to conversing with her," whispered the baroness, her eyes glittering with malice.

The earl took a moment to see that everyone in the immediate vicinity seemed absorbed by their own conversations. "I should think that an unlikely eventuality."

"Why, pray tell, my lord?" Helene hissed.

"Because there is still the matter of the necklace, my lady," he said coldly.

At the same moment, the crowd opened up and he stepped away as Helene's admirer came rushing up. "I thought I had lost you, my dear," he said tenderly.

Helene turned to him with a brittle smile, concealing the rage she felt. She had wanted to tell Sinamor what he could do with the necklace. Fortunately, common sense told her that it was never wise to turn down expensive jewelry, and she had restrained herself. She had been furious when she heard the gossip about his ward, especially when it had been intimated that she had been rejected for a schoolgirl. She wondered now if Sinamor's dismissal of her had been as unpremeditated as she had once thought. I'll get to the bottom of this, she thought, and you shall pay, Sinamor, you shall pay.

Her escort again claimed her attention and they began to make their way through the crowds.

It was some hours later when St. Clair discovered Sinamor at one of the card tables at White's. Catching the earl's eyes, he swept him a gravely mocking bow.

"When your lordship is finished fleecing these gentlemen, I would be honored to have the pleasure of your company."

Young Charles Fitzroy looked astounded at this jesting statement. How could anyone have the audacity to address the Earl of Sinamor in that fashion?"

Lord Ashe caught the bewilderment in the young man's face

and smiled. He leaned over to whisper to him, "These literary fellows get away with a great deal. The rest of us dare not take such liberties."

Sinamor responded with only a flickering glance from his cold blue eyes and with the languid wave of a finger. It was an hour and a half before he rose from the table and went to join his friend.

"A bad night?" he asked St. Clair flatly.

"What indelicate questions you ask," replied St. Clair, amused. "However, you may buy us a bottle of port."

"I already have," said the earl, seating himself with careless grace. "It's not my affair if you wish to buy King a new carriage."

"It's a pity you're rich," St. Clair said. "You obviously don't appreciate it properly. Here you could have the enjoyment of losing vast sums without causing yourself a moment's anxiety, and yet you insist on winning, like a petty merchant who embarks on a venture only for profit."

Their conversation was interrupted by the arrival of a servant with the promised bottle.

St. Clair surprised the earl by making a toast. "To your ward!"

"My ward!"

"Come, come, don't look so surprised."

They drained their glasses and refilled them.

"I have taken a fancy to her. She is something out of the common."

"That much is true," said the earl dryly.

"When do you unleash her on London?"

"I find your metaphor particularly apt. I consider that the city's defenses are not adequately prepared."

St. Clair looked thoughtful. "You may jest if you wish, but I have my reasons for asking."

The earl shot him a sharp glance. "Has there been talk?"

St. Clair shrugged. "There will always be talk. The fact that she is residing with the Dearbornes keeps it from going too far." He glanced at the earl out of the corner of his eyes. "There is talk, also, that the fair Helene has taken a new admirer." The earl said nothing. St. Clair continued, "It is thought by some to be singular that this event should coincide with the arrival of your ward."

The earl sat up abruptly, sloshing port out of his glass. "Damn their black hearts and their lying tongues." He paused for a moment. "What am I supposed to do to prove it is false? Take Harriet Wilson for a drive in the park?"

St. Clair was a little surprised by the vehemence of Sinamor's reaction, though he endeavored not to show it. "I think that the appearance of the girl herself will put an end to these rumors."

The earl shook his head. "I'll go to Winifred's tomorrow to see how she is progressing. Clearly there is no time to be lost."

St. Clair leaned forward, an unexpectedly serious look on his face. "My friend, I would not presume to tell you your business . . ."

"But what?" asked the earl suspiciously.

"But your ward is a high-spirited young lady. I would imagine that when she is pushed, she balks."

A grim chuckle escaped the earl.

"If she is coaxed, she will do much better, and that takes time." St. Clair fell back in his chair with a cynical smile. "We are both familiar with talk," he said. "You would be better off giving her an extra week or two, to see that she has the confidence to carry this off, than thrusting her upon the world before she is ready. The longer there is talk, the greater will be the interest when she finally appears."

The earl looked at him admiringly.

St. Clair continued. "Fortunately, we also have some extra time this year. With the celebrations that are planned for August, I venture to guess that everyone of importance will remain in London for them. I believe this will be a much longer Season than usual." He intercepted the look upon his friend's face and smiled mischievously. "You may repay me by getting us another bottle of port."

True to his resolve, Sinamor drew his smart curricle up in front of the Dearborne residence the next day. As his tiger leapt to the horse's heads and grasped the reins, the earl alighted.

He was starting up the stairs when he encountered an individual coming down.

It might be more accurate to say that he met an individual's fragrance coming down, for the heavily applied scent preceded the man by some paces. The portly gentleman was bewigged, painted, and dressed in old-fashioned knee breeches and frock coat of gaudy hue. He was followed by a timid, less prosperous-looking fellow, clutching a sheaf of music in his arms. The apparition was muttering various imprecations in French as he brushed hastily past Sinamor.

Winifred appeared at the top of the stairs. "Please, Monsieur Fouquet, will you not reconsider?"

He turned to face her. "Madame, I earn my living as a dancing master. I would like to be able to continue to earn my living as a dancing master. Good day!" He made a hasty bow and strode rapidly off.

"Oh, dear," Winifred said.

Sinamor climbed up to where she was standing. "I take it you've lost a dancing master."

"Yes," she replied, discouraged, "the fifth one in five days." She gazed disconsolately after the retreating figure.

"Has Phillipa been indulging in more fisticuffs?"

Winifred glanced at him, startled, and saw that his lips were curling in a suspicious manner. "Don't be odious," she replied acerbically. "He seemed to feel that she trod on his toes once too often."

They turned and went inside the entryway. "Perhaps his scent made her giddy," Sinamor suggested helpfully.

"It's not a laughing matter," Winifred said crossly. "That was the last one I could find."

"Obviously." He paused for a moment. "Can the chit really be that hopeless, Winifred? I've seen her sit a horse."

She shook her head. "She is convinced that she cannot dance, and she has managed to persuade each of these fellows of it. I think if she only could receive some encouragement, or if there were some incentive, other than duty. . . ."

The earl took her hand and patted it.

"I'm at my wit's end, Evelyn."

Their *tête-à-tête* was interrupted by the arrival of a small red-haired fury.

"I am not going to dance with that stinking, greasy old man again," exclaimed Phillipa imperiously. "I do not want to have him near me."

"You may save your tirade," Sinamor told her blandly. "Monsieur Bouquet has departed."

She looked at him incredulously for a moment before erupting into a silvery peal of laughter. "Monsieur Bouquet! That is very good. You met him, then."

"Briefly." The earl gave her a wintry smile. "We are still left with the problem of your dance instruction."

Phillipa affected unconcern. "Lady Dearborne will find me another teacher."

"Lady Dearborne, like the rest of us, is under the constraint of time." His hand shot out and gripped her arm tightly. "I propose that the lesson continue now."

"What?"

The earl nodded curtly at Winifred as he began to drag his charge to the music room. "If you will condescend to play for us, my dear."

"Certainly," replied Winifred, dumbfounded.

"And you might fetch Edmond to help us, if he's here." He paused, consideringly. "The two younger lads, too, while you're about it."

Curiosity was written all over Winifred's face, but she hastily went to obey his commands.

The earl yanked Phillipa into the music room. "We will begin with your curtsy," he said coldly.

"But, my lord, you do not understand," Phillipa said. "I cannot dance; all the dancing masters said so."

"I understand perfectly. You cannot dance, that is why we must teach you."

She shook her head and stamped her foot in exasperation. "You do not understand; I cannot learn to dance."

Those cold eyes held her in their gaze. "Phillipa, you can learn to dance. I can teach you, if you only will try."

Tears began to well in her eyes. "It's no use. Everyuone has already tried."

He held his temper in check and thought of Winifred's words. "Phillipa, I can teach you, but you will need to help. What would make you want to try? A new bonnet?"

She looked mulish.

"A new dress?"

There was little response. He realized that she already had many. He racked his brain for a moment. Jewelry would probably mean little to her either.

"An outing?"

He detected a change in her expression. "Where?" she asked suspiciously.

"Wherever you say." He put up a hand. "Provided it is respectable, of course."

"When?"

"When I am through teaching you all the dances you need to know."

"Whether or not I can do them?"

He sighed. "You will be able to do them." He saw the doubt in her face, "But, yes, yes, whatever you say."

She nodded. "Very well."

The earl drummed his fingers in exasperation. Who would imagine that he, the Earl of Sinamor, would have to bargain with a chit of a girl to persuade her to let him give her dancing lessons? "I must be out of my head," he muttered to himself.

These grave reflections were interrupted by the arrival of Winifred and the three boys. The latter looked at the earl in astonishment. Having had little contact with him, they were accustomed to looking upon him as an awesome and unapproachable figure. The news that they were to assist him in giving a dancing lesson confounded them.

The earl gave them little time to puzzle over it. He conferred quickly with Winifred until they were in agreement on music, then turned to his students and arranged them in two lines facing each other.

"We will begin," he announced, "with the minuet."

"The minuet," Edmond exclaimed in disgust. "But no one . . ." His mother cleared her throat meaningfully. "All right," he said sulkily.

"Now," said the earl, "Edmond, you and . . . William will

be the gentlemen. What is your name?'' he said, addressing the youngest boy.

''Anthony, my lord.''

''Very well, Anthony. You and Phillipa will be the ladies.''

The attitude of respect vanished abruptly. ''Why do I have to be a girl?''

The earl turned icy blue eyes upon him. ''Because I say you do.''

Anthony quailed under the gaze and offered no more objections.

The earl continued. ''Now, gentlemen, you bow, and ladies curtsy.''

He limped forward to Phillipa. ''No, no, not like that. Head up, slowly, gracefully.''

Lord Robert Dearborne, returning home late that morning after having worked through the night, was dismayed to find none of the servants at their posts. He flung himself irritably into the house and saw that they were gathered outside the music-room door. He cleared his throat loudly. After a startled glance or two, the servants evaporated rapidly.

''Bickerstaffe,'' barked Lord Dearborne.

The butler paled. With a look, he directed a footman to relieve Lord Dearborne of his things. ''I beg your pardon, my lord.''

''I should hope so,'' said Dearborne irascibly. ''What's all this. Has someone died?''

Righting himself from his respectful bow, Bickerstaffe regained his composure. ''No, my lord. It is the most extraordinary circumstance, however. My Lord Sinamor . . .''

''Good Lord, what's the man done now?'' exclaimed Dearborne, striding forward purposefully. He was brought to an abrupt halt outside the music-room door. ''What the . . . ?''

The music that was playing had halted. From inside, he could hear Sinamor's voice. ''No, no, Anthony, you must curtsy when William bows to you. Now let's try again.''

The music resumed. Dearborne plucked up his courage and peered inside.

''Good, very good, much better.'' the earl was saying. ''No, no, the other direction. The other way.''

Dearborne could not believe his eyes. Could that truly be the

Earl of Sinamor instructing Edmond, William, and Anthony in the minuet? He rubbed his eyes as if to clear them, but the images did not evaporate.

"I think we had best start from the beginning again," the earl was saying as Dearborne gently closed the door. His brain was too befogged to reason it out. There must be some simple explanation. He'd ask Winifred later.

To say that from this day forward the earl took a personal interest in his ward's progress would be no exaggeration. After another abortive attempt to hire a dancing master, he was resigned to carrying out the task himself. He greatly surprised the Dearborne family by proving himself a capable instructor. Indeed, Winifred thought wearily to herself, it was a pity that all Phillipa's lessons were not going equally well.

She had taken upon herself the task of chaperoning Phillipa while the latter's drawing lesson was taking place. She looked up from her needlework and sighed. The instructor had carefully arranged some fruit in a bowl on the table. Phillipa was herself a study in dedicated concentration, scowling as she poised her charcoal over the paper for a moment, as if to memorize the lines of her subject. Unfortunately, all she had managed to produce so far were some execrable scribbles.

At that moment, the earl appeared in the doorway. Taking in the scene, he murmured an apology for having interrupted the lesson.

Phillipa looked up at him and smiled brightly. "Oh, you are not disturbing us, for I am just now finished." She rose and took her work over to her instructor.

He flushed, muttered something inaudible, and fled the room.

Phillipa's brows drew together in a frown. "I do not think I am doing so well at this," she sighed.

"Nonsense," said the earl briskly. He limped over to her side. "Let me see it."

In spite of himself, his famous eyebrow ascended. Phillipa looked at him questioningly.

"Yes, well, it's very . . . it definitely is very . . . I should say that it is!"

Phillipa dropped her paper crossly. "That is what Edmond said."

Winifred intervened hastily. "Now, Phillipa, you know that you cannot expect to be a Michaelangelo in just a few lessons."

"Michael who?"

"The Italian painter," said the earl absentmindedly.

"Oh. Is he an acquaintance of yours?"

They managed to retain their composure. "No, my dear, he lived a long time ago," responded Winifred gently.

The earl made his way over to the mantelpiece and leaned against it. He drummed his fingers reflectively.

"I'm hopeless, aren't I?" Phillipa said defiantly. "Because I don't know anything about art, or dead Italian painters."

Sinamor drummed his fingers a little more rapidly. Winifred heaved another sigh and turned back to her needlework. Suddenly the earl's fingers stopped.

"That's it!"

Winifred and Phillipa looked at him curiously.

"She doesn't know anything about art. She probably has never been to an art gallery, have you, Phillipa?"

She shook her head wonderingly.

"Get your bonnet. We're going out," he commanded.

Once ensconced in the earl's fashionable yellow-and-black curricle, Phillipa ceased to wonder about their destination and instead settled herself down to enjoy this pleasing new sensation of traveling in an open carriage. She had admired the earl's pair of neat blacks on previous occasions; now she studied the way he drove. He used his whip only sparingly, and then never touched the horses with it. Although they traveled smartly along, he had his horses well in hand and took no unnecessary risks.

"You're a whip, aren't you?" she asked. "That's what Edmond says."

"He's been filling your head with all sorts of fustian, then."

"But I can see that you drive well."

"My dear girl, it takes no extraordinary skill to drive a pair."

"But why should anyone wish to drive a team in town?" she asked, startled.

His eyes met hers in a rare moment of sympathy. ''That's my feeling exactly.''

The moment of sympathy had dissipated by the time they reached their destination. Sinamor began wondering if he had made a mistake. He had discarded the idea of Dulwich as being too long a drive, and instead had decided to call upon an acquaintance renowned for his art collection. Though the gentleman in question was just going out as they arrived, he kindly invited them to remain and view his collection on their own.

Now, after half an hour of examining the works of the masters, Sinamor had not been able to detect anything on Phillipa's face other than polite boredom. He felt like shaking her, but instead asked her quietly, ''Don't you see anything that captures your interest, Phillipa?''

She stifled a yawn, then caught his eye. ''I'm sorry.'' She looked about her hopelessly. Suddenly she espied a painting at the far end of the hall.

''Now, I like that one,'' she said, making her way over to it.

The earl was pleased at her interest. ''That's Stubbs,'' he said, identifying it.

''You can almost see the horse move,'' marveled Phillipa.

''Yes, remarkable, isn't it?''

''That one is good, too,'' said Phillipa, espying a picture of a group on horseback.

''That is Stubbs also,'' the earl said, beginning to be less pleased.

''What beautiful animals,'' Phillipa said admiringly. ''And—''

''Don't tell me, you like this one of the racehorse, too,'' said the earl dryly.

She looked at him, surprised. ''Why, is that Stubbs, too?''

''As a matter of fact, yes.''

''Is something the matter?''

''Phillipa, I challenge you to find a painting that you like which is not by Stubbs.''

She frowned slightly. Taking her chin in her hand, she began to stroll around the gallery. At length, she paused in front of another painting. ''This one is fairly good,'' she said.

The earl came hurriedly up to see that the artwork indeed was by Gainsborough, rather than Stubbs.

"But I don't think his horse is quite as real-looking, do you?" She had selected another portrait of an equestrian.

The earl let out a sigh of frustration. "Phillipa, isn't there a painting here you like that doesn't contain a horse?"

She looked about her slowly. "No, I don't believe so," she said thoughtfully.

When the earl returned her to Hamilton Place some twenty minutes later, he recommended that the drawing master concentrate on equine studies. "For it seems," he said, "she has very little interest in any other form of art."

"Oh, dear," said Winifred, gazing after Phillipa as she disappeared up the stairs, en route to the nursery. "Well, she needn't be accomplished in everything, need she?"

"Fortunately not," replied the earl. He winced slightly. "Tell me, is there anything at which she has shown any promise?"

Winifred smiled at him. "Well, oddly enough, at music—not in playing, she seems to lack the inclination. She has, however, quite a pretty little voice."

"Well, there's one thing, at any rate."

"There is another. You remember that I engaged a French tutor for Phillipa? It was unnecessary; they apparently had an émigré for a neighbor."

Winifred chuckled slightly. "Of course, she knows a great many dreadfully improper expressions . . ." Her face grew more serious. "That is the sum total of her knowledge, Sinamor. It's only fortunate that the girl knows how to read and write. I doubt she's ever read a book."

"My dear, as we both know, that is not requisite for entering society."

6

As the days passed and Phillipa began to show definite signs of progress, Winifred and the earl might have been justified in allowing their hopes to rise. It had to be admitted that she was greatly improved in her overall deportment; even Lord Dearborne was wont to look upon her presence with a kindly eye on the few occasions that their paths crossed. Since Phillipa had won the approval of so severe a critic, both the earl and Winifred were lulled into a false sense of confidence. They were not prepared in the least for the disaster that was to transpire.

The whole affair began innocently enough when young Charles Fitzroy came to see Edmond about the pressing matter of selling his horse. He found him in the gold drawing room, trouncing an indifferent Phillipa soundly in a game of chess.

"No, no," Edmond was saying, "the pawn only moves forward one square at a time, and it captures with a diagonal move, remember?"

Phillipa yawned prettily. She saw Charles and smiled, thinking that at last her tedium would be interrupted.

He was captivated instantly. "Good day, Dearborne," he said, staring at Phillipa.

Edmond glanced up briefly and returned to studying the board. "Good day, Fitzroy."

Charles waited for an introduction, but Edmond remained occupied by the game. Charles coughed meaningfully and smiled at Phillipa.

Edmond looked up at him again. "Oh, this is Phillipa Raithby. She's Sinamor's ward, and she's staying here with us for now. Phillipa, this is Charles Fitzroy."

Charles, who had dandiacal pretentions, swept her a deep

bow. "*Enchanté*, Miss Raithby." He took the hand she proffered and kissed it.

Since Edmond was consumed by the game, Phillipa felt that she must compensate for his omissions. "Won't you join us, Mr. Fitzroy?"

All eagerness, he helped himself to a chair and moved it to her side. He sank into it and regarded her adoringly over the high points of his shirt collar. All thoughts of selling the horse had been driven from his mind.

"Your move, Phillipa," Edmond said.

Hardly glancing at the board, Phillipa pushed a piece carelessly forward. Edmond again studied the board.

Charles leaned forward and addressed Phillipa intimately. "I take it that you have not long been a visitor to London, Miss Raithby, or I know I should have heard of you before now."

She smiled at this flattery. "I have been here but a few weeks."

"Then I take it that you have not had opportunity to see all the sights?"

She laughed the silvery laugh. "I'm afraid that I have seen little of London other than the inside of the dressmaker's salon."

He drew back with an expression of shock. "No!"

"Your turn, Phillipa."

She picked up another piece and moved it.

"I must certainly remedy that. Perhaps we could form an excursion. You could go see the Tower, and the menagerie there. We might to go the Monument, too." He gave her a smile that he fancied was full of devilish charm. "If you're brave, we might even climb it."

Except for her daily sedate ride in the Park under Sinamor's stern eye, Phillipa's time had been divided between lessons and shopping. She had been chafing under this restraint, so Charlers' program sounded doubly entrancing. "That would be wonderful," she said ingenuously, her blue eyes glowing with excitement.

Words failed Charles at the entrancing vision before his eyes. He sat gazing at her dumbly, then coughed to regain his composure.

"In that case, nothing shall prevent me from escorting you there, properly chaperoned, of course." He thought for a moment, then cast a sly glance at Edmond. "We could bring Dearborne, and my sister . . ."

Edmond was oblivious to this scrutiny. He frowned with concentration, then suddenly his brow cleared and he moved his piece. "Yours, Phillipa."

She picked up a piece and moved it.

Edmond pounced upon it. "Checkmate!" He looked up at her. "I wish you wouldn't be so careless about your moves, Phillipa. It's hardly a challenge."

"See here, Dearborne," Charles said excitedly. "We've hatched a famous scheme!"

Upon application, Winifred could perceive no major objections to the proposed outing. She did lift her brows slightly at the mention of their destination, and she suggested that they were likely to encounter a rather common class of people in the City. At the sight of Phillipa's disappointed face, she dismissed this concern and added, "Well, if Lady Fitzroy permits Miss Fitzroy to go, I will not oppose your joining the party, my dear, although I am afraid I will not be here to see you off. I have an appointment at the dressmaker's in the morning."

An ecstatic Charles departed to seek the required permission. An excited Phillipa flew up to her room, to decide which dress would be most suitable for the excursion.

Winifred turned to her son with concern in her eyes. "Edmond, surely it is not possible that she has developed a *tendre* for Charles so quickly, not that I should object to a match—"

Edmond interrupted her, laughing. "You should know Phillipa better by now, Mama. Her one true love has four legs." He stopped laughing as he saw that a slight frown still creased her face. "Don't fret, Mama. It is only one outing, after all. And I will be there to make certain that all goes well." He leaned over, gave her a peck on the forehead, and sauntered out of the room.

Winifred's brow cleared. Edmond was right. Phillipa had

been making a great deal of progress. And, after all, she reassured herself, what could possibly happen during one outing?

Lady Dearborne felt no sense of foreboding as she departed for the dressmaker's the next morning. She had left Phillipa, glowing with anticipation, wearing an appropriate carriage dress in mulberry, with a bonnet and pelisse to match. Winifred might have felt more uneasy had she known that Edmond had succumbed to Charles Fitzroy's persuasions over a bottle of port the night before and agreed to drive the girls in their curricles.

Thinking of the fiasco that his last outing with Phillipa had been, Edmond at first was reluctant to assent to such impropriety. The notion of being able to have Miss Fitzroy to himself and demonstrate to her how he could drive to an inch, proved too much of a temptation to him, though.

"My mother won't like it," he warned Fitzroy.

"Don't tell her," Charles advised him amiably. "I've let my mother think your mother's escorting us." He smiled. "Your mother said she would be gone in the morning, after all."

"I don't know," said Edmond uncertainly.

Charles lifted his hands persuasively. "We'll be in the City. There won't be anyone that we know there." He shrugged. "Of course, if you don't wish to, I can ask my mother to take us."

Edmond could see Charles's point instantly. What an insipid affair that would be. "I'll do it," he said.

Not a single worry disturbed Winifred's peace of mind for the rest of the morning and on into the afternoon. The first misgivings assailed her when she saw Edmond's carriage returning alone, with Edmond and Phillipa inside. She met them at the door and motioned them inside the green salon, out of the range of curious ears.

She looked at the pair. Phillipa was white-faced and tight-lipped. Edmond appeared exasperated.

"What happened?" Winifred asked.

Edmond threw his hat down on the floor. He gestured angrily at Phillipa. "She horsewhipped Fitzroy."

"Oh, dear God," said Winifred, unconsciously sinking into a chair.

"I had to grab it out of her hand."

"Oh, Phillipa!"

"Miss Fitzroy saw the entire scene. It's only fortunate that no one we knew was there."

"Phillipa, how could you?"

"I had to bring her home. Fitzroy said he'd never take her up in his carriage again, and little wonder."

Goaded beyond endurance, Phillipa burst out, "I did not horsewhip him, Lady Dearborne. Edmond is exaggerating."

"Why, I saw it with my own eyes."

"I hit him once, or maybe twice. I didn't hurt him."

"Fitzroy would probably say differently."

"I don't care what he says. He's a liar! And I hate him." Phillipa burst into tears and fled from the room.

"Well, if that doesn't beat everything," commented a bemused Edmond. "Here she caused all the trouble and she's the one who's crying."

One nuance of his speech had attracted Winifred's attention. "What do you mean when you say that *you* had to bring her home, Edmond?"

He had the grace to redden. "Well . . . I . . . er . . . well, that is, Fitroy suggested that we drive them in our curricles."

"Edmond!"

"Well, I'm sorry. Mama, I didn't think—"

"That much is obvious," she said with unaccustomed severity. A thought occurred to her and she looked at him anxiously. "Edmond, you don't think . . . you don't imagine that he took liberties with her—"

Edmond shook his head. "No, besides, he hadn't time."

Winifred frowned. She would have to have a long and serious talk with Edmond. More urgently, though, she needed to find out what was wrong with Phillipa. "You'd better sit down and tell me what happened from the beginning," she told him.

Everything had augured well at the start, Edmond told her. The day was perfect for an outing, the traffic had been light, and they had reached the Tower in good time. Once there, Phillipa had seemed delighted by everything she saw. Miss Fitzroy had been somewhat frightened by the bear in the menagerie, but Phillipa had been intrigued. She particularly had been impressed by the elephant and had wondered how one would do on her farm in Yorkshire. Everyone had laughed, of course.

"And that offended her," Winifred said quickly.

"No, not at all," responded Edmond. "In fact, she seemed grateful when I explained to her that they were only suited to warmer climates."

"But Charles was taken aback by what she'd said?"

"No, he was besotted," said Edmond, shaking his head in disgust. "He said she was 'refreshing.' In any case, all seemed to go well at the Tower. We saw the Armoury and the Traitor's Gate and—"

"Never mind that," said Winifred impatiently. "Did anything significant happen?"

Edmond thought for a moment. "I can't think of anything out of the ordinary," he said finally. "Phillipa seemed to be at her most amiable, and as I said, Fitzroy was besotted."

Winifred frowned. "When did this incident take place, then?"

"We had left the Tower and were on the way to the Monument. They went in his carriage and we followed in ours. Fitzroy put his horse to . . . I suppose he wished to show Phillipa how well he can handle the ribbons, or how well he thinks he can. In any case, we fell behind. As we drove up to the Monument, I saw that they had arrived just before us." He turned to his mother and looked at her squarely. "And then I saw Phillipa snatch the whip from his hand and lash out at him with it."

"Why on earth?"

"I have no idea. As soon as he realized what she was about, he grasped her arm, of course. I was out of my carriage and over there by then. She saw me and she just let me have the whip. I guess she knew what she'd done."

Winifred frowned. "You can't think of any reason?"

"I cannot fathom why she would have done such a thing. Unless . . ."

"What?"

"Unless she thought he was mistreating his horse."

Winifred gasped. "Surely she wouldn't have done that."

Edmond shrugged. "I don't know. In any case, neither of

them was hurt. I asked Phillipa what had happened on the drive home, but she didn't say a word until she spoke to you just now." He frowned suddenly. "I don't know what Miss Fitzroy will think of us."

"I don't know what London will think of us."

He looked conscience-stricken. "I am sorry, Mama. After I promised you . . ."

She rose, still frowning. "We will talk later."

Upstairs, Winifred found that Phillipa was red-eyed, but no longer weeping. She managed to force a little smile to her lips.

"May we talk?"

Phillipa nodded.

Winifred settled herself into the leather-covered fauteuil beside the dressing table. She chose her words carefully. "Edmond has told me what he knows. Do you care to tell me the rest?"

Phillipa pulled her lips together in a grimace that suggested an attempt at self-control.

Winifred tried again. "Edmond said that perhaps you thought Fitzroy was mistreating his horse."

In spite of herself, a tear dropped from Phillipa's eye and began to roll down her cheek. She wiped it away quickly in a determined attempt to master herself. When she spoke, her voice was shaking.

"Do you really think that? Do you really think that I would strike him because of that? After all that you have done for me?" She lifted her little chin and looked at Winifred, who felt her heart softening despite herself.

"My dear, I don't know what to think."

Phillipa heaved a little shuddering sigh, then swallowed. Her chin was trembling. "I am sorry, Lady Dearborne," she said at last. She wiped away another tear.

Winifred's heart melted. She rose and came to sit beside Phillipa on the bed. "I know that you wouldn't have done such a thing unless you thought you had a very good reason," she said softly. "Won't you tell me what it is?"

Phillipa swallowed again. "Lord Sinamor . . . why is it that everyone says such bad things about him?"

Comprehension dawned in Winifred's face. "Is that what it was?"

Phillipa nodded.

"Oh, my dear." Winifred paused. A moment or two passed in silence.

"I know that Charles did not mean anything by whatever he told you," Winifred said slowly. "It is just that sometimes people speak without thinking, and that's very easy to do when you're young."

Phillipa let out another little shuddering sigh.

"It is very easy for a person simply to repeat something he's heard"—Winifred looked squarely at Phillipa—"but whatever he said, it was wrong of you to respond in that way."

"I know." The words were a sob. "It's my awful temper. When he said that about Lord Sinamor, something just overcame me, and he made it worse by . . ." Here she began to weep softly.

Winifred patted her back.

"Why should people say such cruel things about him?" gasped Phillipa at length.

Winifred sighed wearily. "At one time, Phillipa, I promised you that I would tell you about Sinamor someday. I think the time has come now." She rose and walked over to the window, looking out.

Phillipa blew her nose and managed to steady her breathing.

Winifred began to speak, still not looking at Phillipa, and her voice had a faraway quality.

"I have told you what Sinamor was like as a boy. I did not tell you about his parents. His mother was my mother's sister."

She paused, as if marshaling her thoughts, then continued. "My mother's family were simple country gentlefolk, with a small but comfortable estate. They had but two daughters. My aunt's beauty caught the eye of their neighbor, the Earl of Sinamor. When he made her an offer, everyone was delighted."

Winifred shook her head. "She knew no better, of course. She was told that she was a fortunate girl, that no one believed that she might aim that high."

Winifred turned and looked at Phillipa directly. "Of course, what she did not know was that the Earl of Sinamor, for all his wealth and title and lands, was a brute. Not only was he incapable of love, it seems that he also was incapable even of kindness."

Winifred turned away again. "Not that she was the sort to complain. I think that my family never knew the true extent of his cruelty until after she was already dead. I remember her, you see. Although I was only a young child when she died, I can remember how gentle she was, and how kind . . ." Her voice trailed off.

"Did she die when the present earl was born?"

"Yes." The expression of weary cynicism on Winifred's face took Phillipa aback. "My mother always said that perhaps it was the late Lord Sinamor's grief for her that caused him to be so hateful to the child. It was Mama's way of being kind, I suppose. I knew even at that age that love could not cause someone to be so vile.

"The late earl drank. It was a problem that worsened with every passing day. It increased his natural tendencies toward filth and brutality, and in some measure affected his reason. He had no sooner married this pretty, innocent, seventeen-year-old child, than he began to suspect her of unfaithfulness. It was a lie, of course. But when he knew she was to bear a child, his accusations grew more and more bitter. And when the child was born, so beautiful and so frail, favoring the mother rather than himself, it was all the proof this demented man needed."

Phillipa looked incredulous. "Do you mean that he thought his son was illegitimate?"

Winifred laughed harshly. "He didn't just think it, my dear. He told Evelyn at every opportunity just what he thought he was, in the stable-yard language he always used."

Phillipa paled with anger. "How could he be so cruel!"

Winifred sighed. "It was ridiculous, of course. Evelyn has his father's jaw, and those eyebrows, and no one but a Sinamor could be that arrogant." She paused for a moment before resuming. "The talk spread, of course, even though there was no foundation. Evelyn has had to live under that shadow all his life."

Winifred looked up at Phillipa and smiled a wintry smile. "Am I boring you?" Phillipa shook her head, wordlessly.

"Well, then, in brief, though he had this brute for a father, Evelyn had a child's natural desire to win his parent's love. Since his father was a sportsman, Evelyn had to be the most bruising rider, the most perfect shot, a master of the ribbons as Edmond would say, handy with his fives. He took shocking risks, and all for nothing. Of course, that was not the worst; he was beaten regularly, for no reason at all.

"I can explain it best by giving you an example." She closed her eyes for a moment to think. "When I was a young girl, really just a child, I was out riding my pony by myself one afternoon, unchaperoned." She caught the look of surprise in Phillipa's face and smiled slightly. "Yes, at one time I myself was fond of doing improper things. In any event, my pony shied at a rabbit and threw me before running off. I was miles from home and it was not long until dark. I had begun the long walk when Evelyn chanced to see me and came riding up on his pony." Her lips turned up at the memory. "He was just a little fellow, perhaps four or five years old, but he insisted that I take his pony. I wouldn't because we were equally far from Sinamor. He then mounted me on the pony behind him and we rode to my home. It was dark by then, and my mother urged him to stay; she'd send a message to Sinamor House. He refused her offer and also dinner, saying that he must get home. In gratitude, I went to call on him the next day. I saw that he'd been thrashed within an inch of his life for coming in after dark."

She looked at Phillipa earnestly. "Do you see, Phillipa? He had known that the beating was in store for him, but he took me home anyway. He never hesitated for a moment."

Winifred appeared struck by a sudden concern. She crossed the room and sat down by Phillipa again. "I'm telling you this so that you may understand what drives Sinamor to do what he does. I am the only person in London besides Sinamor who knows these things, and you must never tell anyone, especially him, what you know. Will you swear it?"

"I swear it," Phillipa responded seriously. "I still do not understand, though, Lady Dearborne. If he were the only heir to an earldom, how was it that he came to be in the Fourteenth Light and that no one knew his rank, including my father?"

"That is the worst of all." Winifred gave a little shudder.

"He had gone to Eton, as all the Sinamors have. It was a great time for him, because his prowess in sport made him admired for the first time in his life. He also found that he could make friends, friends who could care less about his parentage." She smiled at Phillipa. "St. Clair was one.

"As he approached young manhood, inevitably, he began to rebel against his father. He fell in with a group of young men who were fastidious about their dress, to the point of absurdity sometimes. It was in such opposition to everything his father represented. I think, too, that it was a way for him to get the attention his father had always denied him. Certainly his father did not ignore him any longer.

"I think his new sense of assurance goaded the old earl. We all prayed that one might not kill the other." Winifred shivered slightly. "I was married and gone by this time, but my brother told me about their final break.

"It was Christmas and Evelyn was home on holiday. My brother and sisters had arranged to take him to a party in the neighborhood. He had seemed delighted at the prospect, having no opportunity for social life on his own.

"They arrived at Sinamor the evening of the party. Evelyn was still dressing, so instead they were greeted by the brutish earl. He was in his cups, as usual, but fortunately seemed to lack the energy or inclination to do more than cast them a few dark glances and offer some disparaging words. They wisely held their peace and were relieved to see Evelyn descending the stairs a few moments later."

Winifred smiled slightly. "My brother thought he looked magnificent. They had never seen such London finery in the country before. I can imagine him, fifteen and proud in his tailcoat and knee breeches, ready for his first adult party." Her face changed suddenly. "There was apparently something in Evelyn's manner that displeased the earl. He went rushing up to him and told him that he was an insolent puppy and something a good deal worse, and that he wasn't going to see his son going out of the house looking like a popinjay.

"My brother said Evelyn's face just froze. He looked at the earl coolly and said, 'I've always been given to understand that I was *not* your son, my lord.' The old earl was furious, of course. By way of an affectation, Evelyn was carrying a malacca walking stick. The earl grabbed it from his hand and, before anyone could stop him, smashed Evelyn full across the face with it, breaking it. The ivory knob caught Evelyn on the temple, just above his left eye, and he fell like a stone. The earl muttered something unintelligible and went stomping off up the stairs while my family stood there in horror.

"My brother went to Evelyn, ascertained that he was still breathing, and loosened his stock. My sister found a servant to fetch water and she washed away most of the blood. They bandaged his head roughly with the neckcloth and sat about in confusion for a moment. They were deciding to convey him to a physician when Evelyn's eyes opened. He saw the concern in their faces and managed a little smile.

"My brother said his self-possession was remarkable. He asked them to convey his apologies to their hostess and urged them to hurry on to the party. He insisted that he did not need medical attention and in fact seemed oblivious to his own pain. In spite of all their entreaties, he prevailed upon them to leave. They did so with a sense of dread.

"The next thing we heard was that Evelyn had joined the cavalry. That same night, he had taken what money he had and purchased a cornetcy. He didn't tell anyone of his true rank."

"Did he ever see his father again?"

"No. Oddly enough, his father died just days before he received his leg wound. Evelyn came home in a raging fever, his military career ended, and he awoke to find himself an Earl."

Winifred's words echoed hollowly about the room. She rose with a sigh. "I will never refer to this subject again, Phillipa. I know as well as anyone else that Sinamor is no saint, but neither is he as black as gossip paints him. I hope that you may understand him a little better now."

She then exited the room, closing the door softly behind her as she went. Phillipa was left alone with her own bitter thoughts.

Even Phillipa did not know how long she sat there brooding in the darkened room. Her reverie was interrupted abruptly by the sound of small, shrill voices calling her name loudly. The voices were accompanied by running footsteps, then a frantic knocking on her door.

"Phillipa, Phillipa, come quick!"

She dashed to the door and opened it to see William and Anthony, almost out of breath with excitement.

"Come and see. It's downstairs," they exclaimed.

She allowed herself to be tugged rapidly down the stairs, though she was still uncertain as to what all the furor was about.

The front door stood open. The boys, full of impatience, darted through it, leaving her behind. She crossed the entryway and was herself struck dumb. In front of her eyes stood a magnificent bay horse, pawing at the cobblestones ill-humoredly. He saw her and let out a whicker of recognition.

"Ripon!"

She flew forward and flung her arms around his neck. Ready tears started to her eyes. The horse turned his head around and nuzzled at her gently. She took a step back and wiped her eyes with one hand, leaning on the horse with the other. A rough voice demanded her attention.

"And are ye gang to ignore me, then, Miss Phillipa?"

She looked up to see a familiar figure standing beside the horse. "Mr. McPherson." She flung her arms about him, too, but he proved less receptive than the horse. He peeled her from him with his one free hand.

"We'll hae nane o'that noo, Miss Phillipa. 'Tisn't fittin' for a young lady."

Phillipa stepped back in confusion. "But, how did you, and Ripon . . ."

He laughed. "It seems that the lieutenant—beggin' your pardon—the earl thought you'd be missin' your wee horsie."

"The earl?" As if by a summons, Sinamor's black-and-yellow curricle came bowling around the corner.

"Here he comes! Here he comes," shrieked William and Anthony as they dashed forward to meet it.

In a few moments, Sinamor came up. When he saw McPherson, he gave a genuine smile, an expression that Phillipa had never seen on his face before.

"McPherson," he said. "*Há tanto tempo. Como está a te*?"

"*Bem, obrigado.*" McPherson returned his grin. "I see that your lordship hasna forgotten his Portuguese."

The earl took his hand and wrung it warmly. "The best

forager in the troop. Harry and I would have starved without you."

At the mention of Harry's name, a shadow passed over both the men's faces. "The war ended for you when Harry left, then," said Sinamor softly.

"I couldna let him gang alone when he was sae poorly," McPherson said.

Ripon interrupted this hushed moment by snorting with vexation at his prolonged idleness.

The earl stepped back to examine him with approval. "Don't tell me this leviathan is Phillipa's horse," he said amusedly. "Why, he must be seventeen hands."

"Sixteen and a half, m'lord," said McPherson with a twinkle. "And doesna like anyone on his back save for Miss Phillipa."

At this moment, the earl felt a tug on his sleeve. He had missed Phillipa in the pleasure of the reunion. Now she stood beside him, her eyes filled to overflowing.

"My lord, how can I ever thank you enough?" she whispered brokenly.

For a moment, there was a queer, tender sort of smile on the earl's face, McPherson thought, but it vanished quickly. "My dear Miss Raithby," he said dryly, "I did not want it said that my ward had expired of a broken heart even before she was introduced to society."

"My lord"—a tear or two slipped out as she spoke—"I don't know what to say."

He drew a handkerchief out of his pocket and handed it to her. "Well, I should begin by drying my face, if I were you. Then someone should show McPherson where to stable this beast." He glanced slyly at the two boys.

"We will! We'll show him," burst from their lips simultaneously.

"Now, I think we should inform Lady Dearborne of the new arrival," said the earl, and offered his arm to Phillipa.

"I am afraid, my lord," said Phillipa ashamedly, "that Lady Dearborne will have something she wishes to say to you."

Phillipa was not mistaken in her assumption. As soon as Winifred learned of the earl's arrival, she joined them in the green salon and sent Phillipa out of the room. She then proceeded to give the earl an account of what had transpired that morning. She prudently omitted the reason Phillipa had taken so extreme a course, but said that she believed there was some provocation. To her consternation, the earl did not seem properly taken aback. In fact, as she watched him, his shoulders began to shake and his mouth began to twitch and soon he laughed out loud.

"Evelyn," she exclaimed to consternation, "you cannot mean that you find this amusing."

He started to frame a reply, then collapsed in laughter again.

"I hope that this does not mean that you condone this kind of behavior," said Winifred with all the asperity she could muster.

"I am sorry," he said, forcing down the chuckle that fought to escape him. "It's just that . . . no one has ever had so unusual a ward before, I don't imagine. One can only wonder what will happen next." A brief burble of laughter erupted from him.

"Well," said Winifred, outraged. "Since you're so lighthearted about all this, I'd like to know how you propose to solve this dilemma."

"Phillipa must write an apology to the boy first, of course."

"Do you think that will prevent this tale from getting all over town?"

"My dear"—the amusement still lingered in his face—"do you imagine that any young man would wish it to be generally known that he had been horsewhipped by a young lady?"

Winifred was struck by the truth of this statement. "No, indeed, you are right. But, Evelyn, now her debut must be postponed again."

"That's where you are wrong, Winifred. The Duke and Duchess of Branscombe are having a ball the day after tomorrow and I intend to procure an invitation for Phillipa."

"Why?" Winifred was confounded. In answer, he drew a paper from under his arm and handed it to her without a word. She opened it to where he had marked it and saw that it was dated that same day.

To A Sapphire

A Diamond in its setting may a King or
Prince adore,

But Diamonds upon Diamonds do my jaded
 palate bore.
A single gem, A Sapphire! of the Earl
 of S———
Pales the Diamond by her radiance
Blinds my eyes to other Beauty
Seals my lips from different paeans
Binds my heart forevermore.

A.S.C.

Winifred read it slowly, then reread it. At last she looked up. "St. Clair?"

"Who else?" The earl put a gloved hand to his mouth and yawned in an affected way. "It's not his best work, of course, but it should have the desired effect."

"How kind of him . . . how very kind of him."

"You see why we must act now." He rose, wincing as he did so. "We must be certain that we have not omitted to do a thing. I propose to give Phillipa a dancing lesson now." He looked down at the paper, which she was still holding. "I shouldn't show that to Phillipa, if I were you. I would merely tell her about it. Females are so addicted to sentimental nonsense. Phillipa might convince herself that St. Clair is actually in love with her."

A tiny burden lifted from Winifred's heart at these words, but she only nodded in reply.

A short time later, the company once again assembled in the music rooms. Sinamor stroked his chin thoughtfully as he gazed at his waiting pupils.

"Let's see, we've covered the country dance, the Highland reel, the Irish jig, the rigadoon, the quadrille. What is left?" His eyes lit with a sudden thought. "Of course, the waltz!" Winifred, sitting patiently at the pianoforte, pursed her lips in dissatisfaction. "Sinamor, is it really necessary that Phillipa know all these continental dances?"

"I think it is essential, my dear. If, for example, Phillipa were to develop an interest in a young gentleman of military persuasion, she would certainly be called upon to perform them."

"But the war is over."

"All the more reason. Now that travel to the continent is safe, we must suspect that more people will do it." He nodded at William and Anthony. "Your help will not be required today. Thank you."

Grins of relief on their faces, the boys dashed from the room.

The earl turned to Winifred. "You do have a waltz, I hope." She nodded and began searching through her music. Sinamor turned to Phillipa.

"Now this is the simplest of all dances. It consists of only three steps. You take one long one and two short ones."

He nodded at Edmond. "I think she should be able to follow you. You may begin."

Edmond looked confounded. "But I don't know how to do a waltz or whatever it is."

Sinamor frowned. "You don't?"

"No."

"Winifred, this boy's education is sadly lacking." The earl heaved a sigh. "Very well, then. You begin by facing each other . . . so. Now, take her hand in yours, your right hand. Hold it so. Now your other hand about her waist, not so tightly. You begin, as always, with your left foot, Phillipa with your right."

After half an hour or so of instruction, the earl was almost ready to profess himself defeated. Edmond was frustrated, Phillipa was bored, and even Winifred was beginning to show the first signs of rebellion.

"It's really very easy," Sinamor was saying in an irritated way when the clock on the mantelpiece chimed four.

"I beg your pardon, my lord," Edmond said hastily, "but I've just remembered a pressing engagement. If you will excuse me . . ." He bowed quickly and exited.

The earl frowned after him.

Winifred stood and sighed. "Well, I suppose that ends the lessons for today."

The earl's frown deepened. "It's only one dance—and so simple. Why, I could practically do it myself."

He whirled around with an unexpected smile. "Sit back down, Winifred. I will teach Phillipa the waltz."

Winifred looked at him inquiringly, but she obeyed his command.

"Come here, Phillipa," said the earl. "I may be lame, but I think I can manage to convey the idea of what this dance is about."

Phillipa stepped up to him obediently. She was unprepared for the sudden shock that went through her as he took her hand and drew an arm about her waist. She was abruptly aware of the muscular strength of his body. She looked up into those cool blue eyes and felt as if she might drown in them. The air seemed suddenly too thick to breathe. She began to tremble.

As if from a distance, she heard the earl's voice. "Now, Win," and they began swirling about the room. Her body followed his through the dance as if it had been born to do so. She was conscious of feeling light-headed. Her eyes remained fixed magnetically on his face. She seemed to read something new in his eyes, something she had never seen there before. She was trembling more violently now, but oddly enough she felt no dislike of the sensation. She felt a new, strange, urgent desire to be pulled even tighter into those powerful arms. She couldn't be sure, but wasn't he breathing her name?

As if a spell were broken, the music ended with a resounding chord. She was breathing far harder than the exertion warranted. The earl stepped away and bowed as Winifred applauded. Phillipa felt as if she were awakening from a dream.

"Bravo! You performed that beautifully," Winifred was saying.

"Credit must go to my fair partner," Sinamor replied coolly. "I knew that she would catch on, but I didn't know how swiftly." The indifference in his voice acted like a pail of cold water on Phillipa. Had she been imagining what had passed between them?

"In any case, my dear," said the earl, turning back to Phillipa, "you have certainly earned your outing. Where is it to be?"

Phillipa's shock prevented her from speaking.

"Phillipa?" asked the earl. He paused for a moment before continuing smoothly, "Of course, if you have not decided, there is no need to settle on any one place yet. When you know London better you may."

Phillipa swallowed hard. Her pride came to her rescue. "Indeed, my lord," she said with as much composure as she could muster, "I settled on a place when you first made me the promise. I wish to go to Astley's."

"I might have known," murmured the earl.

"Astley's Amphitheatre?" asked Winifred puzzledly. Abruptly, her brow cleared. "Oh, William and Anthony."

"Is there something the matter?" asked Phillipa loftily.

"Not at all," the earl assured her. "We will go tomorrow night, if you like." Phillipa's smile sprang to her face. He held up a hand to show that he had not finished, "But tomorrow afternoon, we will go for a drive in Hyde Park."

"As you say, my lord." She swept them a grand curtsy and left the room.

Winifred turned to the earl with anxiety in her eyes. "Evelyn, is this wise?"

His lips curled in something approaching a smile. "My dear, I think it better that she see the social lions roaming free in their habitat before she attempts to beard them in their dens."

7

''What a great many people there are, to be sure,'' exclaimed Phillipa with interest.

Lady Dearborne tugged her back into her seat. ''My dear, fashionable young ladies do not lean out of their carriages to gawk about them. It is a sure sign that one is a rustic.''

''How very dull,'' Phillipa said, but she remained settled back among the velvet squabs. She glanced enviously at Sinamor, who rode alongside them on his black. ''I do not see why I should not be able to ride also.''

Winifred sighed. ''Ladies do not ride in Hyde Park at five o'clock. It simply isn't done.'' As she observed the cloud that was beginning to gather over Phillipa's brow, she added gently, ''Besides, you've already taken one ride in the park today, haven't you?''

Mumbling a reluctant assent, Phillipa continued to brood for a moment on this injustice. Irresistibly, her attention was reclaimed by the panorama passing around them. She had never seen such beautiful equipages before, with the powdered footmen in their liveries, the bewigged coachmen, and the beautifully matched horses. She also noted that the gentlemen that rode about the park were mounted on some of the most magnificent horses she had ever seen. So this is why Edmond wants a new horse, she thought shrewdly.

''What's that?'' In her surprise, she almost sat up, in direct violation of Lady Dearborne's admonition.

Winifred shushed her, though she could well understand the girl's surprise. Coming from the other direction was an unusual curricle shaped like a scallop shell, drawn by a beautiful pair of white horses. As the carriage approached, one could plainly see that on its door was the picture of a cock with wings outspread, which bore over it the motto "While I live, I'll crow."

"That is only Mr. Romeo Coates. He is not an acquaintance of ours."

Phillipa's attention was attracted by another carriage, this one all in black, drawn by four superb black horses. "How gloomy that looks," she commented.

"That is Lord Onslow," replied the earl, overhearing her, "and I daresay he takes nearly the interest in horseflesh that you do." The earl then nodded slightly at a gentleman driving a chocolate-colored coach four-in-hand, approaching from the other direction. He anticipated Phillipa's next question. "That is 'Ball' Hughes, my dear. One of the wealthiest men in the kingdom, but you will not see him at the ball tomorrow night."

A familiar figure came riding up beside their carriage on a handsome chestnut horse. "St. Clair," Winifred said gladly.

He tipped his hat politely at the ladies. "Good day to you all." He nodded at Sinamor. "What a fortunate man you are to have the prvilege of escorting such beauty."

Sinamor was eyeing his horse. "You know, that looks like Montgomery's nag."

"It was." He shrugged his shoulders. "Fortune was kind enough to smile on me last night. If you will excuse me."

He nudged his horse into a position beside the carriage. Soon Phillipa's silvery laugh could be heard as St. Clair murmured various absurdities to her. Lady Dearborne was well-pleased by his attentions. It could only benefit Phillipa if the world saw that St. Clair deemed her worthy of his interest.

After several minutes' conversation, he bid them a courteous farewell and rode off. The earl resumed his place beside the carriage, his gaze a little icier than usual.

"St. Clair seems to have the knack for amusing you."

"Yes," replied Phillipa, "and he made me promise to save him a dance tomorrow night. Oh, I shall feel so much better, knowing that he is there," she exclaimed impulsively.

The earl frowned slightly, then was startled by a gasp from Winifred. He glanced over his shoulder to see where she was gazing and saw a carriage approaching. St. Clair's lure was pulling in a very big fish, indeed.

Phillipa started as she received an unexpected poke in the ribs.

"Whatever you do, be at your most amiable now," Lady Dearborne said.

"My lord Sinamor, and Lady Dearborne, how do you do? Such a pleasant surprise to see both of you here." As the carriage drew nearer, the dark-haired woman sitting in it leaned forward to peer at Phillipa with undisguised curiosity.

"Lady Jersey, will you allow me to present my ward, Miss Phillipa Raithby?"

As soon as the introductions had been completed and the necessary pleasantries murmured, Lady Jersey glanced up at Sinamor with an arch look.

"So this is the sapphire with which St. Clair has been tantalizing us. It was naughty of you to keep her hidden for so long." She looked back at Phillipa, who contrived to hide her resentment of this peremptory examination. Lady Jersey laughed suddenly. "It's evident what St. Clair sees in her."

She glanced back at the earl flirtatiously. "And just when I was beginning to think that this Season was becoming dull. Trust you, my lord, to provide some spice. Shall I send you vouchers for Wednesday night? I think I must!"

"How very kind of your ladyship," Lady Dearborne was murmuring eagerly.

The earl managed a graceful half-bow in the saddle. "I am, of course, your ladyship's most devoted slave."

She laughed again and signaled her coachman to drive on. "Good-bye."

Phillipa turned to Winifred questioningly, but a warning pressure on her arm kept her mouth shut until Lady Jersey was well out of hearing.

"What a talkative lady," Phillipa said in as mildly curious a tone as she could contrive.

"That, my dear, was the Countess of Jersey, one of the patronesses of Almack's," Winifred breathed, "and you have just been given a privilege that many young women would happily commit murder to obtain. To be offered vouchers to Almack's upon your first meeting! Oh, heavens, who could imagine it?"

Sinamor gave a cynical smile. "I suspect that we owe it all to St. Clair. I can't imagine what he's been telling her, but it was evident that her curiosity was piqued to the utmost."

"This all seems very silly to me," grumbled Phillipa.

"My dear," Winifred spoke in a tone of the greatest gravity, "you must never say such a thing again!"

Not quite knowing what to reply, Phillipa fell silent and turned once again to perusing the fashionable throng about them. Her attention was attracted by the sight of a magnificent yellow carriage. The shield and armorial bearings on its side confirmed to Phillipa's mind that this must be the conveyance of a great personage.

"Who is that?" she asked.

"No one," snorted Lady Dearborne in disgust.

The earl seemed amused by her question. "That is a prominent moneylender, my dear."

"Oh," said Phillipa, embarrassed. Another carriage approached, containing a strikingly beautiful woman who seemed to be looking their group over appraisingly.

"Phillipa, do not look at that dreadful creature," Winifred said. Phillipa found it hard to tear her eyes away. The woman studied the earl as she passed, and flashed him a provocative smile.

"My lord, is that lady a friend of yours?" Phillipa asked innocently.

Winifred was seized by a choking fit.

The earl maintained his composure. "I am afraid that she is no lady, and, no, we are not acquainted."

Phillipa's face reddened. She resolved to keep her mouth firmly shut for the duration of the ride. Accordingly, they rode along in silence for a while, interrupted only by their acknowledgment of acquaintances and the passing along of such information they thought necessary for Phillipa to know. She was beginning to feel weary and rather bored.

Sinamor unexpectedly took pity on her. "See that carriage?" he asked.

She could not help but notice it. The body of the carriage, the harness, the horses, even the liveries were all brown.

"That is Lord Petersham. He once was in love with a widow named Browne and this is the result."

Phillipa could not suppress a giggle.

Winifred looked at him crossly. "Really, must you feed the child such gossip?"

The earl continued imperturbably. "He is a noted connoisseur of snuff and tea."

Phillipa chuckled at this fresh absurdity.

The earl consulted his watch. "And his presence here is a signal that it is past six o'clock. Shall we return home, ladies? Phillipa and I would not wish to be late for Astley's."

Even Winifred could have no objection to this scheme and accordingly they turned toward home.

When the earl arrived at Hamilton Place that evening, ready for the long-anticipated outing, he saw to his surprise that three companions awaited him, rather than the expected one. William and Anthony, their faces freshly scrubbed and beaming with excitement, rose with Phillipa as the earl entered.

"What's this?" Sinamor asked coldly. "I do not recall bargaining for a party of three."

William and Anthony's faces fell.

"Oh, but, my lord," said Phillipa, "they have been so very good about helping me with my dance lessons."

The earl was studying the two dejected little figures before him, dressed in their best dark-blue tailcoats and pantaloons. He was assailed by a new and unfamiliar emotion.

"And I never would have heard of Astley's except for them. Why, I just assumed you meant to take us all," Phillipa continued.

"Never mind, Phillipa." William was doing his best to keep his voice from trembling. "We would not wish to impose on Lord Sinamor's kindness, would we, Anthony?"

His younger brother, not trusting his voice, only shook his head.

William made a wooden little bow. "If you will excuse us, then, my lord, we will let you be on your way." He looked up at Sinamor bravely, his eyes bright.

"My lord . . ." There was a pleading note in Phillipa's voice.

The corner of the earl's mouth curled up in a smile. "I didn't say they couldn't come; I merely said I hadn't bargained on them. By all means, if you really wish for the company of these two young jackanapes, I have no objection."

He was rewarded by three explosions of delight. Anthony so far forgot himself as to give forth a whoop of excitement. Catching the earl's stern eye, he immediately retreated into bashful silence.

"And where is Edmond, then?" asked the earl.

"Oh, he's far too top-lofty to go with us," Phillipa assured him. "He says that Astley's is children's fare."

Sinamor began to draw on his gloves. "Well, if this is the entire party, we might as well be off." He looked Phillipa squarely in the eye. "You're sure there's no one else that you've invited whom you've neglected to mention? There aren't thirty or forty people waiting out in the hall, for example?"

Phillipa blushed red and would have protested hotly, but Anthony saw the telltale curling of the mouth. "He's only roasting you, Phillipa," exclaimed Anthony, then he roared with laughter.

"Enough of this talk," said the earl with mock severity. "We wouldn't wish to miss the acrobats."

"Or the conjurers," William added.

"Or the clowns," put in Anthony eagerly.

"Or the horses," Phillipa said.

Any number of the *ton* would have been justifiably amazed to learn that the arrogant Earl of Sinamor was spending his evening escorting a nursery party to Astley's. No one could be more surprised than the earl himself, however, by the fact that he was enjoying it.

The children's frank pleasure in the unsophisticated entertainment was in itself a form of diversion to the earl. As the boys doubled up in amusement at the antics of the clowns, it was hard to prevent smiling at the picture they presented. Phillipa was laughing joyously, too, so overcome that the tears began streaming down her face. An unexpected chuckle escaped the earl, and then another. Soon, unnoticed by his companions, he was laughing with an ease that might have astounded those who knew him best.

Through the rest of the performance, he found himself studying the faces of his companions rather than focusing on the acts themselves. He felt an odd sensation as he observed the look of wonder on the boys' faces as they watched the conjurer or the acrobats.

The highlight for Phillipa was, of course, the equestrian performance. Her eyes sparkling as she watched, she appeared to savor every moment of it. She gasped appropriately at the sight of the intrepid riders performing pirouettes atop the backs of their saddleless mounts.

Sinamor felt a sharp pang as he watched her. Somehow, under his very nose, she had blossomed into quite a taking young lady. He could not doubt that there would be offers, many of them—and soon. He could not analyze why he felt a stab of pain at the thought. She has made my life more interesting, at least, he admitted to himself. It would all seem just a bit dull when Phillipa was gone. He smiled grimly to himself. Here he was, carrying on like a maudlin fool, worrying about Phillipa's nuptials when there wasn't even a suitor in sight yet.

He settled back in his seat to watch the rest of the performance, unaware of Phillipa's scrutiny. She had glanced at him once or twice, to make sure that he was appreciating the finer points of the performance. Now he sat there, withdrawn, a bitter smile on his face. What an odd man he is, Phillipa thought.

He maintained his usual cool reserve on the drive home while Phillipa and the boys excitedly discussed what they'd seen. As the drive progressed, however, first Anthony's, then William's eyelids grew heavier, and by the time they had reached Hamilton Place, both were sound asleep.

The earl charged a pair of footmen with the task of conveying the boys upstairs, then turned to bid Phillipa good night. She grasped his sleeve with an unspoken urgency. Her hesitancy showed in her face. It was singular, thought the earl, how beautiful those eyes were as they shone in the moonlight. It would be fatal to say so, of course. He must not betray any weakness.

"Well?" he asked icily.

"My lord, I just wished to thank you for taking me and the boys. It meant so much to them, I do not think that you can know. . . ."

He detached her hand from his sleeve gently. "Do not imagine that I am a philanthropist, Phillipa. It did not discommode me to bring the boys tonight, that is all."

"But I know that you—"

"If you will excuse me, my dear, the hour is late and my leg is rather uncomfortable. I appreciate your thanks, but they are unnecessary." He stepped into his carriage. His eyes glinted at her. "If you feel that you must repay me, you may do that best by doing Lady Dearborne and myself credit at the ball tomorrow night."

"I will try," Phillipa said brokenly, and turned so that she would not see the carriage driving off. Her eyes smarted. Why should she care what he thought? She hated him; she had from the beginning. He was nothing but an arrogant, overbearing man who cared little for anything or anyone. She slipped a handkerchief out of her reticule and dabbed quickly at her eyes. She was a fool if she permitted herself to care about him, even if he was her guardian.

By the next evening, a sense of excitement had overpowered Phillipa's feelings of grievance against the earl. Her pride came strongly to her rescue also. She could see Lady Dearborne's nervousness on her behalf and determined not to betray any herself. An angry voice inside her said, "They both expect me to fail," and accordingly she resolved that she wouldn't.

Her maid was not infected by Phillipa's apparent steadiness of nerves. Ever since her rescue, she had regarded her new mistress as something more than mortal. Now, as she finished her handiwork, she stepped back and gasped with pleasure.

"Oh, Miss Phillipa, you're so beautiful. You look like a princess."

Phillipa examined her reflection in the mirror. The maid was exaggerating, of course. She never actually would be beautiful, but at the same time, she could not help but be pleased by what she saw.

She was wearing a modish gown of net over a sapphire-blue satin slip. Lady Dearborne had objected to the gown's color, saying that it was too vivid a hue for a young lady, but the dressmaker had championed Phillipa's choice. She had argued that not only was the color perfect for Phillipa, but also that Phillipa was right to set herself apart.

Phillipa did have to admit that the color became her. The vivid blue made the creamy skin exposed above the high-waisted bodice seem even more lustrous. Her eyes looked enormous, accented by the shade of the gown. Again, Madame Couteaux had designed the gown with utter simplicity, forsaking many of the fashionable furbelows in favor of one deep flounce at the hem and a few knots of ribbons on the sleeve. Her hair, reflecting the candlelight, shone with red fire. Sapphire kid slippers and evening gloves completed the ensemble.

Lady Dearborne poked her head in the room curiously. "My dear! You are a vision!" She smiled kindly at the maid. "And that's a lovely job you've done with her hair, too, Mary."

The young servant curtsied, obviously gratified by praise from such high quarters.

Winifred stepped in to examine Phillipa more closely. "All that is wanting," she began critically, "are the proper jewels, child."

Phillipa raised a hand, protestingly, to her neck. "But I am wearing my mother's pearls."

"Hmm! Well, it shall have to do," said Winifred dissatisfied. "Come along, then; Sinamor has arrived and it would not do to keep him waiting too long."

Winifred was looking very smart herself in a yellow silk gown, her head topped by a fashionable toque of yellow gauze. Phillipa ventured to compliment her.

"Heavens, child, no one will notice me with you there," exclaimed Winifred good-humoredly as they made their way down the stairs.

As Phillipa caught sight of Sinamor, a small gasp escaped her. She had not anticipated how superb he would look in full evening dress. From the sober black cutaway, without a wrinkle in it, to his form-fitting pantaloons, he presented a magnificent sight. She marveled at the snowy perfection of his cravat with the beautiful diamond pin nestled in it. He epitomized the ideal of understated elegance as he stood there. The impeccability of his dress was mirrored by his air of cool detachment. The illusion of perfection was complete to Phillipa, but it shattered as he took a limping step toward them.

He complimented them in a dispassionate way upon their appearance and led them to the waiting carriage. Phillipa was determined to match his poise with her own. She kept up a flow of inconsequential small talk, in order to show that she, at least, was not worried about the evening before them.

She did find it rather hard to maintain her composure during the forty-five-minute wait they encountered after reaching the area of their destination. As if sensing her distress, Lady Dearborne patted her arm sympathetically.

"The carriages always have to wait in this sort of line if it is a function at all worth attending. I am afraid it is a part of life in London." She thought for a moment, then added, "Besides, it is a good sign. One never wishes to arrive before the other guests."

Sinamor stifled a yawn behind one gloved hand. "Perhaps this is an opportune time for this, then," he said enigmatically as he extracted a long, slender case from his waistcoat and handed it to Phillipa.

She looked at him in confusion.

"Open it."

She did so, and beheld a large and gloriously beautiful sapphire suspended from a chain of diamonds. Winifred uttered a little surprised cry when she saw it. Phillipa held it in her hands, speechless.

The earl took it from her, leaned forward, and calmly unclasped her pearls. He then fastened the sapphire about her neck. He surveyed the finished picture critically. "Perfect." He shot Lady Dearborne an inquiring look. "Don't you think so, Winifred?"

She could only nod in silent agreement.

Phillipa put one hand up to her neck. "M-my lord," she stammered.

He caught her hand, gave it a tiny squeeze, and returned it to her lap. "After all St. Clair's hard work, it is only fitting that my ward should live up to her sobriquet."

She was beginning to protest again, more hotly this time, when the carriage came to a final stop and a liveried footman opened the door. She gave up. "Thank you," she whispered, then turned to take the footman's arm.

Winifred was surprised to see the oddly tender look that passed quickly over the earl's face. He seemed unaware of her scrutiny. She turned to exit the carriage. Perhaps she had imagined it.

The sparkling jewel hanging from her neck somehow banished the nervousness Phillipa had been concealing. She stood, erect and serene, in the entryway as their names were announced. There was no mistaking the sudden lull in conversation or the hundreds upon hundreds of curious eyes that turned upon her. She remained seemingly indifferent to it all, greeting her host and hostess with a charming smile and expressing her appreciation for being included.

My word, thought Lady Dearborne, who had never seen this side of the girl before, she has the composure of a queen.

As they proceeded into the room, Phillipa scarcely had time to notice the magnificent surroundings or to enjoy the spectacle of hundreds of people clad in their finest silks and satins. There was a surge in the crowd, and soon she was surrounded by a swarm of young gentlemen. She bestowed upon each of these gallants a bewitching smile as he was introduced, and it was not long before her dance card was entirely filled.

Winifred, standing beside her, was delighted with her charge's social dexterity and with her success. She was beginning to feel that nothing could happen to mar her enjoyment of this evening when she spotted the Fitzroys. Charles looked to be in a very sullen mood, indeed. Winifred sent a little prayer heavenward that nothing untoward might occur.

Phillipa, looking up, saw the object of her companion's gaze. Before Winifred knew what she was about, Phillipa had excused herself prettily from her throng of admirers and was heading in Charles' direction. Unwilling to make her fears obvious by chasing Phillipa, Lady Dearborne could only watch with a feeling of doom. She looked on in horrified fascination as Phillipa met with an icy greeting. She saw the girl holding out her hand in an open way and murmuring some words with a smile on her face. The hand was at last taken, reluctantly. A few more unencouraging words were offered. Still Phillipa persisted. Winifred could see that the boy was not avoiding looking at her as much as he had before. His sister, too, seemed to join in the conversation, and there was no rancor in her face. After a few more minutes' work, incredibly, a smile spread across the boy's face and he began to talk in an animated fashion. Winifred judged it to be a prudent time to intervene.

After exchanging the necessary chitchat with the Fitzroys, she bore Phillipa off. There was no question but that Charles' eyes followed her with interest.

"I don't know how you did that, child," she whispered, "but thank God that it worked, whatever it was."

Phillipa shrugged indifferently. "Oh, my father always was used to say there was nothing anyone liked better than a frank, direct apology." She smiled mischievously. "And the fact that my dance card was already filled didn't hurt."

Their conversation was interrupted by the appearance of St. Clair. After greeting them and murmuring polite encomiums to their beauty, he turned to Phillipa with a smile.

"And has the Sapphire kept her word and saved me a dance as she promised?"

She held out her card to him ingenously. "I saved you my very first one."

"Excellent." He smiled at Winifred. "Lady Dearborne, I hope that you will grant me one also?"

She laughed. "Shameless man. You know very well that we matrons do not dance."

"Matrons, no. But surely someone as young and as lovely as yourself would not forgo that pleasure."

Winifred smiled and shook her fan at him. "Go on with you. I hear the musicians beginning."

He bowed and offered his arm to Phillipa. "I will return her to you safely," he promised.

St. Clair was, as Phillipa soon discovered, an exceedingly graceful dancer. Although she initially laughed at some of the absurd compliments he was paying her, her mind was not entirely upon her dancing. St. Clair observed the way those beautiful eyes roamed about the room, and at the next opportunity he asked her quietly, "Who is it that you are seeking?"

She looked back at him and blushed for her poor manners. "I am sorry. It's just that I haven't seen the earl since we arrived."

St. Clair had no need to ask which earl. With a little smile, he said, "He is standing near the corner of the floor, observing you discreetly."

She blushed even deeper. "You must think me a perfect idiot. It's just that I—"

"Not at all," said St. Clair evenly, though his eyes sparkled with an inexplicable sort of satisfaction.

With that worry from her mind, Phillipa was able to devote her attention entirely to her partner and the dance. Her spritely figure attracted a certain amount of scrutiny, as did the great blue eyes, which shone with pleasure.

"That's a fine-looking girl," commented a slightly overweight, corseted young man in a coat with ridiculously padded shoulders and enormous silver buttons. "Who is she?"

His companion shrugged. "The new ward of the Earl of Sinamor. I understand she's lately of Yorkshire. The name is Raithby."

"Raithby?" pondered Viscount Wakehurst, frowning beneath his pomaded hair. "I wonder why that should sound so familiar to me."

"They say she has a considerable fortune."

"Oh, really?" Wakehurst asked with interest.

Another observer was watching Phillipa with equal interest, though far less admiration. "So that's Sinamor's ward," said the Baroness Serre in a hostile way. "Not a beauty, is she?"

Lady Joseph giggled maliciously. "I suppose not, but she seems to hold his attention rather well."

From their vantage point, the ladies could see that the earl was keeping a sharp eye on his ward.

Helene paled with anger. "I can't believe that he's taken with that drab little creature."

Lady Joseph giggled again. "There's little you can do about it if he is."

Helene looked at her companion with cold fury in her eyes. "That's where you're wrong. If it is this insignificant chit he's interested in, there is a great deal that I can do about it. And I will, if only to pay him back in his own coin!"

Lady Joseph looked about them nervously. "Please, keep your voice down, my dear Baroness."

Phillipa was happily unaware of the malevolent stare that was being directed at her. She was finding, to her surprise, that balls could be very pleasurable with so many young men importuning one for one's hand. Dancing was not nearly the trial it had seemed to be. It was, after all, no very great hardship to have young men continually whispering agreeable things into one's ear.

Winifred had been observing Phillipia's flirtations in growing amazement. When the earl came limping casually up, she turned to him in shock.

"Can you imagine, Sinamor? Our Phillipa is a coquette!"

The earl smiled slightly at her. The dance was ending and Phillipa's latest partner was escorting her back to Winifred. They could see the youth bow his head to listen to Phillipa and then explode with laughter at something Phillipa said. Winifred shook her head.

As Phillipa walked up, their group was joined by Lord Malling. He bowed corpulently to the ladies.

"Sinamor," he said elaborately, "your diamond is justly famous, but now I see that it is your Sapphire who is creating a sensation."

The earl's expression did not waver. "Lord Malling, may I present my ward Miss Raithby to you. Miss Raithby, Lord Malling."

He took the hand she offered and kissed it fulsomely. "Ah, such a radiant vision." He glanced at Lady Dearborne belatedly. "To have the company of two such beauties must be—"

"Yes, very," said the earl shortly.

Lord Malling looked at Phillipa with a glimmer of curiosity. "Miss Raithby, have I met you somewhere before?"

Phillipa's heart sank within her at these words. In panic, she looked at the earl. He gave a tiny shake of his head. She looked back at Lord Malling and gave him an ingenuous smile. "No, I think not, my lord. I surely could not forget having met you."

Another man might have been put off by the obsequiousness of the compliment, but Lord Malling puffed himself up visibly.

"Nor I you, my dear—nor I you."

Her next dancing partner had joined them and was looking at Phillipa impatiently. The earl waved a languid hand at them. "We will detain you no longer, my dear." With their departure, Lord Malling also excused himself.

Winifred let out a long breath. "I thought that the fat was in the fire that time," she whispered.

The earl took her hand and patted it. "Phillipa will be fine as long as she keeps her head."

8

In fact, Phillipa kept her head so very well indeed that all parties agreed that her first public appearance had been an unequivocal triumph. Not a soul in the house regarded this victory with indifference. Even Lord Dearborne, who sleepily encountered his wife in her celebratory mood, had the grace to own that he had thought all along that Phillipa would manage the thing. He yawned and added tiredly, "I suppose we'll need to plan our own ball for her next."

Winifred's eyes sparkled. "Why, I hadn't even thought of it. Where can my mind be? Dearest!" She flew to him and planted an enthusiastic kiss on his cheek.

He grumbled and turned over.

Despite the hour, Lady Dearborne was still too full of excitement to sleep. She opened her secretary and began to write down her plans.

Phillipa, oddly enough, was not affected by a similar restlessness. She felt the exhaustion of having passed through a hazardous trial. As soon as her preparations were finished, she fell into bed into instant sleep.

It was probably this fact that enabled her to rise, dress, and go down to the stable at her usual hour of half-past seven. McPherson was waiting for her there, with Ripon saddled. He had been given the word of Phillipa's success, but he was doing his best to hide his pride under a gruff exterior.

He thought she was an elegeant picture in her dark-blue riding habit, but he concealed it with a scowl. "So ye've come for a ride, then. I thought certainly ye'd be abed half the day, since ye're keepin' the hours of these city folk."

She gave him a devastating smile. "Then why did you have Ripon saddled?"

He shifted uneasily. "Och, well, that's me order, Miss Phillipa. Just because yer horse mon stand here for hours."

She patted Ripon on the neck. "But he didn't, did he?"

"I doot ye'll hae mich time for 'im in future, poor creature."

Phillipa, who knew full well from the thickening of his accent that McPherson was in a mawkishly sentimental mood, only gave a little laugh as she swung into the saddle.

"I shouldn't make any wagers, if I were you, Mr. McPherson. I imagine that we have lost Lord Sinamor, though."

McPherson began to walk over to his own dependable mount. An icy voice came from behind Phillipa. "And why, pray tell, should I choose not to honor you with my company today?"

Phillipa gritted her teeth. How exasperating he was. She had made a perfectly innocent remark and he had twisted it to sound as if she were plotting against him somehow. She had wanted to thank him for his gift and his unspoken support last night. Now all she wished to do was to plant him a facer. She contrived to hide her irritation.

"Good morning, my lord," she said coolly.

The ride passed, as usual, in stony silence. She was unaware that the earl was taking the opportunity to study her covertly. Her success the previous night had surpassed his expectations. He felt foolishly proud of the little, trim girl beside him, who had taken the beaux by storm.

Ripon started at a sudden noise. Phillipa managed to quickly fight him down. She then spoke soothingly to him and patted his neck. His eyes still showed white, but it was apparent that he trusted her.

The earl watched this little display in admiration. She was a wonderful horsewoman and the bond that she had with the big animal was undeniable.

She caught him looking at her and her eyes flashed in indignation. "You needn't concern yourself, my lord," she said coldly. "I have this animal under control."

His words of approbation froze on his lips. Why must the chit still insist on perceiving me as her enemy? he thought angrily. So, instead, he turned his gaze from her and said indifferently, "The world would think me a poor guardian if I allowed you to break your foolish neck, Miss Raithby."

She was tempted to put her heels to Ripon and leave the earl far behind. Only the knowledge that he was capable of putting her back on the placid mare stopped her. It required an act of iron will, but she closed her lips firmly and kept them closed for the rest of the ride.

As they returned to Hamilton Place, they were surprised to see Edmond cantering in ahead of them. He greeted them cheerily enough, though Phillipa privately thought that he looked a fright. She had never seen him with his stock tied carelessly and his hair untidy. She had no chance to comment upon it, for he was busy congratulating her upon her triumph.

"Lord, Phillipa. I wish I'd been there," he said frankly. "How I should have laughed to have seen them all making idiots of themselves over you."

Oddly enough, this sincere compliment did not seem to please Phillipa overly. "I did not know you liked to go for early rides, Edmond," she said.

He flushed and spoke a little too quickly. "Why, yes . . . marvelous exercise and all that, you know. Why look at how fat old Prinny's gotten since he gave it up."

The earl's quelling look was turned upon him and he flushed and reverted to his former topic.

"I don't know how you did it either, Phillipa, but Fitzroy was mooning over you like a great calf last night."

"Last night?" she said puzzledly. "You mean after the ball?"

A cough from Sinamor interrupted her.

"By the way, that's a magnificent horse . . ." Edmond was beginning somewhat desperately when the earl cut him off. "Will you permit me to say farewell, Miss Raithby. I have business to which I must attend this morning."

She dismounted. "Very well. Are there any more lessons?" She looked at him challengingly.

"Phillipa, my lessons for you are through," he said in a tone that suggested both weariness and amusement.

She nodded a farewell and went inside the house.

Edmond had dismounted and was preparing to follow her when the earl spoke abruptly. "A word, young Dearborne."

Edmond turned to face him with a sigh.

Sinamor looked at him coldly. "You are not to make my ward

privy to your nocturnal activities, do you understand me?''

A little shiver passed along Edmond's spine as he squirmed under that basilisk stare. ''Lord, couldn't you see that I was trying to keep it from her?''

The earl's glance never wavered. ''Trying will not be sufficient.''

Edmond fidgeted uncomfortably. ''Lord, you'd think I'd committed a crime, or . . .'' He suddenly turned beet-red. ''Well, if that's what you think, you're mistaken, my lord,'' he said hotly. ''I did nothing more than have a few games of cards with Fitzroy and Sutcliffe and then later with some fellow named Wakehurst and a few others. I admit that we might have drunk a bit more claret than we ought, but I assure you, my lord, that I've done nothing of which *I* would be ashamed.''

The emphasis he had placed on the word ''*I,*'' leaving no doubt as to his implication, at the very least normally would have earned him a sharp set-down from Sinamor. Instead, the earl was looking at him with narrowed eyes. ''Did you say Wakehurst?''

''Yes,'' said Edmond sullenly, ''and he has the devil's own luck, too.''

Edmond suddenly realized the precarious position in which he had placed himself. ''My lord, you won't . . . you won't tell Mama, will you?''

The earl's face relaxed into the usual cool mask. ''What you do is a matter of supreme indifference to me. My only concern is for my ward. I wish her to be treated with the delicacy that befits any young lady of rank.''

Edmond opened his mouth and shut it again. ''Yes, my lord. Thank you.'' He stood there in bewilderment as Sinamor rode off. Why, from the way Sinamor talked, you'd think that he, Edmond, had committed some heinous crime. Treat Phillipa with delicacy? The thought made him smile bitterly. He at least had never horsewhipped anyone. As if he were going to boast to Phillipa about how he had been befuddled and thoroughly bested in the card game last night!

McPherson gave him a look of sympathy as he prepared to lead Edmond's horse away. He felt pity for the young sprig, for McPherson himself had been at the receiving end of one of the earl's trimmings more than once.

"Never mind, then, lad," he said in a kindly way, "he's daft for the lass."

"Sinamor?" Edmond's face was expressive of shock and total disbelief.

McPherson only chuckled as he departed.

Edmond puzzled over his words. Surely there could be no truth in it. Sinamor had never been in love with anyone, as far as he knew. All the same, it was fortunate perhaps that he hadn't told Sinamor about the outcome of the card game. He himself had felt a great deal of relief when Wakehurst had offered to cancel his debt in exchange for an introduction to Phillipa. It had seemed a small thing to ask. He shivered slightly, thinking of the look on Sinamor's face. No, it would be better if the earl did not know about it.

Phillipa, meanwhile, was startled to discover what seemed to her to be a veritable mountain of flowers in the hall.

Winifred, coming down the stairs, smiled at her surprise. "It seems that you have won yourself quite a few admirers."

"But who could possibly . . .?" began Phillipa, stripping off her gloves to begin examining cards.

She opened an envelope attached to a very pretty bouquet of white roses. "Why, this is from Charles Fitzroy," she exclaimed in surprise.

She opened another envelope and smiled delightedly. "This is from St. Clair. He offers me his congratulations."

'How kind of him," murmured Winifred, taking the card from her to examine it.

Phillipa turned to a beautiful little nosegay of violets. "Oh, how sweet these are." She opened the card and saw the single, bold signature, "Sinamor." In her shock, the card fluttered from her hand.

Winifred stooped to retrieve it. "How thoughtful of Sinamor," she said in a matter-of-fact voice. "What lovely taste he has." She glanced sharply at Phillipa to see that she was standing motionless, as if mesmerized.

"My dear, I know it was all a very great triumph," Winifred

said, "but I beg you to go upstairs and change your clothes immediately. We have a great deal of work to do today."

Phillipa started and looked at her uncomprehendingly.

"Go on," urged Winifred.

Phillipa went up the stairs to do her bidding.

Within the hour, the two ladies were ensconced in the gold salon. Winifred happily was discussing her plans for Phillipa's coming-out ball, while Phillipa somewhat boredly assented to them.

"And I don't think we can possibly arrange everything in less than three weeks' time, but it would not do to delay much longer, for after the celebrations are over, I doubt that anyone will wish to remain in town."

Phillipa agreed with a tiny yawn.

After forty-five minutes or so of this, Phillipa could only be relieved to have the footman appear and announce that she had a visitor.

"Who is it, Fredericks?" asked Winifred.

"Miss Middleton, my lady."

A militant look leapt into Phillipa's eye.

Winifred glanced warningly at her. "Very well, show her up."

Marianne came into the room with no less confidence than before.

She greeted them both and stepped up to Phillipa, proffering a volume. "I went by the lending library this morning and decided to bring you a novel."

Phillipa took it unwillingly.

"It's one of my favorites. I do hope you haven't read it before."

"No, I haven't," Phillipa said coolly. At an emphatic glare from Winifred, she added belatedly, "Thank you. It is most kind of you."

"Not at all," said Marianne, delighted to have accomplished her purpose. "I am persuaded you will love it, as I do." She assumed a look of seriousness. "And I feel that reading improves the mind, as I am sure Lady Dearborne would agree."

Winifred was forced to murmur a polite assent, though she didn't see how reading Mrs. Radcliffe's novel was going to improve anyone's mind. "Won't you have a seat, Miss Middleton?" she asked. "Would you care for tea?"

Miss Middleton refused the offer politely and, sitting, turned to Phillipa. "Actually, I wished to have an opportunity to see you, because I heard that you were to attend Almack's. Naturally, being from the country, it must seem very frightening, and I thought that, since I have attended an assembly there already, I could give you advice on how to conduct yourself and whom you must be careful to conciliate and . . ."

Winifred almost gasped at the effrontery of the chit. To treat Phillipa so patronizingly when she knew full well about her triumph last night. She looked at Phillipa's face, expecting to see murder in her eyes.

Instead, Phillipa was saying in an unusually languid way, "That's really too kind of you, Miss Middleton, much too kind, in fact. It is so generous of you to wish to help me. I'm afraid that I find all of these social obligations rather tiresome, however, and I wish to waste as little time thinking about them as possible. Thank you for your sweet offer, though."

Bravo, thought Winifred as she watched Marianne sputter and slowly turn purple with rage. A little demon inside her prompted her to say, "Oh, Miss Middleton, I am so glad you mentioned that. Do you know, Phillipa and I have been so busy this morning planning a ball that I completely forgot all the invitations to which she needs to respond today."

Phillipa managed to achieve a creditable pout. "How tedious. And I thought we might go shopping later."

Winifred could not resist helping her. "I'm afraid we'll be busy most of the day, my dear."

Phillipa opened her eyes wide and said innocently, "But I must have a new pair of kid slippers. Mine were completely ruined at the ball last night." She turned to Marianne confidingly. "Dancing all night is so hard on one's shoes, don't you find?"

Marianne could only mutter a stifled affirmative. With a fixed smile on her face, she rose and said she had to be on her way.

Polite protestations were made, but Marianne overruled them, departing after Phillipa finished her profuse thanks for the loan of the book.

Marianne stalked out, leaving the two occupants of the room breathlessly silent. As soon as the front door closed, they both broke into suppressed giggles.

"Oh, Phillipa," gasped Winifred, "that was too naughty of you."

"I know, but she deserved it. She wished to make me feel like a bumpkin. I only turned the tables."

"Oh!" Winifred was stung by a new thought. "I know she pestered Sinamor for months to procure that Almack's invitation for her, and then for you to say it was tiresome . . ."

Despite her brave assurances to Marianne, Phillipa felt a certain amount of trepidation as Wednesday night approached. Winifred had been very careful to impress upon her just exactly what success or failure at Almack's could mean. She had also spent hours going over all the rules, which if transgressed, even unknowingly, could mean social ostracism.

Winifred had also helped her select which dress to wear. It was of white lace over white satin, with a simple double flounce of lace at the hem. White kid slippers and gloves completed the ensemble. The only touch of color was provided by the glowing gem at her throat.

Winifred examined her with approval. "Very good," she said, "*jeune fille*, but with a difference. Perfect."

Although Phillipa had been warned about this rule, it was still somewhat of a shock to come down the stairs and see Sinamor and Edmond in their knee breeches and silk stockings, with their chapeaux bras under their arms. Edmond looked slightly uncomfortable, but the old-fashioned formality of the costume seemed to suit Sinamor. She found it hard to tear her eyes from that figure, who still bore himself with a military erectness. Suddenly, she could picture him as he must have looked in his cavalry uniform. How handsome he is, she thought. At that moment, her eyes met his and she colored.

He did not know the reason, but he thought how the touch of pink in her cheeks became her.

Phillipa could not have said why, but the mere presence of the earl was a comfort to her. His very nonchalance gave her confidence to face the ordeal ahead.

She was to discover that it was less of an ordeal than she had imagined. To begin with, the rooms themselves had disappointed her. She had expected something worthy of a palace. She also found the refreshments shockingly bad. She had to make an effort not to grimace when she tasted the stale cake brought her by one adoring swain.

It seemed very silly to have to decline the many offers for her hand in the waltz, but Winifred had assured her that she must on no account take part in it. She also was constantly irritated by the jostling of the crowd. Combined with the heat, it made her feel as if she could not breathe. More than once she felt like dashing outside for some fresh air, only to be aware that eyes were upon her, constantly assessing and judging her for defects in manner, speech, or decorum.

There were a few bright spots to make the evening more bearable. First, St. Clair had materialized as if out of nowhere to request the first dance from her once again. He had spent a good bit of time chatting with her and making her laugh, which seemed to attract the notice of the patronesses.

Also, when she was beginning to be tired of declining offers for the waltz, Sinamor came to stand by her and engage her in quiet conversation. This seemed to hold many of her would-be partners at bay. She wondered if the earl had done it purposely, for he moved away just as the next dance was beginning. She felt a sense of gratitude to him in either case.

She felt fortunate, too, that her dance card was filled as quickly as it had been the last time. She did not disdain the attention she was receiving from these beaux, though privately she thought most of them rather young and silly. There were those also, of course, who were old and silly.

In fact, she derived a certain amount of entertainment from observing the foibles around her. As she relaxed, she became more free to appreciate the follies of speech, manner, and dress all about her. There was nothing to rival it in all of Yorkshire, she was certain.

The most interesting part of the evening for her was when Edmond introduced a friend of his, the Viscount Wakehurt. She had not been impressed by this plump sprig of fashion despite his handsome face, thinking his expression fatuous and his clothing absurd. She had not immediately connected his name with her mother's family. When he asked a few probing questions, therefore, she was surprised when he concluded that he was her cousin.

Startled, she looked into his face and saw confirmation of his words there. Although he had dark eyes and the lines of his face were somewhat softened by his extra weight, the Wakehurst nose was there plain to see.

"I had no idea that I had a cousin, a cousin your age, I mean," stammered Phillipa.

"Delightful, isn't it? I am an only child also," he said.

Phillipa did not hesitate for a moment. "I understood that your family did not wish to associate with mine," she said frankly.

For some reason, this remark amused him greatly. "You certainly believe in plain speaking," he said when he had finished chuckling.

There was no answering smile on Phillipa's face.

He assumed a serious expression. "Please don't misunderstand me. My grandfather—our grandfather, that is—was very much an old tartar. He died only three years ago, and we had no way of knowing your whereabouts. Believe me, my father and mother will be just as delighted to meet you as I am."

Phillipa, not knowing of the letter her father had written, accepted his words at face value.

"It's nice to find a relation," she admitted. "Now that Mother and Father are both gone, there is only me."

His face was alight with sympathy. "No one on your father's side at all?"

She shrugged. "A great-aunt who lived with us. She's rather old now. I do have some cousins, but they are busy with their own families." She omitted to mention that her cousins had been among those who laughed at her for seeming more a boy than a girl.

"Well, I want you to consider me family now." He gave her hand a little press with his warm, sweaty one as the dance ended. "I hope I may call on you—to see if I may be of service?"

She felt a physical repulsion toward him, but tried to be

charitable, thinking of the kindness of his words. "Yes, that would be very nice," she said.

The earl did not mention the subject until they were riding the next morning.

"By the by," he said casually, "who was that young corseted tulip I saw you chatting with so earnestly last night?"

Phillipa smiled. "That is the Viscount Wakehurst, my cousin."

The earl's expression did not alter. "Did he tell you that?"

She looked at him, surprised. "Yes. Why? Isn't it true?"

He shook his head. "No, I believe it is true."

Phillipa lifted her chin a little. "Well, he was very nice. He told me that when his grandfather died three years ago they had no way of knowing how to contact us."

"Oh," said the earl enigmatically.

Phillipa's eyes began to flash dangerously. "And he said that his parents would be delighted to meet me and he asked if he could call and I told him yes!"

"Hm," said the earl.

"Is there something wrong with that?" she asked defiantly.

"No, not at all," said Sinamor in an expressionless voice.

Wakehurst, in fact, was as good as his word, calling upon Phillipa that very day.

Winifred, knowing the family's history, was not inclined to look upon his suit with a kindly eye. She tolerated his presence since Sinamor had not seen fit to enlighten Phillipa and since the girl took such obvious joy in the discovery of this new relative.

Because Wakehurst treated her with such respectful deference, Winifred could voice no real objections to the boy. Listening to his rather humdrum conversation, she thought that at least Phillipa could not form any lasting attachment to him. In fact, thought Winifred, observing the couple with narrowed eyes, he may prove useful to us. If Phillipa spends time with him, she can't spend it with a more dashing, more dangerous young blade.

Winifred was to observe at least one disturbing effect of Wakehurst's presence. The single-minded devotion Wakehurst was to show in the ensuing weeks was to irritate Edmond in the extreme. When accidentally confronting him in the hall of the green salon, Edmond was at his most frostily polite. He also made a habit of excusing himself rapidly from any expedition they proposed. Phillipa was hurt by his behavior and told him so after one of Wakehurst's visits.

"I wouldn't have anything to do with the fellow, if I were you, cousin or not," Edmond advised her.

She looked at him puzzledly. "But Edmond, you were the one who introduced us. You commended him to me as your particular friend."

For some reason, this answer seemed to enrage Edmond. "Honestly, sometimes you've no more sense than Arthur."

Phillipa's eyes were beginning to sparkle angrily. "Well, at least when I have a little tiff with someone, I don't go around telling everyone else not to associate with them."

"A little tiff! Well, if you think I could be that petty . . ."

"I think you could be more petty! Why, if I were to tell you what I knew—"

"Go ahead, tell me. Make me laugh!"

"Gervase warned me you would be like this. Don't even try to reason with him he said."

"Gervase! So we're on a first-name basis now, are we?"

"He told me that you would never forgive him because he came into that gamester's hell and found you foxed and tried to keep you from continuing to play."

"What absolute gammon. Don't tell me you swallowed that."

"And you wouldn't forgive him for discovering you in that condition, even though he was trying to help you."

"I was wrong. You've far less sense than Arthur," said Edmond contemptuously.

Her eyes blazed at him. "What reason would Gervase have to lie to me? And you forget, I saw you ride in that morning!" She stood there glaring at him.

Edmond's face was still angry, but there was a sudden thoughtfulness in it. "All right," he said. "If this fellow is so altruistic, why was he in this den of iniquity?"

Her mouth dropped open in outraged shock. "Because you

had told him you were going there, and he was concerned for you."

"That's rich." Edmond laughed scornfully. He looked at her face and saw that she did not believe him. "I have never been in a so-called gaming hell in my life, Phillipa, and I need not add that the expressions you're picking up are most unladylike."

Phillipa might have felt an inclination to trust his word, but the second half of the sentence made her furious again.

"Well, I am sure that this will surprise you, but I am capable of choosing my language and my friends without any help whatsoever from you!"

They stood there facing each other belligerently for another moment, then Phillipa spun around and walked briskly away.

From this moment on, a silent war began between Edmond and Phillipa. Each was icily polite to the other when necessary and the rest of the time pretended the other didn't exist.

Winifred was worried by this rift and terribly afraid that it might have been caused by jealousy on Edmond's part.

She attempted to approach Phillipa about it and was gently but firmly rebuffed. She had no more success with Edmond. Lord Robert envinced disinterest in such trivial proceedings and Sinamor was no more helpful. It seemed that the problem lay beyond her grasp.

The revelation came one day after Phillipa had departed on an outing with Wakehurst and a party of other young people. Edmond had arrived at home just in time to see them depart, and his face revealed his scorn. He gave them the scantiest of greetings before disappearing inside the house. He found his mother in the gold drawing room, perusing a letter.

"My dear, isn't it delightful? Francis has written from Eton saying that he will be home next week!"

"Mother, I'm surprised at your letting her go like that."

Winifred smiled at him tolerantly from the chair she was occupying. "What a nice sense of propriety you've developed. Really, my dear, there can be no objection to Phillipa's joining the party—they are well-chaperoned."

"I'm not talking about that," Edmond said in exasperation. "I'm talking about that . . . that cousin of hers."

Lady Dearborne sighed. "Edmond, we have discussed this before. I know you dislike him, but he is Phillipa's cousin, and the only relation she has in London. You must remember that—"

He cut her off. "But the fellow's a scoundrel! Surely you could forbid him to see Phillipa, or at least tell him to come less often."

"My dear, that is her guardian's place, not mine. I am not that fond of the young man myself. Surely you must know Phillipa better than that by now. The best way to get her to do anything is to tell her not to do it."

"Sinamor could make her."

"But he isn't." She looked at her son with concern. "If there is something that we should know about Wakehurst please tell me."

"Well, they say he hasn't a feather to fly with and . . ."

"And?"

He struggled for words for a moment, wondering if he should make his confession. It was too late, he decided morosely. "Nothing really, I suppose. It's just that there's something about him I don't like."

Winifred decided to break it to him gently. "My dear, I know that in these few months, you and Phillipa have become rather close."

He turned to her, his face uncomprehending.

"But you must consider that she is the first young lady whom you have known so well. I promise you, there will be others who—"

He frowned at her in shock. "Mama, have you gone mad? Don't tell me you think I have a *tendre* for Phillipa?"

Winifred gazed at him in equal surprise.

"I'd rather marry her horse," he said frankly. "At least his temper is a little less vile."

9

If Edmond had conceived an antipathy for Phillipa, it seemed that he was the only one in London who had. Invitations, flowers, and callers flowed in at an astonishing rate. The earl had been forced to decline more than one offer for her hand, a circumstance he thought fit to mention to Phillipa as they took their morning ride.

"Who was it this time?" she asked disinterestedly.

"Young Edwards. I hope that you had not conceived an attachment for him."

She sniffed in disgust. "Him! Why, he can't tell one end of a horse from another. Have you ever seen what he rides?"

The earl looked thoughtful. "You mean the animal that looks as if it should be hitched to a plow?"

She giggled. "Exactly. Now, how could I marry someone like that?"

"My dear, had you ever considered that a knowledge of horseflesh is perhaps not the best criterion for choosing a spouse?"

"It is not only that." Her eyes began to sparkle dangerously. "I do not wish to marry anyone who does not ask me first whether I wish to be married."

"Possibly he is just old-fashioned," the earl suggested.

She shook her head angrily. "I don't believe that. He is very willing to sit there and tell me that my eyes are like stars and all the rest of that nonsense, but he doesn't have the nerve to even hold my hand. I scare him, I know. I am formidable."

The earl's lips began to curl suspiciously, but fortunately Phillipa was staring straight ahead and did not see it.

"I know why they all wish to marry me, anyway." She heaved a little sigh. "Gervase told me that by acknowledging our connection, he was in some ways doing me a disfavor. He warned me that there would be only too many young men who would wish to marry me in order to become related to the Wakehursts."

A dark scowl descended upon the earl's face.

Phillipa did not notice it. She tried to assume a lighter tone. "So you see, my lord, if I am to be married for my birth and my fortune, I at least should have the right to demand a husband who knows how to sit a horse."

The low, menacing tone of the earl's voice took her by surprise. "Phillipa, while I am your guardian no one will wed you merely for your birth or your fortune, I promise you."

She was startled by the seriousness in his expression and didn't know quite how to respond. She fell silent, and the topic was not alluded to again.

Despite Sinamor's evident earnestness, Phillipa could not feel reassured. Her social triumphs had begun to seem hollow to her when Gervase had explained how matters stood. It was plain that no one would wish to marry her if she were only Phillipa Raithby, a soldier's daughter. It quite oppressed her spirits to think about it.

Upon their return, Sinamor took the opportunity to closet himself with Winifred. That good lady's sense of outrage was keen.

"How could he be so wicked? Evelyn, I have never trusted that boy, and you see what happens. What are we to do? I certainly could not receive him now."

Sinamor frowned broodingly. "I am afraid you cannot refuse him," he said at some length. "At this point, it is my word against his, and Phillipa has never trusted me."

"Oh, Evelyn," Winifred began to protest, but he silenced her with a hand.

"She is not alone in feeling the way she does. It is a pity in this case, for I am afraid that it renders her vulnerable."

"What do you mean. What do you suspect?"

His eyes glittered icily. "I think he intends to convince Phillipa that all other offers for her hand are insincere, thus paving the way for himself."

"But surely Phillipa realizes—"

"She is clever enough to know that there is some truth in what he is saying. Unfortunately she lacks the sophistication to determine the extent."

Winifred scowled. "And when I think of all St. Clair did to bring her into the fashion, and this creature acts as if it were nothing." She suddenly looked up at Sinamor with a stricken face. "Evelyn, is there nothing at all we can do?"

He shrugged. "Trust Phillipa's good sense, I suppose. If the situation becomes impossible, I can always remove her to Sinamor, but that will cause talk, and it is unlikely that she should submit tamely."

"To Sinamor? But, Evelyn, you hate it so." She halted abruptly. A queer sort of noise was beginning to reach their ears. "What on earth?" Winifred's eyes met his in dismay. Instinctively, she started to rise.

He motioned her to stay. "I'll see what it is."

As he stepped out into the hall, he could hear the noise more clearly. It was apparently an unmusical attempt at singing. He limped toward the door and opened it to observe a reeling figure making its way up the street. The words of the song became intelligible to the earl.

". . . *It is not fit the wretch should be, in competition set with me*," sang Edmond lustily as he approached. "*Who can drink ten times more than he*!"

He reached the bottom of the steps and met the earl's cold eyes. He executed a deep, if somewhat ramshackle bow and seemed to have a little trouble righting himself.

"Benefit of your training, m'lord," he offered handsomely.

"Young Dearborne," began the earl icily as Edmond put up a protesting hand.

"Firs' mus' finish the song, later the minuet." He opened his mouth and began bawling, "*Make a new world, ye powers divine! Stocked with nothing else but Wine—*"

His song was interrupted when the earl rushed down the stairs and hurriedly clasped a hand over his mouth. "Quiet, you young fool. Do you wish the whole street to know you're jug-bitten?"

Edmond tried to protest as the earl began to hustle him up the stairs. "I am not!" he mumbled indignantly. He glared at the earl balefully as Sinamor struggled to get him inside. "You think I'm overtaken, don't you? Damned insulting, I call it."

The earl gave an exasperated sigh. "I should keep my voice down if you don't wish your mother to know."

Edmond's eyes widened and he began to do his best to assist the earl in achieving a forward motion. He put a finger to his mouth. "Ssssh," he hissed loudly.

Winifred opened the door to the hallway. "Edmond!"

"Ssssh," Edmond told her.

"He apparently had rather a full evening," said the earl dryly as Bickerstaffe directed a footman to relieve him of his charge.

"I am not," Edmond said, following the statement with a loud hiccup.

"Oh, dear," said Winifred, watching anxiously as her son was half-carried up the stairs.

Sinamor limped to her side and gave her hand a reassuring squeeze. "He'll be himself again after a few good hours' sleep, the young whelp." He looked in her eyes and saw that her anxiety was not relieved. "What is it, my dear?"

She motioned to him and he silently followed her into the green salon. As soon as the door was safely closed, she began.

"I'm worried, Evelyn. Dearborne says every young man has to sow his wild oats, but it's not like Edmond to behave in this fashion."

The earl's eyebrow ascended quizzically.

"Now, you know I have never coddled my boys," said Winifred hotly. "It's just that, well, this is not the first time he's come home in this condition."

"I must confess that I take Dearborne's view," said the earl. He smiled. "How shocked he would be to know that I agreed with him in anything."

Winifred was shaking her head. "I cannot concur. This all began when that Wakehurst fellow began calling on Phillipa."

Sinamor's interest was caught. "Wakehurst, is he a particular friend of Edmond's?"

"No, Edmond hates him. I thought perhaps Edmond was jealous of him, but I found I was wrong."

"Hmm."

"I think something is eating away at Edmond, but he won't tell me what it is."

The earl's expression was enigmatic. "He's probably just fallen in with a set of rascally fellows. I will look into the matter, however."

They were interrupted again, this time by a great bustling in the hall.

"What can it be this time?" wondered Winifred.

As they rose to go and see, the door was flung open and a tall, thin schoolboy stood there for their inspection.

"Francis!" Winifred flung her arms around him joyfully. "I did not expect you so soon."

As she gave him a kiss, he reddened with embarrassment. "Mama, I am not a child anymore," he protested.

"Very well, then," she said, leaving an arm about his shoulders. "Say how do you do to Lord Sinamor, then."

Francis scraped a hasty bow. "My lord," he murmured.

This opportunity for conversation was cut short as William, Anthony, and Arthur dashed into the room, Phillipa on their heels. Francis immediately was surrounded by an enthusiastic throng, busy pumping his hand enthusiastically, admiring his clothes, and pestering him with every sort of question in the world.

"Francis," said Winifred. "This is Miss Phillipa Raithby, the earl's ward. She is staying with us for the time being."

Francis bowed hastily again and looked shyly at Phillipa. He was dark-eyed, with brown curly hair, like his brothers. He was tall, also, already a head above her. He was thinner than his brothers, though, with a serious, diffident expression. Phillipa liked him immediately.

"Phillipa's champion at battledore," Anthony volunteered.

Arthur stretched out his arms and Francis picked him up. "Do you want to play spillikins with us?" Arthur asked ingenuously.

Had anyone been observing the earl's face, they might have been surprised to see it entirely devoid of its usual glacial expression. All eyes were on Francis, however. The earl realized that his presence must be superfluous and made his excuses.

Winifred looked at him, stricken. "Oh, dear, I forgot to discuss Phillipa's party with you, and it's only a week away."

"As I said before, my dear, I have implicit faith in your

arrangements." He bowed and left the happy family group behind him.

Although Phillipa's spirits had been lifted temporarily by this new arrival, they had plummeted again by that evening. Her head had begun to pound by the time they arrived at Countess Lynton's musicale. The prospect of hearing Catalini sing would at one time have delighted her, but now she found herself wishing that the evening were already over. She found oppressing the red satin damask with the gilt trim that lined the walls of the salon. The magnificent luster, with its crystal and ormolu, did not excite her admiration either; its sparkling presence hurt her eyes. Her admirers seemed more inane to her than ever, and she found it hard to receive their fatuous compliments politely.

St. Clair, upon his arrival, perceived her look of discontent and made his way to her side. He cast a disdainful glance at the young beaux about her and they parted respectfully as he led her away.

"Now, what could possibly bring a frown to that beautiful face?" asked St. Clair gently.

She broke into a relieved smile. "Oh, you have no idea how tiresome this all is. I have spent the past thirty minutes wishing I were somewhere else."

He stopped and regarded her quizzically. "Surely you cannot have tired of this attention so quickly?"

She smiled a tight little smile. "You're right to censure me. I know I must sound a conceited person."

He said nothing. She shrugged bravely. "I suppose, I suppose it's hard to adjust to city ways after living in the country all one's life."

The feebleness of this excuse must have surprised him very much, though he said nothing. She suddenly could not bear that kind inquiring gaze any longer.

"There's my cousin Wakehurst. Pray excuse me, sir."

He relinquished her arm and bent gracefully to kiss her hand. "Only exceedingly reluctantly, my dear."

She hastened away from him, unwilling to let him see the moisture that had sprung to her eyes. His solicitousness was harder to bear than scorn. Wakehurst had warned her away from St. Clair, too, avowing that he was an inveterate gamester.

"For though he has no need of your name, coz, I fear that your fortune might render you attractive to him. I do not mean to advise you; you know your own business best. I only wished to warn you, as a concerned family member."

She had denied his accusations hotly at the time, but now that she thought of it, it was true that St.Clair had always distinguished her by his attentions. She surreptitiously wiped away a tear, then smiled courageously at her cousin. He might not be a leader of fashion, but at least his liking for her was genuine.

St. Clair strolled casually over to the corner of the room where the earl was standing. After exchanging the barest of greetings, St. Clair glanced around to make sure that no one could hear, then said in a low voice, "My word! What ails your ward, Sinamor?"

The earl's face grew icier than ever as he gazed across the room at Phillipa and Wakehurst. "I am afraid that her cousin had been generous-minded enough to inform her that all her admirers are either forutne-hunters or social climbers."

St. Clair paled. "Why, the young blackguard! And she believed him?" He looked keenly at his friend. "You have not spoken to her about it?"

Sinamor shook his head slightly. "No. With the opinion she bears of me, I must have evidence to back my claims."

St. Clair looked at Wakehurst with narrowed eyes. "I shall be delighted to assist you, my lord." He nodded and moved off in another direction.

This whole interchange had not gone unobserved. Helene's eyes were riveted to the earl's handsome face. "This is working out much better than I thought," she whispered to her companion.

Lady Joseph looked puzzled. "But the way he's looking at her—surely he is in love with her?"

Helene laughed bitterly. "I don't doubt it. What you are not observing, my lady, is that his ward seems taken with that plump puppy of a cousin. My God, this is too rich."

"I don't understand."

"Don't you see? She's going to break his heart, and over a conceited, impecunious, young cardsharp. I couldn't have planned everything better myself."

Lady Joseph looked uncertain. "I can't imagine Sinamor's heart breaking over anyone."

Helene lifted her chin. "Don't worry, I mean to try those waters."

She was as good as her word, for in a few minutes she materialized by the earl's side. She put a caressing hand on his sleeve and smiled at him provocatively.

He gave her a bored look. "What are you doing here, Helene?"

She laughed as if he had paid her an extravagant compliment. "I merely came to congratulate you on the success of your ward, Sinamor."

His eyes narrowed. "What do you mean?"

She gave him an innocent pout. "Why, I have no hidden motives, my lord. After all, we are old friends, are we not?"

"You're about as subtle as a cavalry charge," he commented dryly.

"So, when will the announcement take place? She is a fortunate girl indeed. A Wakehurst! I never dreamed she might aim that high."

He did not respond to this verbal thrust; instead, his jaw tightened as he stared at her with coldly glittering eyes. She patted his arm with simulated affection. "*Au revoir*, then, my friend." She walked away with a satisfied smile on her face. He has told me what I wish to know, she thought.

Phillipa had not missed this interchange. The earl always attracted a certain amount of feminine attention, but it was disgusting how that woman threw herself at him—pawing at him in that way. It was a wonder that he bore it.

Wakehurst cleared his throat gently, in order to attract her attention. At her request, he had procured seats for them at the back of the room.

"I thought you liked concerts," he said a little crossly.

Phillipa shook her head. "How can one enjoy them when all you can hear are people gossiping about you and rattling their cups as if there were no performance in front of them? I find it most tiresome."

His face assumed a look of concern. "But you did not enjoy Drury Lane last night, either?"

She shook her head. "I cannot understand what all the sensation is about. Such an ill-favored little man."

"That's true, but Kean—"

"And how boring to have to sit for hours listening to a bunch of idiots jabbering on a stage." She saw that she had shocked him and attempted to laugh. "You mustn't mind me; my temper becomes fierce when I have the headache."

He smiled at her in a sympathetic way. "Well, you may be as cross with me as you like. I often weary of these pleasures myself." He looked at her and saw that he did not have her attention. He cleared his throat again. "Did you see Edmond today?" he asked in an undertone.

"No. Should I have?" Phillipa responded carelessly.

His voice was grave. "I was with him again last night. I'm afraid it was worse. He had a great deal too much to drink and lost heavily. I fear he is becoming a confirmed gamester."

Phillipa turned to him, irate. "Why could you not have prevented it? I very much dislike your going and encouraging him in that way."

He began sputtering in protest. "Well, if that is all the thanks I get! You know how he resents my interference. If it weren't for you, I should have washed my hands of him, and then who knows what might have befallen him? Why, the proprietors of these establishments sometimes murder young gentlemen all for the sake of a few guineas."

Phillipa's face reflected her horror.

He continued. "I was forced to join in a few hands myself, just to allay suspicion. And I have told you before how I abhor gambling."

She was apologetic. "I am sorry, my lord."

"Please, you know I prefer you to call me Gervase."

Phillipa's discontent persisted through the next few days. It did not pass unnoticed by the Dearbornes. Phillipa was aware of the anxious gazes she inspired, but did not feel that she could confide in Winifred, since it was her son who was causing the greater part of Phillipa's inquietude.

She could not enter wholeheartedly into the plans for the ball. Winifred thought her apathy alarming. Phillipa, meanwhile, was busy trying to devise a way to aid Edmond. Try as she might, no scheme presented itself to her.

Sinamor noticed her introspection also, but ascribed it to a different cause. The information St. Clair had obtained on Wakehurst was alarming. The earl studied Phillipa with concern. He hoped her heart was not too involved.

Winifred knew that matters were serious indeed when Phillipa refused to join the family on a trip to the confectioner's in preparation for the ball. Even Francis did not deem himself too grown-up to accompany the expedition, though he claimed he only wished to help his mother manage the younger children.

Phillipa wondered if anyone had seen Edmond since the night before, but she did not have the courage to ask. She bid the party farewell and settled herself in the gold drawing room with the novel Marianne had lent her.

She read for about half an hour and had concluded that it was all simply nonsense. She had just laid it down in boredom when Edmond suddenly opened the door and swept into the room.

"Edmond!" She could not keep a feeling of relief from her voice.

He looked rather disheveled, but it did not appear that anyone had been making attempts on his life. "Your servant," he said, his words slurring slightly.

"Oh, Edmond, you're in your cups again—and in the middle of the morning."

"Morning." He grinned foolishly. "That's the song." He proceeded to render it for her, "*This very morning handy my malady was such, I in my tea took brandy And took a drop too much!*"

Phillipa had her hands over her ears, but fortunately his own performance delighted him so much that he was unable to continue and instead burst into a fit of the giggles.

Phillipa watched him in exasperated silence.

At length, looking up, he caught sight of her serious face and endeavored to assume an air of gravity. "Miss . . . Miss Raithby," he said formally if a little unsteadily, "I have a beg to a boog to . . . a bog to ben . . ." He collapsed with laughter for a moment, then struggled to right himself. He leaned on a nearby table for support. "I have a favor to ask you."

She waited.

"I need to borrow your horse, just for the morning."

"Absolutely not."

"Why? If I had one, I'd lend him to you. Dashed unhandsome of you, I call it."

"Why do you want to borrow him?"

"A race." He nodded. "A race, and"—he laid a finger on the side of his nose and nodded again knowingly—"and a wager."

Phillipa's breath exploded from her. "He'd kill you, you, you Bedlamite!"

Edmond drew himself up. "Madam, you have insulted me!"

"Well, you can't have him, and that's that."

A look of cunning came into his face. "Doesn't matter," he said. "I'll go to Tattersall's today and buy a horse that makes your nag look like a cockhorse!"

Phillipa rose in alarm. "Edmond, don't."

"You'll be sorry for laughing at me, then."

She walked up and put a hand on his sleeve. "I'm sorry now," she said earnestly. "Oh, Edmond, please don't do this."

She saw that her appeal had some effect. "Well," said Edmond gruffly, "a fellow doesn't like to be laughed at."

"No, of course not," she said, leading him to the sofa. "I'll ring for some tea."

"But the race," protested Edmond.

"Now, you know you'll only break your neck if you try to ride when you're half-seas over."

"Half-seas over!" This was uttered in a tone of extreme indignation and Phillipa saw that she had made a fatal mistake. "That does it!" He turned and made his way to the door.

An idea occurred to her. "Edmond, won't you tell me where the race is so that I may come watch?"

He paused for a moment, as if considering the idea, then turned to her disapprovingly. "You won't gull me so easily. I know you, you'd peach!"

"I will anyway," she said hopelessly.

"Don't care. Matter of honor."

"Why not let Sinamor help you choose a horse? He'd be happy to, and in your condition you're likely to get a—"

"Women," he exclaimed in a tone of extreme disgust, and exited the room.

Phillipa stood alone in the salon in despair. She glanced out of the window and watched as Edmond pulled a bottle from the depths of his greatcoat and took a swig out of it.

"What am I to do?" she exclaimed aloud.

Her mind began sorting quickly through the possibilities. She could wait for the family, but Winifred had said they had several errands to do and by then it would probably be too late. She could ride to fetch Lord Dearborne, but she didn't even know where his office was. There was Sinamor. Her heart leapt with hope at the thought. She realized abruptly, however, that during their ride he had told her he would be attending a cricket match today and he had not mentioned the location.

Clearly, it was all up to her. Edmond was in very real danger if he tried to ride in that condition. She wondered angrily for a moment who could have been so thoughtless as to challenge him. She dismissed the thought and turned back to the problem at hand.

There did not appear to be any way that she could find out where the race was being held. She could follow him and try to stop him, but she already had achieved little success in that department. Besides, he had been gone for several minutes. He might almost be there now.

What could she do? She knew quite well that females were not allowed in Tattersall's. To appear there could only create a scene. Probably, I should let him break his neck, she thought angrily.

The germ of an idea came to her. It was ridiculous, she told herself, but the idea began to grow and blossom. It was, after all, a solution. She would be taking a fearful risk, but it would be worth it if she were able to rescue Edmond.

"I'll do it," she said decisively, then she gathered up her skirts and went dashing out of the room and up the stairs.

Once in her room, she rang for her maid. "Mary," she said, "fetch me one of Francis' outfits, and a greatcoat, and a bottle of claret."

"Miss?" Mary's eyes almost started from her head in shock.

"And, if you know where one is to be found, a wig."

Mary stood gazing at Phillipa in bewilderment, her jaw hanging slackly open.

"Don't stand there like a gaby," commanded Phillipa imperiously. "I have to save Edmond."

"Yes, miss." Recognizing the voice of authority, Mary flew off to do her bidding.

A short while later, a stealthy little figure made its way down the back stairs. As Phillipa stepped away from the house, she congratulated herself on having made such an inconspicuous escape. She glanced behind her to make certain that no one was watching, and almost bumped into the sturdy figure of McPherson. She took an involuntary step backwards as she met his disapproving gaze.

"And if I may be so bold as to ask, *Miss* Phillipa," he said, dourly, surveying her outlandish garb, "just where do you think you're going?"

10

Edmond, not having an inkling of what was occurring at Hamilton Place, was feeling quite in charity with himself and with the world at large. This feeling possibly was intensified by the bottle of claret he had consumed on the way to Tattersall's. He felt a warm glow of satisfaction at having bested Phillipa so easily. Interfering female. Well, he'd had the last word.

He leaned over the walls of a horse box to examine its occupant. The horse turned around to gaze inquiringly at him. As if recognizing an acquaintance, Edmond doffed his hat and hiccuped cheerily.

"Tol de rol iddly pol," sang Edmond under his breath. He saw that a gentleman was staring at him disdainfully. "Good day to you, sir," said Edmond, bowing politely.

The gentleman muttered something to his companion that Edmond did not catch. He bestowed a bleary smile on the pair of them and continued on his way, looking at each horse in turn and commenting, "Fine-looking animal that," at the sight of each one.

Edmond decided that it might be wise to claim a column to lean against. His legs were becoming somewhat unreliable. He smiled happily to himself. What foresight he had shown. To arrange a race for the day that Tattersall's had its auction.

He could not be sure how long he stood like that. The passage of time had become quite immaterial, but he was impatient for the auction to begin. When at last it seemed as if matters were beginning to organize, he was distracted by a tugging on his sleeve. He looked down with some curiosity and saw a black-haired youth in an oversized greatcoat. The youngster's face was fairly obscured by the hat he had pulled down over his face.

Edmond sought to remedy this by lifting it. A pair of hands snatched it down again firmly, but not before he'd had a chance to see a pair of imploring sapphire-blue eyes.

"Edmond," whispered a voice.

He stared incredulously for a moment.

"Phillip . . . uh." A sharp poke in the ribs kept him from completing the word. "Ow." He rubbed his ribs tenderly.

"Please," hissed the voice.

He began to laugh. "This is the worst trick you've ever . . . Ow!" A small booted foot had trod firmly on his. "You've ruined the finish," he complained.

"You mustn't give me away," whispered Phillipa. "People were beginning to stare."

He looked around suspiciously. "You might as well go home, you know. You won't talk me out of this."

Phillipa gave an exagerated sigh. "I'm not here to talk you out of this. I'm here to help you."

"Well, I don't need your—"

"Listen. Doesn't even Sinamor acknowledge that I am an expert on horseflesh?"

"Yes," he admitted sulkily.

"Well, you want to win the race, don't you? Why shouldn't I help? Why, I can sometimes tell if a horse is to go lame before it does."

"Well," said Edmond, not entirely convinced.

"And no one here knows me or knows what I am; no one will know you didn't pick out the horse all by yourself."

This appealed more to Edmond. "You won't tell?" he asked.

"I swear it," Phillipa said. She stealthily drew the bottle of claret from under her greatcoat. "We'll have a drink to seal the bargain."

Edmond's eyes lit up appreciatively. "By gad, I've misjudged you."

"Sssh," said Phillipa, "we mustn't let them see us. Here, let's go back in this corner."

Edmond followed her readily enough, ignoring the signs that the auction was about to begin. He took a few pulls on the bottle as the crowd began to bid on the first horse. He frowned in some confusion.

"Wait, must get back to the horses."

Phillipa shook her head. "I had a look at that one. You wouldn't want it—too short in the leg by half."

He accepted her word, but after a few more pulls he shook his head at the offered bottle. "No, mus' get back to business."

He walked unsteadily back to where the current animal was being led around while Phillipa followed him desperately. The horse was a fine-looking big grey, and Edmond fairly beamed at the sight of it. He was about to raise his hand and make a bid when a small strong, hand closed about his arm.

"You don't want that one either—knock-kneed, do you see it?"

Edmond was not seeing anything too clearly at this point, but he was not about to confess that to Phillipa. He peered at the animal. "Ah, yes, now that you mention it, I do."

A buyer was soon found for the animal and a bright chestnut was led in. Edmond was on the point of making a bid when he felt a tug on his sleeve. He looked down and saw a small head shaking at him. "No?" he asked.

"Goose-rumped," she said.

He again made a pretense of staring at the animal. "Oh, I see it now. I couldn't tell until he moved it that way."

The sequence went on in the same pattern for the next few horses. This one was too spiritless, that one lacked depth in the chest, another she suspected strongly of having thrush.

Edmond was finally becoming impatient. "I say, just when are you going to let me choose a horse?"

Phillipa was beginning to feel desperate. She whispered to Edmond that perhaps he'd care for another drink, as the next few looked to be a sorry lot.

"No, I don't care for a drink," Edmond was saying rather loudly when a gentleman joined them.

"Young Dearborne, isn't it?"

With dread, Phillipa recognized Lord Malling's voice. She slouched and pulled her hat down a little further.

"Here to select a horse, are you, lad? Well, I'd be happy to be of assistance." He looked with some curiosity at the little figure beside Edmond.

Edmond caught his gaze and followed it. "My lord, permit me to introduce . . ."

Phillipa felt an icicle of fear travel down her spine.

"Phillip." Thankfully, the name ended with a hiccup.

"Some relation of yours?" asked Lord Malling with interest.

"Relation?" Edmond asked blearily. Phillipa poked him discreetly. "Ah, yes, cousin."

Lord Malling smiled at Phillipa in an inquisitive way. "You must be one of the Baldridges, then."

Phillipa nodded hastily.

"I should have known from the dark hair. How is your dear mother?"

"Fine," said Phillipa in the lowest register she could manage.

"I'm glad to hear it," Lord Malling said, drawing near to her. "And your eldest sister, lovely girl. What's her name?"

Phillipa was seized by panic. She looked at Edmond for help, but he was busy gazing at the horses.

"I have the name on the tip of my tongue," said Lord Malling.

Winifred had mentioned the Baldridges before. It was her husband's sister's family. What was it she had said about them? Phillipa suddenly remembered. They all had royal names.

Lord Malling was staring at her curiously. "I am afraid I cannot recall it."

"Elisabeth, my lord," growled Phillipa prayerfully.

He smiled. "Oh, yes, that was it. I never can remember those ordinary sort of names."

Phillipa breathed a sigh of relief as Lord Malling turned back to Edmond.

"As I was saying, I can be of service to you in the matter of a horse. I myself am disposing of several. My doctor recommended that I ride for exercise, but I find that it doesn't agree with me."

"Most kind," said Edmond.

"I have several fine animals, and I will be happy to advise you."

"Thank you."

"It's nothing at all, I assure you. Why, if I had a lad of your age, I would wish for someone to advise him when he made such an important purchase.''

A groom was leading a white-faced black up.

''Ah, here's one of them now. I paid well over four hundred pounds for that animal, a very sweet little goer indeed.''

''Is that so? Well, my lord, if you say—''

Edmond was interrupted in making his bid by a firm tug on his arm. Phillipa stood on her toes to whisper in his ear.

''What's that?'' asked Lord Malling, obviously puzzled.

''My cousin is of the opinion the animal's a little straight-shouldered,'' Edmond said amiably. He concluded with a yawn.

''Why, you young—'' Lord Malling's face was turning purple.

''Yes, honestly I don't think the nag looks that bad,'' Edmond said helpfully, pulling Phillipa out from behind him, where she had sought refuge.

They were beginning to attract attention.

''Of all the ill-mannered young cubs,'' Lord Malling was saying as another gentleman stepped forward.

''Is there some sort of problem here?'' asked the gentleman helpfully.

''This young rapscallion has the nerve to criticize a perfectly good horse—''

Another gentleman walked up to them. ''What's this discussion about?''

Lord Malling began a loud and resentful explanation, assisted by helpful interjections from the first gentleman. As the bidding on the horse concluded, several more heads turned their way.

It seemed to Phillipa that a hundred pairs of eyes were focused curiously on her. She tugged pathetically on Edmond's sleeve, but his eyelids were drooping and he was beginning to sway in a suspicious manner.

''This young whelp badly needs a lesson in manners,'' Lord Malling was saying angrily when suddenly a muscular arm shot out to grasp Phillipa's wrist. She gasped with pain and fear. Discovery was inevitable and imminent. She had dropped her head in order to hide her face as much as possible, but the owner of the cruel grip was drawing her inexorably toward him.

"Causing mischief again, then, my lads?"

The voice was Sinamor's. Her knees buckled with relief. She might have fallen except for his firm grasp. Edmond had no such support. He had been swaying in ever-increasing circles and he went over suddenly.

The earl gave a realistic snort of disgust. He released Phillipa and bent over to Edmond, loosening his cravet. "I don't know how I'll explain this to your mother when you get home. A fine pair you are!"

Lord Malling's face was alive with mistrust. "Young Dearborne said the other was his *cousin*."

"Did he?" asked the earl indifferently as he continued to minister to the unconscious Edmond. "I don't doubt it. What a lecture his mother will read him when she learns how he's corrupted his brother, fresh from Eton." He shook his head carelessly in Phillipa's direction. "Help me lift him to his feet, Francis."

The other men had begun to turn away, chuckling to themselves. Lord Malling still looked dubious. "But he said the boy's name was Phillip."

"Yes," the earl grunted with the effort of heaving Edmond to his feet. "I've no doubt that he's fed you all sorts of taradiddles, but I am afraid that I don't have time to listen to them now. I must get this lad out."

Edmond made a choking noise in his throat. Lord Malling stepped back in dainty haste.

"Quick, Francis." Sinamor and Phillipa hastened Edmond outside, followed by amused smiles and laughter.

They rode home in the earl's curricle, Edmond propped up limply in the front seat and Phillipa having usurped the tiger's place. She did not dare to speak to the earl. She had meant to thank him, but had been frightened by the anger that blazed from those blue eyes.

When they arrived home, the earl had seen that Edmond was attended to, then he turned to her.

"I can explain," she began lamely.

"No, you could not possibly explain. Go upstairs and change immediately."

She started up the stairs, all too aware now of the curious

eyes of the staff. What a picture she must present. She was surely sunk beyond reproach this time. Even Wakehurst probably would hate her if he knew. With these and many other self-pitying thoughts she went trudging slowly up the stairs.

"Phillipa!" A little voice sounded above her head. She looked up to see Arthur. He came running down the stairs toward her. "Not so fast, sweetheart," she was cautioning him when he suddenly tripped and came flying down the stairs headlong. Reacting instinctively, she reached out to catch him. In stretching out, she lost her own balance and went tumbling with him down the bottom flight of stairs.

Lady Dearborne had walked into the hall in time to witness the whole performance. Her scream of fright brought everyone running.

The earl was the first to reach the ball of human flesh. Somehow, Phillipa had managed to wrap herself around Arthur, so that she absorbed most of the shock. Arthur poked his head out of her arms and began to cry in fear. His mother took him in her arms and, ascertaining that he was all right, began to speak to him soothingly.

The earl was still bent over the pale, motionless form of Phillipa.

"Phillipa," he said anxiously. There was no reply. He loosened her stock and felt her neck for a pulse. "Thank God, she is sitll alive," he said.

Everyone had began to gather around.

"Fetch a physician," Winifred ordered a servant. She handed Arthur to a stunned nursemaid and bent over Phillipa. "I think she's coming 'round."

The long dark eyelashes fluttered. Her eyes slowly opened to focus on the earl's face, staring down in concern. Blue eyes locked into blue eyes for a moment, then Phillipa gave a faint smile.

"That's my brave girl," he uttered with a hoarse sort of tenderness.

The spell was broken by the intrusion of Winifred, who had obtained a dampened handkerchief from the ever-efficient Williams, and who now made herself busy sponging Phillipa's brow.

"Is Arthur all right?" Phillipa asked in a weak little voice.

"Yes, my dear, you saved his life," said Winifred.

Phillipa managed a short laugh. "No, I bungled it properly."

She attempted to sit up, but Sinamor restrained her. "No, you must lie still, my love. We have sent for a physician."

She frowned. "I do not like physicians, and besides, I am perfectly all right." She struggled to rise again. She turned her head toward the earl. "You're making this difficult, you know."

At a warning look from Winifred, he withdrew his hands. Phillipa sat up gingerly. "Why, I've taken worse spills than this on Ripon." She shakily attempted to rise to her feet. "Umph." She grunted and fell down.

"What's the matter? Are you in pain?" The earl and Winifred hovered solicitously about her.

She winced. "I'm afraid that I must have twisted my ankle as I fell."

Without a moment's hestiation, Sinamore picked her up and carried her over to the green salon. Two of the footmen sprang forward to relieve him of his burden, but at a signal from Winifred they fell back.

Despite her pain, Phillipa felt a thrill go through her as she was picked up in those strong arms and pressed against that surprisingly powerful chest. She experienced a sense of security also, as if she were being protected from the world and all its dangers. She surprised herself by being disappointed when he deposited her tenderly on the couch. He knelt by her and took her hand, and she could feel her cheeks begin to pinken.

Perhaps he saw it, for he dropped her hand hastily, and as everyone came into the room, he began to strip off his exquisite neckcloth in a businesslike way.

"Fetch me a good, stout knife," he told a servant. To Phillipa, he said, "Do you have pain anywhere else?"

She shook her head bravely. "None to speak of."

"Very well, then."

"What are you doing, Sinamor?" asked Winifred, but he paid her no heed.

The servant returned with the knife and handed it to him. He looked Phillipa in the eye. "If I am hurting you, please tell me, and cry out whenever you feel like it. No one will care."

Phillipa met his eyes resolutely. She was determined not to make a sound.

She could not prevent herself from giving a stifled groan of pain as he began to cut the boot off her leg. His brows drew together, but otherwise he seemed not to notice it.

She clamped her lips tightly together in order to keep from betraying herself further. The earl worked quickly and efficiently, and only Phillipa could see the beads of perspiration standing out on his forehead.

As soon as the boot was off, he pulled the strap of the pantaloon up behind her heel and stripped off her stocking. He then proceeded to bind her foot expertly with his neckcloth. As he cinched the ends together, he looked up at Phillipa. "Is that uncomfortable?" She shook her head. He turned to Bickerstaffe, who was hovering behind him. "Fetch some brandy, will you?"

His lips curled apologetically. "I am sorry that I could not give it to you before, but I wanted to make sure that you could tell me if I were cutting into you."

She managed a tight little smile in return.

When the brandy arrived, he poured a glass and gave it to her. She took a sip and coughed as the liquor burned down her throat. She would have put it down, but at a look from Sinamor she raised the glass again and obediently took another little sip. This time it was more bearable.

"Drink it up," Sinamor said briskly. He rose and turned to Winifred. "I have some matters to discuss with you."

At his signal, she followed him into the next room, closing the door behind her. She did not speak but instead looked at him hopefully, trusting that he had a way to bring them out of their predicament.

He seemed to sense her mood, for he proceeded right to business.

"Did you run into many acquaintances today, Win?"

She shook her head. "No, although Lady Beresmond did step up to our carriage to greet me."

"More pertinently, then, did anyone else see Francis?"

"Only the shopkeepers, as far as I know."

He let out his breath in relief. "Then there is a chance we may pull this off." He led her to the sofa, sat down, and explained his plan.

A few hours later, Phillipa sat fretting in a post chaise upon Tyburn Turnpike. The earl's preparations had seemed elaborate to her, and though she could not protest against the need for caution, the arrangements were not necessarily accommodating to a recently invalided young lady. She heard a carriage approaching and leaned to peer out the window, only to wince in pain as she accidentally put weight on her injured foot.

"Is your ankle troubling you, Miss Phillipa?" asked the maid respectfully.

"It's nothing," Phillipa lied.

"Then, if I may suggest it, you'd be doing better not to show your face at the window." The earl's insistence upon secrecy had made a great impression upon Mary, who had never been involved in such cloak-and-dagger adventures before. She found it all very exciting. "We're supposed to wait for Mr. McPherson to tell us to move."

As if summoned, that individual appeared at the door of the carriage. "That wasna him, Miss Phillipa. I knew you'd be frettin' yourself." He gave her a stern glance. "And I should pull the veil down again, if I were you."

She gave an exasperated sigh. "But there's no one here to see me, and besides, I can hardly breathe with the thing on."

He pursed his lips. "And if anyone does see you, then they'll know o'course that you have been in London these past two days and not gone, like the earl says. But then you're not worried about causing the earl more trouble than you already have."

With a disdainful sniff, Phillipa pulled the veil down again. McPherson grinned and moved away from the carriage. Mary stared in wonder. She was very much in awe of her young mistress and she didn't know how Mr. McPherson dared to speak to her like that, let alone got her to obey him.

"It's sprinkling rain," Phillipa said. "Oh, I wish he would come!"

As if in response to her request, there came the sound of hoofbeats. This time Phillipa refrained from peeping out the window. Her self-control was rewarded when McPherson reappeared.

"It's his lordship," he said gruffly.

In a few minutes the earl appeared at the door. "Are you ready, then?" he asked.

"What took you so long, my lord?" asked Phillipa crossly.

"I had to pick up your trunks, didn't I?" he replied, stepping up into the carriage.

Phillipa could not be persuaded to relinquish her foul mood. She was tired and miserable and her ankle was hurting her abominably.

"I've forgotten, why did I not take them with me when I left London two days ago?"

"Because you were so anxious to see your ailing great-aunt, who, it was rumored, was at death's door. You took only a bandbox or two with you." He pulled her to him easily, miraculously avoiding undue pressure on her ankle.

How wonderful those arms felt about her. She mustn't let him know it.

"And what is to happen with my ball?" she asked, maintaining a veneer of vexation as he swung her into his arms and lifted her free of the carriage.

"Winifred is busy writing everyone, explaining this unforeseen tragedy. It's fortunate your aunt lives in such a remote area."

It was delightful being carried by him again. She could no longer maintain her pretense and instead dropped her head comfortably onto his shoulder. She saw that he had driven a phaeton and four, as well as bringing his traveling carriage. She gave a little squeal of delight and lifted her veil to observe it better.

"Oh, my lord, may I ride with you?"

"You certainly may not," he said firmly, limping toward the other carriage.

"But . . . but please, my lord."

He stopped in his tracks for a moment. "It is damp and you have an injured ankle. I am persuaded you would be more comfortable in a closed carriage."

The sapphire eyes turned upon him pleadingly. "But that is why I should go with you. With your team, you may reach Sinamor hours before the other carriage does, and it is not raining now and I have on my pelisse."

He stood there for a moment, undecided. Her bottom lips trembled slightly. "My ankle is bothering me, and the sooner I get to bed, the better."

He hesitated, then began to walk away from the phaeton. "I cannot take you so far unchaperoned."

"But it is not likely we should see anyone, and besides, I have my veil."

"Which you should have down," he reminded her sternly.

There was a look of bitter disappointment on her face. "Very well," she said in a tight little voice before pulling the veil down.

McPherson was staring at them curiously. "Can I lend you a hand, my lord?"

The earl did not answer for a few seconds. Then he raised his voice. "She'll be riding with me in the phaeton." With an air of decision, he walked over to the dashing equipage and lifted her in.

McPherson could not prevent a look of surprise. It was lucky the post chaise had departed already. This would surely have caused talk.

The earl tucked some robes about Phillipa. His groom, John, at the horse's heads, regarded him with disapproval, though he silently obeyed the earl's forthcoming order to raise the phaeton's top.

"I think it would be best if you joined the others in the closed carriage, John," said the earl quietly. "It is too wet for you to ride in the back all that distance."

John was deeply offended. "My lord . . ." he began protestingly.

Sinamor's eyebrow flew up quizzically.

John endeavored to swallow his disgust and nearly choked on it. One did not answer back to the Earl of Sinamor, even for his own good. "Very good, my lord," he muttered resentfully.

The earl lifted himself into the carriage. "We'll see you at Sinamor. Let 'em go."

With a shake of the reins they were soon flying over the ground at a spectacular rate.

Phillipa was delighted. "Why, we shall be there in no time at all."

He never took his eyes off his team. "If we were on the new Holyhead Road, that would be true, for it is one of the best in England. We have to take the older road, though, via Southhall and Uxbridge. From High Wycombe to Sinamor, it's little more than a cart track and it has probably worsened since I saw it last. Unfortunately, we are not renowned for the quality of our roads in Buckinghamshire." He glanced briefly up at the sky, which was ominously overcast. He hoped he hadn't been foolish for allowing Phillipa this treat. He simply found it hard to resist her.

Phillipa had no such gloomy thoughts. She was busy admiring the earl's horses. "What prime 'uns. How I should like to have a turn at the ribbons!"

"Absolutely not." The earl's flat denial reminded her forcibly of her own words to Edmond what seemed like weeks instead of hours ago. She realized that she had never offered Sinamor an explanation for her actions. After all he had done for her, he was certainly entitled to one.

"My lord," she began hesitantly, glancing at the stern visage beside her.

"Yes?"

"I wished to thank you . . . for . . . pulling my chestnuts out of the fire today."

His right eyebrow ascended in surprise, but since she was seated on his left side, she saw no alteration in his countenance.

"I appreciate all you've done for me, and I wished you to know that, and to know why I did what I did today."

He did not respond.

"I know it looked very bad, but I was just trying to get Edmond to drink enough so he'd fall asleep and not buy a horse."

The earl flicked his whip to catch his leaders' attention as he negotiated a turn at speed with only inches to spare. Phillipa's eyes shone with admiration.

"You are a dab hand, aren't you?"

"It was nothing," he said carelessly. "You were just telling me why the gentlemen at Tattersall's would wish to sell their cattle to an obviously raddled young gentleman of nineteen."

He heard her draw in her breath suddenly at the thought.

She put a hand to her mouth. "You're right, they wouldn't, would they?"

"I should think it highly unlikely," he said dryly. "You see, Phillipa, if you would just pause to think before rushing to entangle yourself in this sort of coil . . ."

"But that wasn't all," she said meekly.

He sighed.

She paused for a moment, but when he didn't say anything, she continued. "He had come home to borrow Ripon from me. Someone had challenged him to a race. Tattersall's was his next idea, but he could have taken Lord Dearborne's hunter from the stables, or hired a horse, or . . . I was afraid he would break his neck."

The earl did not know what to reply. If Phillipa's actions still did not seem reasonable, at least they were more understandable.

"Why didn't you come get me, Phillipa?" he asked wearily.

"Because there wasn't time, and I didn't think you were home. How did you find out where I was anyway?"

"McPherson managed to catch me as I was leaving."

"He promised not to tell!" she said, outraged.

"Before you get too angry, need I remind you what might have happened if I hadn't come?"

A little shiver passed up her spine that was not due to the dampness and the chill in the air. She dropped her head and clutched the robes more tightly about her.

"No," she said with a new and not unbecoming humility. Her attention was suddenly caught by a tingle on her face, followed by another and yet another. She lifted her face and stared ahead of them.

"It's beginning to rain again," she observed.

The earl's face became a little grimmer. He tightened his grip on the reins. "That's what I feared. I'm afraid we may be in for an unpleasant journey."

11

The next half an hour of their drive passed in silence. Sinamor was filled with concern at the steadily increasing precipitation. Phillipa was simply delighted to be in the country once more.

The rather flat landscape of London had given way to wood-covered hills. Here and there she saw a timbered cottage or a brick-and-flint manor house of a type that seemed to be peculiar to the area. Some might have considered the landscape bleak, but to Phillipa it was a welcome change from the noise and the congestion of the city. They were approaching a picturesque village when she gave a little sigh.

"How pretty it is!"

The earl shot her a quick glance of surprise.

"It's just that I enjoy being in the countryside again."

As the rain had increased to a steady downpour, Sinamor had slowed the horses and was proceeding at a more cautious pace.

"What do they call these hills?"

"The Chilterns."

Phillipa looked at the earl. "Is something wrong, my lord?"

"I am debating whether we should stop at what passes for an inn here, or whether we should attempt to go on to Sinamor."

She lifted her chin. "I am not afraid of a few drops of rain, my lord."

"Your bravery was never in question, my dear."

This was said in such a dryly ironical tone that a lesser soul than Phillipa might have been daunted. She persisted, however. "How far are we from Sinamor?"

"About ten miles."

"Well, I don't see why we shouldn't continue on, then. It is not such a great distance, and inns are such uncomfortable places." He did not appear to be convinced by her arguments, so she decided to play her trump card. "Besides, it would be most improper."

She was taken aback by the chuckle that escaped him. "You will forgive me, I hope, but I consider you the last person on earth to read anyone a lecture on propriety."

"Well!" Her eyes were beginning to sparkle with anger. "It may surprise you, my lord, but I consider *you*—"

"Peace!" He gave his head a little shake. "We lack the leisure to be quarreling about trifles, you little goose."

Phillipa sat in affronted silence as they approached the village. "I have considered what you have said. I do think the inn here likely would be devilish uncomfortable, and there is your ankle to think about"—the corner of his mouth curved suspiciously upward—"as well as your reputation."

Phillipa was pleased by this victory, but endeavored not to show it.

"If the road proves absolutely impassable, I suppose we can always manage to turn the horses around somehow."

They passed through the village and continued on for about half a mile. The earl then swung his horses into the wood. Phillipa now saw that he had not exaggerated the quality of the road. Lined with beeches, it was somewhat overgrown and only wide enough for them to pass. Several days of rain had reduced it to a quagmire. The earl's face became even grimmer.

The phaeton hit a submerged hole, jouncing its occupants as it did so. Phillipa could not prevent a stifled gasp of pain as weight was brought to bear on her injured ankle.

"Are you all right?" Sinamor asked concernedly.

She nodded. "I am fine." She was quiet for a few moments, then she added, "I am sorry, my lord."

"You did not cause this weather, Phillipa."

Her cheeks, already made rosy by the chill in the air, deepened their color. "No, but if I had not been selfish and insisted you take me with you, you would have had your groom here. You both might have stayed at the inn, or he could have turned the horses around for you. Instead, you have a useless invalid on your hands. I have put us both in a predicament."

He gave a curiously tender smile that would have surprised Phillipa if she'd had the nerve to look at him.

"Do not blame yourself overmuch. I was well aware of what I was undertaking." He added in a rallying tone, "Besides, I do not see that our situation is so bad. A little uncomfortable for now, that is all. We should reach Sinamor within the hour."

Unfortunately, his brave words were followed by a sudden violent jolt of the carriage and then a loud crack. The phaeton lurched forward and downward and stopped abruptly, nearly throwing its occupants from it.

The earl cursed under his breath and climbed down to soothe the horses.

Phillipa, whose injured limb had been jostled painfully, had to bite her lip to keep from crying aloud in distress.

Confusion reigned for only a few moments. After calming the horses, Sinamor hobbled over to examine the phaeton. What he saw made him swear loudly. He looked up and caught Phillipa's eyes. She was calm, though a little pale.

"I apologize." He grimaced.

"It does not signify," she said. "I suppose we can go no farther?"

He shook his head angrily. "The front axle is broken. Damnation!"

Phillipa's military upbringing had inured her to this sort of language. She waited patiently for his commands.

He had glanced about him quickly, but there were no signs of life in the silent woods. To complicate matters, twilight was beginning to descend rapidly. They would be trapped in darkness soon, and the temperature was falling as the light faded away. Since no one expected them, no help would be forthcoming. The other carriage would be hours behind, if they hadn't already stopped at an inn for the night. He made his decision in an instant.

He limped his way to the front of the carriage and began to unhitch the horses.

"Can I help?" asked Phillipa.

"You can't stand," he reminded her savagely.

She did not seem bothered in the least by his foul temper.

Instead, she wisely gathered the robes about her to ward off the damp as he worked.

She watched him with concealed admiration. He was surprisingly good with horses, she thought. In fifteen minutes, he had accomplished his work expertly and with little fanfare.

Phillipa ventured to make only one suggestion. "Aren't we going to take them all with us? We can't leave them out here."

The earl felt like retorting that it was going to be hard enough to manage her on a bareback horse. He cast a caculating eye at the animals, damp with a mixture of sweat and rain. They could have taken a chill already.

"Very well."

He led one of the horses over to the phaeton. He stepped up and lifted Phillipa from it, then swung her onto the horse's back. It snorted in protest at this unaccustomed burden and shied away from the phaeton, but soon the two had it under control. The earl then swung himself behind Phillipa and put an arm around her.

"Shouldn't we each take a horse, my lord?" she asked, uncomfortably aware of his closeness.

"I think it best to double up, since the animal's probably never been ridden before. With two of us on his back, he may think harder before unburdening himself."

He drew the reins of the others from where he had tied them, and wound them around his wrist. He clucked gently to the horse and they set off slowly.

"He seems gentle enough," Phillipa said, patting the neck of their mount.

"He's the steadiest of the lot, which is another reason we both should ride him."

Phillipa raised no more protests. There was a part of her that wished nothing more than to remain in such proximity to the earl. A little shudder of delight ran up her spine. He pulled her to him more tightly.

"This is no time for misshishness," he said coolly. "We must keep each other warm. It's still a good ride from here."

"Yes, my lord." She did not quite trust her voice. She basked in the feel of that strong arm about her, of that firm torso behind her. Her cheeks flushed. She was glad he could not see.

Sinamor himself was not unaffected by the situation. He felt absurdly protective of the little figure he was clutching to him so tightly. He could not tell her the real reason he had insisted on sharing a horse. With pools of water obscuring the pitfalls, he knew there was a danger that the horse could take a misstep. The last thing she needed now was another fall. He was aware that her ankle had taken a thrashing when the phaeton wrecked. Still, she had not cried out, or complained, or fallen into hysterics as any other female of his acquaintance would. He felt a sudden rush of tenderness. It was a dream, he knew that. They were too many years apart in age and . . . in experience. He smiled bitterly to himself. At least he could console himself with the knowledge that he had behaved honorably in this one circumstance. Phillipa herself would never suspect.

Darkness had fallen, and as they traveled, it became complete, unrelieved by a hint of a moon or stars. Their progress was slowed by the need to pick their way around the brush, which had been knocked down by the storm. The beeches, which had seemed to hold a somber kind of beauty a few hours before, now seemed oppressive to Phillipa. An animal rustled in the bushes, causing their mount to flinch and jostle them uncomfortably. The only positive note was that the rain had begun to lessen and finally stopped falling.

Phillipa had never been subject to fancies, but as they at last turned up the drive to Sinamor House, she shivered slightly. It was too dark to receive an overall picture of the house, but from the few candles burning, she received an impression of a vast, brooding structure. The impression was not at all alleviated when they finally alighted and spent what seemed like hours ringing the bell. They finally managed to rouse an elderly servant in his nightcap and robe. He peered at them in undisguised dismay.

"Who is it?" he called in a quavering voice.

The earl stepped forward into the light of his candle. "Sinamor."

This seemed to startle the old servant more than their untimely arrival.

"My . . . my lord," he stuttered, awkwardly trying to execute a bow.

Sinamor swung Phillipa into his arms and entered, brushing past the fellow. "My ward and I will require accommodations." He glowered at the servant. "*Separate* accommodations."

"Yes . . . yes, milord."

A plump woman in a mobcap bustled into the room. "Who is it, Tom?" Sinamor turned in her direction and raised a quizzical eyebrow. She gasped audibly. "Your lordship!"

Phillipa had seldom seen him look more arrogant. "As I was saying, my ward and I require accommodations."

"But, my lord, we had no idea that—"

He sighed. "I am sorry I was unable to inform you of my coming. It is late and we are tired. Just do the best that you can."

"Yes, milord." The woman seemed to regain her equilibrium. "Tom, go wake Rose and tell her to make the master's chamber ready and—"

"Not that one." He spoke sharply, startling even Phillipa.

"Milord?"

"Any of the others will do," he said, relaxing into his usual cool hauteur.

"Yes, milord." She curtsied. "Tom, tell her the blue and the gold bedchambers, then. Tell Ned to take care of the horses, and send Joseph down too. Hurry now," she said, giving him a little push as he began dazedly off.

"Now, milord," she said, "if you would care to take the young lady into the drawing room there, I will send Joseph in to start a fire for you. I imagine you're a bit peckish after your journey." She began to usher him in the direction of the room, lighting the candles on the wall as she went.

"We haven't anything but simple fare, but hunger is the best sauce, after all. There, milord." She stripped a dustcover from a blue silk damask sofa. The earl laid Phillipa down tenderly. The housekeeper leaned over to help Phillipa remove her sodden pelisse.

"Now, would the young lady care for some tea? And your lordship a bottle of claret or some brandy?"

He was looking at Phillipa tenderly. "I believe we could both use some brandy." He gave the servant one of his rare smiles. "I don't think you were here during my time. It is good to know we are in such efficient hands, Mrs.—?"

She lifted her chin, but her eyes betrayed her pleasure at his words. "Mrs. Tiddingford, sir. Mr. Fenwick hired me when the old housekeeper couldn't carry on."

"Very good," said the earl.

She curtsied again and bustled out of the room.

Phillipa raised her eyes to the earl protestingly. "I have no wish for brandy, my lord. You'll make me into a sot."

"Hardly." His expression was enigmatic. "I ordered it because your ankle is paining you."

Phillipa was both surprised and touched by his concern. She didn't know where to look or what to say. Fortunately, the earl did not seem to notice her confusion. He limped painfully over to a sturdy-looking winged chair and settled himself in it. Phillipa realized with a sudden burst of conscience that the jolting carriage trip and the long ride after in the cold and damp must have had an injurious effect on his leg.

"Does it hurt you very much?" she asked softly.

His eyebrow flew up in a coldly quizzical way. "Don't tell me you're concerned for my welfare. That is an unusual preoccupation for you, isn't it?"

He had the satisfaction, if one could call it that, of seeing her lower her eyes in confusion. He smiled bitterly to himself. She must continue to think of him as an ogre, as something less than human. He must not betray his weakness.

Phillipa was hot with shame. Here she had driven him to a place he hadn't visited in years, in the dead of night, in inclement weather. He had shown nothing but solicitude for her the entire time, and she had never thought of the physical demands she was making on him. She had not once considered his comfort, being too preoccupied with her own. Would she ever learn to be less selfish?

Tears welled in her eyes, but she was rescued by the entrance of a footman, who started to lay the fire. As he was at work, the older manservant came in with a decanter of brandy and two crystal glasses. He poured the glasses and then exited, the younger man following behind him.

The earl handed Phillipa one of the glasses. The brandy warmed her deliciously, and by the time the meal arrived, she found that she was well able to do justice to Mrs. Tiddingford's pigeon pie, boiled tongue, and cold roast mutton. Her eyelids were growing heavy and she was only half-aware that it was the earl himself who carried her up to her bedchamber and ordered Mrs. Tiddingford to make her comfortable.

Phillipa was sleeping so deeply that at first her brain could make no sense of the sounds. As she opened her eyes, she saw that her room was still dark, except for the glowing embers of the fire. She was abruptly aware that someone was screaming in anguish. She stood up quickly, put on a wrapper, and lit a candle from the fire. She rushed out into the hall as the screams died away. She proceeded in the direction from which they had been issuing. She saw a group of people in the hall. Mrs. Tiddingford was taking charge.

"Go on back to bed, all of you. Everything's fine. Just a nightmare, that's all."

Pale-faced and muttering, the little group began to disperse to make their way upstairs once again.

Phillipa strode boldly up to Mrs. Tiddingford. "Is there anything I can do?"

The woman took her elbow and drew her away from the doorway, with a motion for her to be silent.

"Old Tom says the earl's had bad dreams ever since he was a little fellow. He's in there with him now." Mrs. Tiddingford looked at Phillipa seriously. "I don't mean to tell you your own business, miss, but Tom says the earl's a proud man and he doesn't like folk to know of his weakness."

It was on the tip of Phillipa's tongue to make a haughty reply and then to rush in and help Sinamor. She saw the woman's kindly worried expression and hesitated. She gave a small cold smile.

"Thank you, Mrs. Tiddingford. I will take your sound advice. Good night." She lifted her chin and set back on the way to her chamber, thus missing Mrs. Tiddingford's look of surprise.

She's in love with that devil, thought the housekeeper wonderingly.

"Did you sleep well last night?" Phillipa looked up from her eggs and gammon the next morning to see the earl's eyes boring into her. It was an idle question, but she imagined that she could detect a faint anxiety in it. She patted her mouth with her napkin, then smiled at him guilelessly. "I'm afraid that with the brandy, nothing could have woken me last night."

Did she imagine that slight relaxation of his shoulders? He nodded coolly at her and sat down at the table himself. "That's good." He glanced at her plate. "It appears that Mrs. Tiddingford is a a woman of considerable resourcefulness."

Phillipa smiled. "She is. See what she found for me." She held up a heavy walking stick of thorn. The earl's face blackened.

"It's so I don't have to depend on others to get about," Phillipa said uncertainly, unsure why he would be scowling so.

Mrs. Tiddingford interrupted them by bringing in a plate for the earl. She apologized as she set it before him, saying that her larder was not properly prepared for his visit.

He gave her a wintry smile. "You have done an excellent job with such little notice, Mrs. Tiddingford."

She contrived to hide her pleasure. "Milord, if I may be so bold?"

He looked at her, but made no response.

She plunged ahead bravely. "If I might know whether you and the young lady are planning an extended visit? I should like to have the proper amount of provisions, and also to know whether I should open the rest of the house."

"We should be here for a few weeks at least. I will also require accommodation for my aunt, Lady Wensley, who should arrive within a day or two."

Mrs. Tiddingford did not appear to be at all taken aback by the news of this expected arrival, or by the earl's description of the retinue of servants who must also be housed and fed. She merely nodded her acquiescence and excused herself.

Phillipa stared at the earl in surprise. "Your aunt?" she asked.

He had taken a bite of his breakfast and so took a minute to respond. "My Aunt Ondine, actually my father's cousin." He glanced at Phillipa with a hint of amusement. "Surely with your concern for decorum, you did not imagine that you could remain here unchaperoned?"

"But will it not inconvenience her to remove here at this time of year?"

He gave a tiny yawn. "Anything that occasions her removal from Bath is of the greatest inconvenience to Aunt Ondine."

With these reassuring words, he turned back to his breakfast, leaving Phillipa to brood over this new concern.

This first day of life in the country was to prove less idyllic than Phillipa had imagined. To begin with, word of their arrival had somehow filtered to the earl's estate agent, Mr. Fenwick. He had lost no time in presenting himself and soon he and Sinamor were closeted together in the library, leaving Phillipa on her own.

In normal circumstances she would immediately have gone for a brisk ride. Unfortunately, the only horses in the stables were the carriage horses they had brought with them. With her injured ankle, she knew she should not attempt strolling about the grounds. She had never been a great reader, and the notion of curling up with a good book disgusted her. The only option left was to explore the house itself. She set off to do this at a slow and painful hobble.

The impression of gloom she had received from first viewing the house was not dispelled by her tour of it. She tried to make allowances for the dust sheets covering the furniture and the general air of disuse, but still there was a depressing quality to it.

It offered none of the gothic horrors of the castle in the novel Marianne had lent her. Phillipa was no authority on architecture, but she judged that this structure could not date back further than the earl's grandfather's day. Since she prized simplicity, it was odd that these rooms should seem so disagreeable to her. She had a difficult time analyzing why they should be so. She finally decided it was their very cold perfection that made them so uncomfortable. There was no warmth, no life, no humanity anywhere in the house, as far as she could tell.

The one room that she found interesting was the long gallery upstairs. It was filled with portraits of Sinamors, going back for generations. Examining his ancestors, she could see that Winifred was right: the remarkable brows were an inherited characteristic. She paused before a portrait of the late earl, painted while he was still a young man. Although the artist had done his best to flatter, there was an evil glint to the earl's eye that Phillipa could not quite like. She turned to the next portrait, which was obviously of the present earl's mother. There was a great deal of resemblance: the same classical, delicate features; the same dark curls and fair skin. Her eyes were even the identical shade of blue, but unlike Sinamor's, hers were alive with warmth and humor. The artist had captured her in a state of high excitement. A faint shading of pink rested on her cheeks and her mouth was parted in a smile. She looked very young and free from care.

It must have been painted before her wedding, thought Phillipa. She felt rather sorry for the happily expectant young girl on the wall before her. She was just my own age, thought Phillipa sadly. She felt no inclination to linger longer over the portrait and instead turned to one of the present earl. It had been painted when he was a youth of only twelve or so, she guessed. Clad in hunting garb, he stood, one leg crossed carelessly over the other. His right hand rested on the shoulder of a hugely magnificent black horse. There was hauteur in his manner already as he gazed down at her. Did she imagine it, or was there also pain at the back of those young eyes?

"Phillipa!" A voice interrupted her reverie. "What are you doing up here?"

She flushed and spun around a little too hastily to face Sinamor. She could not prevent a grimace of distress.

He scowled at her. "I should have thought you'd know better than to try walking about on a twisted ankle."

"I was using the stick," she protested.

"Of all the shatterbrained notions," he said, scooping her up in his arms.

She held herself away from him. "My lord, this cannot benefit your leg."

"My leg will survive," he growled.

Phillipa was enjoying to a dangerous extent this sensation of being carried by the earl. She struggled against it. "My lord, I refuse to rely upon you as transportation."

"If you would remain on the sofa for a few days, you might not need to rely upon me."

Her face colored. She could think of nothing to add. They had reached the stairs and Sinamor was beginning down them when they heard the sound of a carriage driving up to the house. They had almost reached the bottom when the front door was flung open and a tall, imposing figure came sweeping inside.

"Sinamor! What are you doing?"

Phillipa had nourished hopes of the earl's aunt being a plump kindly grandmotherly sort of person. These were quickly dashed. Instead, Phillipa saw an amazon with iron-gray hair and imperious brown eyes that at the moment snapped with anger.

"Put that creature down this instant."

He ignored this command and, without pausing, carried Phillipa into the drawing room. Lady Wensley had no choice but to follow. Sinamor laid Phillipa gently on the sofa and turned to greet his aunt.

"Hello, Aunt. We did not expect you so soon," he said dryly.

"Obviously not," she said with angry disapproval.

Sinamor turned his coldest gaze upon her, but Phillipa could see that it did not affect her. "This is my ward, Miss Raithby," he said expressionlessly. "Her ankle is injured."

"A likely story." She snorted in disgust, strode over to Phillipa, and stood towering over her menacingly. "You're just a poor little dab of a thing, aren't you? I must say, I expected better."

Phillipa's own eyes were now flashing with anger.

The earl started to speak, but Lady Wensley cut him off. "Raithby." She gave another unladylike sniff. "Common sort of name. Who were your parents?"

Her eyes sparkling, Phillipa had risen to a sitting position on the sofa. "My father was Major Harry Raithby—"

"In the infantry, no doubt."

"Of the Fourteenth Light Dragoons."

The two combatants glared angrily at each other.

"Hmph. And who was your mother, then?"

"Lady Phillipa Farnborough."

Lady Wensley was momentarily taken aback. "Wakehurst's daughter?"

"Yes."

The older woman recovered quickly. "The Wakehursts were ever a spendthrift lot."

The earl intervened forcefully. "Then it will please you no doubt, Aunt, to hear that Miss Raithby is a considerable heiress, although I don't know what business it is of yours."

"What business it is of . . . ?" His aunt was almost rendered speechless with indignation. "And whose more so than mine, then?" She did not allow time for a reply, but instead turned back to examine Phillipa with gimlet eyes. "You're younger than I expected, too."

Phillipa's hands were clenched into fists. "And you're more ill-bred than I expected, your ladyship." The last part of the sentence was uttered in as bitingly sarcastic a tone as Phillipa could muster.

Surprisingly, this thrust, instead of offending, caused Lady Wensley to look upon her with the first vestiges of approval.

"Well, she has spirit anyway," said Lady Wensley grudgingly. "But you needn't think that's enough to win me over." She turned to the earl. "The chit's unsuitable in every way, Evelyn, and that's my final opinion on the matter."

Phillipa was ready to explode with fury.

The earl looked coolly amused. "Unsuitable for what exactly, pray tell?"

She shook her head. "So that's the way it is, then. You're thoroughly besotted." She gave Phillipa a glance of reluctant respect. "I own I did not expect such wiles in one so young." She addressed Phillipa directly. "I'm afraid all your schemes have come to naught, Miss Raithby. You have no family to protect you and the word of a Sinamor carries a great deal of weight."

Phillipa was both resentful and confused. She was itching to flatten this old lady's nose. Both she and the aunt were surprised by the unexpected sound of the earl's chuckle. They stared at him, puzzled.

"Don't tell me, Aunt, that you think that Phillipa . . . that she . . . that she has entrapped me into a proposal of marriage?" He chuckled louder.

Lady Wensley stared at him in surprise. "What else

could it be? You would not ask me here if she were merely your . . ." She paused; Phillipa's sense of humor had also responded to the absurdity of the situation and both she and the earl began laughing aloud. The look of perplexity on the older woman's face only added to their amusement.

"See here. This is very bad of you. I wish you would explain to me what is going on."

Wiping his eyes, the earl responded, "And I wish you might explain to me how you came by such an addlepated notion."

Covered by confusion, she stammered, "Well, I'd heard talk—yes, even in Bath—about you and this red-haired woman, and I knew very well you never had a ward. And when you wrote to me and said you wanted me to chaperone her at Sinamor, well, naturally I assumed she had convinced you to do the honest, the right thing by her."

He broke out into a fresh paroxysm of laughter.

"Sinamor, this is not like you, and I certainly don't see what is so humorous about all this. It would only be natural for you to retreat to Sinamor to announce your betrothal and avoid all the gossip in town—even have a quiet wedding here, if that were necessary."

He looked up, suddenly unamused. "I think it would be best if you did not go on about your conjectures, Aunt, although it certainly is edifying to know the opinion my own relations have of my character. Miss Raithby is truly my ward, owing to an unexpected set of circumstances, and she has been staying with the Dearbornes until yesterday, when we removed here. I think that you owe her an apology."

"I beg your pardon, Miss Raithby," Lady Wensley said, very much mortified.

"Just how did you come to be here, Aunt?" asked the earl.

"When I received your letter of last week, with what I had already heard, I thought I should take no time in posting up to London to see if I could bring you to your senses. It was a rude shock to find that you had already departed just a few hours before my arrival. I managed to worm out of that butler of yours the information that you had already gone to Sinamor. I decided to follow on your heels as quickly as I could."

"How very providential. I sent a letter just yesterday requesting that you join us here immediately."

Phillipa took pity on her sadly defeated opponent. "Lady Wensley, you must be tired after your trip. Would you care for some tea? Or would you rather have someone show you to your room?"

All of a sudden, Lady Wensley had become a tired old woman. She accepted Phillipa's olive branch gratefully.

Tea somewhat restored her spirits, and by the time it had been completed, she was busy quizzing Phillipa about how she had come to be the earl's ward. The two women were fast on their way to developing an understanding.

12

Within the matter of a few weeks, Aunt Ondine's opinion of Phillipa underwent a total transformation. She had begun to regret her own officious behavior upon arrival, for, in her eyes, Phillipa was exactly the sort of a wife that Sinamor needed.

As soon as her horse had arrived and her ankle had somehwat healed, Phillipia was out in the saddle, covering the estate from one end to the other. Soon she was more familiar with the estate's tenants and their affairs than Sinamor himself. She was not afraid to add her voice to Mr. Fenwick's in urging that a certain area might be cleared for pasture or that this tenant's cottage needed roofing. After Mr. Fenwick had departed, she spent extra time explaining the advantages of agricultural methods such as crop rotation to the earl.

Sinamor listened unwillingly to all this, but with a growing respect for her. More than once he was heard to joke that if Mr. Fenwick ever left him, he'd consider hiring Phillipa as his replacement.

In Aunt Ondine's eyes, it was all for the good. She had long despaired of finding a way to force Sinamor to take a proper interest in estate affairs. This little girl bullied him into it as naturally as if she'd been doing so her entire life.

Phillipa had a good way with the tenants and with the servants, too, commanding not only respect but affection. Her air of self-possession was remarkable for one so young.

Even more important, since Phillipa had recovered from her accident, Ondine could see that she boasted the rude health requisite for a Countess of Sinamor. Even her somewhat hoydenish manner could be forgiven in one who would be so highly placed. All in all, Ondine thought to herself, Sinamor could do far, far worse.

Phillipa fortunately had no inkling of that good lady's ideas as she merrily charged about. She was almost giddy with her newfound freedom. Her life changed abruptly from a monotonous existence to a busy and worthwhile pursuit. She fell enthusiastically into this routine, delightfully familiar except for a change in the cast of characters. She most certainly was meddling in matters that were not her concern, but fortunately she had no idea of it and everyone else welcomed her interference. Sinamor was just an absent London landlord to his tenants. It was a relief to be able to pour their troubles out to someone who not only understood them, but also had the earl's ear.

The weeks turned into months, and fall changed into winter, but the passage of time went almost unnoticed by the inhabitants of Sinamor House.

Sinamor threw down a letter from Winifred that he'd been perusing, and gave a bitter laugh. He didn't know what society would find more amusing: his new role as responsible landlord and friend to the needy or the fact that he was hopelessly besotted by a seventeen-year-old chit who despised him. He had hoped that the months of increased proximity might serve to give him a disgust of her; instead, he became more attached with every passing day. The situation could not continue. It was time to think of returning to London. The sooner she was married, the better.

He rose and limped from his desk. He was in the hall before he heard the music. It was an unexpected sound and he was drawn to it.

First came the tinkling of a harpsichord, then followed the voice, low and sweet. "*Since first I saw your face I resolved to honor and renown you. If now I be disdained . . .*"

He stepped up to the door of the music room, listening.

"*I wish my heart had never known you.*"

He cracked the door open and peered in. Phillipa was seated at the harpsichord. The lightheartedness of the tune provided a sharp contrast to her face, which was filled with a sadness he had never witnessed before.

"*What I that loved and you that liked, shall we begin to wrangle*?"

He opened the door softly and stepped inside the room.

"*No, no, no, my heart is fast . . .*"

Sensing his gaze upon her, she looked up and closed her mouth abruptly, crashing her hands down on the keys.

"You needn't stop on my account. I was enjoying your performance. You have a lovely voice."

She rose immediately. "No, my lord. I mean, thank you, but . . . but the instrument is out of tune."

He walked closer to her, his face enigmatic. "You have a very expressive voice also. Are you unhappy, Phillipa?"

She could not meet his eyes. "No, my lord."

He was only a foot away from her now. She felt a magnetic tension between them and strove to resist it.

He picked up her chin with one hand. "But you are! I can see that."

There was a surprising tenderness in his voice. She looked up and met his eyes and read something new there. For a moment it was as if a spark passed between them. He dropped her chin abruptly and she looked away again.

"I have been selfish, keeping you here so long while I put the estate in order. I received a chiding letter from Winifred only today." He managed to assume a light tone. "An elderly woman cannot be very much company for you, especially after the gaiety of London. You must wish for the society of persons your own age."

A part of Phillipa wished to scream a denial at him, to tell him that his society was all that she required for the rest of her existence.. Pride came to her rescue.

"I do miss Lady Dearborne and her family."

She could feel Sinamor's eyes boring into her, and so she hastily added, "And my cousin, of course."

"Of course." These words were said in a particularly chilly way, but Phillipa did not notice. "I will go and confer with Aunt Ondine, then, and see what she thinks would be a proper schedule for our return."

"Yes, my lord." Phillipa waited until he had left the room,

then went running out to the stables. She found her way to Ripon's stall, flung herself on his neck, and indulged in a fit of weeping. Ripon turned his head around to nose at her curiously. She looked up at him, her face streaming with tears.

"I love him, I love him, and I shall never have him. Oh, what am I to do?"

The horse butted her gently with his nose. She collapsed on him again.

When the actual time for departure came, Phillipa was able to conceal the despondency she felt at leaving Sinamor. The servants were not able to put on equally brave faces. For the first time, someone had been able to make the earl take an interest in the estate, and now she was going. Mrs. Tiddingford was the only one who seemed unmoved by the exodus.

Young Joseph looked at her in amazement, for his wife, Rose, had not even been able to bear the spectacle of departure and had fled inside with well-reddened eyes. It was Tom who had the boldness to put the question to her.

"Aren't you sad to see her go, then? Knowing she's never coming back?"

Mrs. Tiddingford allowed herself a small, smug smile. "We'll see about that."

Aunt Ondine, who had decided to do what she could to promote a romance, had informed the earl privately that she would be willing to stay in town as long as she was needed. Sinamor had accepted her offer with only a few qualms. It might be more difficult for him to have Phillipa living with him in Berkeley Square, but at the same time it would allow him to discourage suitors such as Wakehurst.

Phillipa had similarly mixed feelings about living in the earl's home. A part of her was delighted at the opportunity to remain in such proximity to him. A colder, more rational side argued that it could only mean more pain for her.

Apart from the change in residence, Phillipa's life settled quite easily into its old routine upon their arrival in town. The earl let it be known that Phillipa's great-aunt had made a miraculous recovery, so that Phillipa was once again free to receive callers and invitations. Even though the Season had not yet begun, she found herself once again caught up in a social whirl she had not missed.

She was delighted, of course, to see St. Clair, one of her first callers. He observed her closely and thought she was more lacking in spirits than when she had left, but was tactful enough not to comment upon it. He amused her instead by flirting outrageously with Aunt Ondine, a pastime that formidable lady thoroughly enjoyed. Phillipa was amazed to see the color that remained in the older woman's cheeks even after St. Clair had departed.

"What a young scoundrel he is," commented Aunt Ondine, fanning herself briskly. "La! He makes me feel twenty years younger."

Phillipa managed to conceal her smile.

Phillipa was glad also to see Charles Fitzroy and his sister, who lost no time in calling upon her and inviting her to tea. Phillipa thought to herself that it was pleasant to know that at least one young lady of her acquaintance possessed some sense. Marianne Middleton had been annoying her daily with her attentions ever since she divined that Phillipa was now residing with the earl.

By far her happiest reunion, however, was with Winifred and her family. They had arranged for her to have dinner with them upon her return. It was a mark of their esteem for her that the only family member absent was Francis, who was back at Eton. Even Lord Dearborne had dragged himself away from his work in order to see Phillipa. He greeted her warmly when she arrived.

"Never had a chance to thank you, my dear. Lady Dearborne told me what you did for Arthur."

Remembering the events of that day, Phillipa turned a tomato-like shade of red as she murmured, "It was nothing."

He clapped her on the shoulder. "Well, Lady Dearborne tells me this arrangement with Sinamor is best for you now, but I wish you to know that you have a home here whenever you wish it."

Her inarticulate words of thanks were interrupted by the precipitate arrival of a small figure in nankin trousers. "P'lippa . . . P'lippa," Arthur called.

She caught him in her arms and swung him up in the air. He shrieked with delight. His brothers were not far behind. William and Anthony were more careful of preserving their collective dignity, for they merely offered her their hands, although their eyes betrayed their excitement.

Edmond was the last of the group to enter. Phillipa was pleased to see that he was clean-shaven and clear-eyed. He gave her an apologetic look as he joined the company.

"Wished to thank you," he was mumbling, but Phillipa would not let him continue. She pressed his hand warmly.

"No, it's all behind us. I've forgotten it, if you have."

He smiled at her. "Now that you mention it, so I have."

Winifred herself could not conceal her delight at Phillipa's return. She smothered her in a fond embrace. "My dear, we all have missed you so."

Lord Dearborne offered Phillipa his arm and escorted her into dinner as the guest of honor. The rest of the family followed. Even Arthur, Anthony, and William were afforded the privilege of dining with the family on this special occasion.

Winifred kept up an almost unceasing flow of questions about Phillipa's journey to Sinamor House. how she had found it and how she had liked it. Winifred exclaimed with pleasure at hearing old familiar names, queried her about new ones, alternately wondered at the changes that had occurred since her youth, and marveled at everything that had remained the same.

Phillipa was kept so busy answering her and remembering what details she could that she never noticed how narrowly Winifred was watching her. Winifred was of much the same opinion as St. Clair. Phillipa definitely lacked the exuberance she'd had before she left for Sinamor. Her face showed faint signs of strain also, and a swift, unhappy look was wont to pass over her face whenever she mentioned Sinamor. Winifred had cherished secret hopes that this enforced period of time together might bring them to an understanding. It seemed that it was not to be.

Phillipa felt a sense of guilt that her first meeting with her blood relation, Lord Wakehurst, was a great deal more lack-luster than the reunion with her adopted family. He greeted her with an enthusiasm that demonstrated that his feelings had not altered. She, on the other hand, felt a rush of her old aversion to him, and it required her greatest efforts to conceal it. His rather high, lisping voice grated on her ears. She shrank from the clasp of his warm, sweaty palm. The scent of his pomade made her head ache.

Still, she knew it was wrong to scorn someone with such kind intentions. He did his best to amuse her in his unimaginative way by telling her who had gone abroad and recounting scandals that had occurred in her absence.

Aunt Ondine regarded him with a steadily disapproving eye. Phillipa ascribed it to the fact that Wakehurst had not St. Clair's ease of manner, and furthermore that he had made no effort to ingratiate himself with the older woman. Provoked by Ondine's reaction, Phillipa showered her cousin with little pleasantries, exerting her charm to the utmost. When his visit had come to a conclusion and he asked if he might call again, Phillipa issued him an invitation with defiant alacrity. As soon as he had left, she swung around, ready to wage verbal battle with Aunt Ondine. That woman fortunately by now had months of experience in dealing with Phillipa and so refused to allow herself to be drawn.

Wakehurst himself was filled with elation at these new developments. His ambitions had been shattered by Phillipa's sudden departure. They had revived with her unexpected return. His prospects had seemed gloomy when she had left without a word, but now she seemed determined to throw herself at his head. She had never shown such warmth during their previous acquaintance. The time was ripe to bring his parents to London. A pity all the furbishings had been stripped from their London house. Well, he could always say that it was in the process of being redone. Something would be arranged.

Sinamor, meanwhile, contrived to see as little as possible of Phillipa in the days following their arrival. He reverted to all his former occupations, spending a great deal of time at his tailor's and an inordinate amount at his club. He found the play wanting in its usual spice, though he did not lack his customary good fortune. The beauties, who in former days might have provided some amusement, now cast their lures out to him in vain. Sinamor was unaware of being the object of St. Clair's scrutiny night after night, and that gentleman took care not to share his observations with him. The grimness about the mouth, the abstraction: these were things that the world at large could not notice, but they worried St. Clair. The earl would be the last to confess whatever was bedeviling him, as his friend well knew.

Phillipa was too tortured by her own feelings to have much awareness of a change in Sinamor. Perhaps he was somewhat more distant, but they were back in London, after all. He considered her no more than an obnoxious burden, as he'd often made clear. Any kindness he'd shown her was simply out of duty to her father. In a way, it was a great relief that he no longer accompanied her on her morning rides. It was tormenting to be near him—and all the worse since she knew his opinion of her.

The only times that Phillipa saw Sinamor were when he escorted her and Aunt Ondine to various social functions. It was true, as Wakehurst had said, that many people had removed to the continent, but London, as always, offered much in the way of gaiety. A case in point was Lady Raymond's assembly. Upon their arrival there, it was clear that London was hardly deserted. Phillipa did not welcome the idea of mingling in this crush of people, but she bore it with good grace, greeting acquaintances amiably and responding coquettishly to repartee from even the most inane of her admirers.

Ondine, on the other hand, was genuinely enjoying herself. Having secluded herself for years in the no longer fashionable resort of Bath, she took great pleasure in seeing old friends and catching up on all their news.

Sinamor deserted the ladies immediately, but oddly enough he was not to be found in the card room with most of the other gentlemen. He made desultory conversation with those who hailed him and in all seemed to be his usual remote self. Only a close observer would have noticed how he managed to keep Phillipa within his sight and how often his eyes strayed to her.

Unfortunately such a close observer existed in the person of Helene, who also noted angrily that Phillipa's glance seemed drawn to the earl with equal frequency. She had been perturbed when she had heard that they had left town at the same time.

She had never known the earl to spend time at Sinamor, and there was certainly no reason for him to attend Phillipa's ailing great-aunt, if such a person existed. Now, her worst fears were confirmed. What else could it be but a love match? It made her absolutely furious just to think of it. She didn't know offhand what she could do about it, but she swore to herself that she'd find some way to destroy them. She watched, her spleen rising as the two pairs of blue eyes met accidentally and quickly looked away. She saw the telltale blush on Phillipa's cheeks, despite her affected unconcern.

"You shan't have her Sinamor, I swear it," she muttered.

Winifred was also scrutinizing the earl and Phillipa, but she had come to an entirely different conclusion than Helene. She saw Phillipa's flirtatious response to her beaux and the earl's apparent boredom, and she heaved a little unconscious sigh.

Ondine, who was standing beside her, looked at her curiously. "Whatever is the matter, my dear?" she asked.

Winifred shook her head. "Nothing to signify, I assure you."

Ondine had keen eyes of her own. "Is it Phillipa who concerns you, or Sinamor?"

Winifred gave a tight smile. "It is only a foolish fancy of mine." She saw that her companion was waiting expectantly. "I suppose you will think me a complete dolt, but at one time I hoped that Phillipa and Sinamor might make a match of it. I don't know why I imagined anything so improbable. They have wrangled from the moment they met, and from what I have seen, they still are."

Ondine smiled knowingly. "Of course, my dear, there could be no surer sign of an attraction."

Winifred's head jerked around with surprise as she stared at her companion. "Do you really think so?"

Ondine nodded, but looked grave. "They are both such stiff-necked imbeciles, though. There is nothing one can do."

Winifred's considering frown returned to her face.

Despite these ladies' hopes, circumstances did not alter between Phillipa and the earl. Phillipa was seeing a great deal too much of her cousin, in Ondine's opinion, and she said so to Sinamor. He assumed an expression of boredom.

"I dislike the fellow just as much as you, but I have no reason to forbid him the house, and it would only set up Phillipa's back."

Ondine gave an exasperated snort. "Well, surely you could tell her to spend time with other young gentlemen."

His eyes glittered icily. "You may have noticed by now, Phillipa does not hold a high opinion of me or my advice."

"Nonsense, you're her guardian!"

"And so must do as I see fit. I am afraid, Aunt, that you must respect my wishes in this matter and leave it to Phillipa's good sense."

"What good sense? Why, the chit's seventeen!"

He coldly ignored her outburst.

Drat him, thought Ondine, can't he see that he's driving her into the arms of that young rogue?

The earl himself had some qualms on that score, but the information that St. Clair had obtained was based on gossip alone. Sinamor knew better than to try to confront Phillipa without concrete evidence. It was clear whose side she would take in that argument. He had hoped that the fact that she was living in his own house, under his own protection, might have scared off Wakehurst. With such encouragement from Phillipa, though, it was possible that nothing would. No, he must continue to bide his time and to hope that Phillipa might come to see Wakehurst for what he was.

Wakehurst himself, astonished by his own good fortune, was proceeding busily along with his plans. He had persuaded his parents that it was of the utmost urgency that they come to town. He had seen them established at Grillon's. It might be a frightful expense, but at least it obviated the need for a retinue of servants. Besides, it was most important that Phillipa and Sinamor should not suspect their true financial situation. Fortunately there was always some unsuspecting young nobleman about who was ripe for a fleecing.

In one respect at least, Grillon's was an admirable choice, for it was renowned for the quality of its dinners. Wakehurst had impressed upon his parents the need to conciliate Phillipa. He now felt the time had come for a meeting.

Phillipa could not help but be gratified by the invitation to dine with Lord Wakehurst and his family at their hotel. She was both curious and apprehensive about meeting her mother's brother. Wakehurst drove away any lingering doubts she had by assuring her of his parents' fervid desire to be acquainted with her. She supposed that the little her father had told her could have been tinged with the bitterness resulting from her mother's death. At the very least, she owed it to her cousin to meet them.

As they rode in the carriage toward Grillon's that evening, Phillipa for once was grateful for Aunt Ondine's presence. Even though she still looked disapproving, she had the good sense not to say anything against the plan, for which Phillipa was grateful. Phillipa found herself wishing that Sinamor had seen fit to accompany them: her nervousness was increasing by the minute and she badly wanted his support. He had found some excuse to cry off from the evening. Maybe it was better that she learned not to rely on him.

Phillipa had cherished some vague hopes that in the Wakehursts she would find a new family, and in this she was soon to be disappointed. She could trace a resemblance in Lord Wakehurst's face, it was true, despite his corpulence. Although he made an evident effort to be amiable, there was such hauteur in that visage and such condescension in that manner that she could not help but take him in dislike. His wife, whose face still bore the faded remains of a formidable beauty, was more personable, but Phillipa was put off by her vanity and the malice with which she slandered most of her acquaintances.

Phillipa found it necessary to conceal her feelings, though, for she was aware that Gervase was watching her constantly. It would not be fair to wound him by showing her antipathy toward his parents. After all, it surely was kind of them to wish to heal the family breach. Perhaps they improved upon closer acquaintance, though Phillipa had no great desire to see if it was so.

She managed to act her part so cleverly that Gervase had no notion of her true feelings. He frankly could not have imagined that she would be anything but overawed at being accepted back into the Wakehurst family. It was easy, therefore, for him to accept her delight as genuine, and when the evening concluded, he felt entirely pleased.

Aunt Ondine was not so easily taken in, though she kept to innocuous topics on the carriage ride home.

"I thought the potted lobster was excellent, didn't you?"

Phillipa murmured an assent.

"Though I considered the daubed goose a trifle overdone."

Phillipa made a faint sound.

"But the pastry was simply marvelous. I can understand the Wakehurst's preference for dining there."

Phillipa kept silent, wishing that her companion would be quiet.

"Is something the matter?"

Phillipa gave a little wave of dismissal. "It is nothing. I think the champagne has given me the headache."

Ondine had never known Phillipa to suffer from such an ailment, but she was careful to betray no surprise. "I am sorry, my dear. I'll send my maid up to you with some lavender water when we reach home."

Phillipa gave a tiny shake of her head. "It's not necessary, I assure you, though I appreciate your kindness."

Ondine drew a deep breath of satisfaction. Sinamor had been right. The silly fellow was hanging himself with his own rope and he didn't even know it. Matters definitely were looking up.

13

All of Ondine's fond hopes and imaginings could not have caused her to anticipate the dramatic turn that events were soon to take. It all began most quietly one day when Phillipa paid a visit to Hamilton Place. She had found some consolation in remaining there to enjoy the support of her adopted family and to forget her sorrows for a few hours in an enthusiastic game of jackstraws. Winifred, while delighted to have Phillipa's company, also saw this as an opportunity to put the finishing touches on her protégée's education. Accordingly, this afternoon was spent on a lesson in assigning places at table.

"I'm finished," Phillipa announced, having arranged the names to her satisfaction, while Winifred was engaged in needlework.

Winifred rose and went over to examine the sheet of paper. She eyed it critically, looking for possible faults. "Very good," she said at length, "but I see one problem here. Lord D. should not have the Duchess of L. sitting beside him." She had assigned initials to each individual for discretion's sake.

"Why not?"

"My dear, you are absolutely correct in terms of rank, but Lord D. is a social lion, as you well know. You can't seat him next to a deaf widow of eighty. He would be bored and would never return to your home."

"I might prefer that," scowled Phillipa.

Winifred shook her head as she resumed her work. "This is a theoretical problem that I am posing. You must solve it to the best of your abilities."

Phillipa frowned for another moment. Suddenly her brow cleared and she quickly switched two names. "I'm through," she said triumphantly.

Winifred came over to see the sheet and could not prevent a gasp when she had done so. "Phillipa!"

"It is correct in terms of rank, isn't it?"

Winifred was horror-struck. "Phillipa, you cannot seat them together. You know very well that they are . . ."

Phillipa gave Winifred her most engagingly mischievous grin. "Well, at least he will not be *bored.*"

Winifred could not resist her charm. "You minx. You'll be London's most original hostess." She regretted her unthinking words, for a cloud of gloom immediately descended over Phillipa's features.

"I have no wish to be a hostess," Phillipa said flatly. She looked up and saw Winifred's troubled expression. "Though I do appreciate your efforts on my behalf."

Winifred smiled. "It is no effort." She assumed a lighthearted tone. "Do you wish to accompany me? You know that we have resumed our plans for the ball. I promised Arthur that he might go with me to the confectioner's."

"Where are William and Anthony?"

"Edmond took them somewhere. I only hope it's not to a mill!"

Phillipa gave a wan smile. "I think it would be best if I returned home. Aunt Ondine might be wondering what has become of me."

Phillipa did remain long enough to greet Arthur before setting out on foot with her maid. Winifred had offered to drive her by Berkeley Square, but Phillipa had declined, for it was a fine day, despite a gusty wind.

She was preoccupied as she started out, and only vaguely registered the sounds of Winifred and Arthur being handed into the waiting carriage. She did hear a loud voice call "My lady!" and turned to see Bickerstaffe hurrying out to the carriage. Whatever he had to say apparently was of some urgency, for Winifred stepped down and went back inside the house.

Phillipa turned back and continued on her way. Since she was walking away from the house, she did not see the coachman step away from the carriage for a moment to ask the footman a question. Neither had she any way of observing as Arthur discovered the newfound freedom of being alone in the landau.

He climbed stealthily onto the coachman's box. The incident might have gone no further had not a puff of wind caught the hat of a gentleman across the street. The hat sailed up into the air and went skittering up to the carriage, startling one of the horses. He snorted with fright and bolted just as Arthur made an unsuccessful grab for the reins.

Phillipa heard the cry of alarm and the sudden pounding of hooves. She had a vague impression of seeing a familiar equipage rounding the far corner as she turned and beheld the driverless carriage headed toward her, with Arthur bouncing about alone on the box. She acted without a moment's hesitation, running to intercept the carriage. Her maid watched, horrified, as she dashed practically in front of the oncoming horses yelling and waving her hands. It seemed there was nothing to prevent her being trampled under their hooves.

Mary had not figured on Miss Raithby's dexterity, however, for as the horses refused to slow, Phillipa stepped aside adroitly and grabbed at one of the dangling reins. In the next moment, Mary gasped as the small, pelisse-clad figure was lifted off her feet to fly through the air. Mary closed her eyes in fear. When she opened them, the carriage had stopped, miraculously blocked by another, and Phillipa was standing at the horse's heads soothing them. In the same instant, everyone came pouring from the house.

Winifred came running up as the footman handed Arthur down to her. She clasped him to her bosom with tears. He was chuckling with pleasure at his unexpected joyride.

Sinamor's tiger, still a trifle pale after the near collision, jumped down from his perch to hold the horses as the earl descended from the curricle and limped over to Phillipa. The coachman had relieved her of the reins and she turned to the earl in some confusion.

"You damned little fool. You might have been killed!" He spat the words angrily at her.

She had little time to fret over his words or to worry about the blazing fury in his eyes, for he took her crushingly in his arms and kissed her violently. It was entirely unexpected and completely delightful. Phillipa did not have time to analyze her reactions. She simply melted into him, her arms snaking about him receptively, her lips returning his kiss with equal passion. They remained locked in the embrace, lost to all propriety, for almost a minute. They were recalled by the pleased laughter of an interested bystander.

Sinamor released Phillipa immediately. She flushed and put a hand to her face as the laughter increased, several more onlookers joining in the merriment.

A little smile played about the earl's lips. "I think we had better go inside, don't you?"

She nodded mutely and they joined the procession in returning to the house, disappointing their audience and leaving the coachman and tiger to deal with the horses.

Once inside, Winifred hugged her thankfully, then disappeared discreetly, murmuring something about tea. Phillipa hoped the earl might have forgotten his anger by now. She was mistaken.

"Phillipa, you saw I was approaching. Why couldn't you trust me to stop the carriage?"

Unexpectedly, her eyes began filling. "I didn't see you—at least not in time—and I had to save Arthur." Her lower lip began trembling.

The earl saw it and softened. "There, there, my love, don't cry."

She promptly burst into sobs.

He took her and folded her in his arms, stroking the back of her head tenderly.

She continued to sob painfully as her overstrained nerves abruptly gave way.

The earl clasped her to him and murmured soothing words to her.

At length, she looked up, red-eyed. Unasked, he provided her with a handkerchief. She blew her nose in an unladylike manner, but this did not seem to excite his disapproval.

"You have been quite a brave girl today," he said, "and I think that you should go home and rest now. All right?"

She nodded and he led her from the room.

Winifred came up to them in the hall. She began to pour effusions of thanks on Phillipa's head.

Sinamor gave her an admonitory look. "Yes, she has been

quite heroic and you may praise her all you wish tomorrow, but for now she must go home and recover from all this.'' With an arm about Phillipa, he led her outside and then helped her into the waiting curricle.

She was surprised to see that night had already fallen. ''My maid?'' she asked.

''I sent her home so that Aunt Ondine might know what had become of us.''

Phillipa rested her head on Sinamor's shoulder as he drove them back to Berkeley Square. A part of her recognized that this was improper, but she was simply too tired to care.

When they arrived home, he descended from the carriage and helped her out. She took a step and found that she was trembling violently. Without a word, he swung her into his arms and began to carry her up the steps.

The butler met them at the doorway. He held a note on a silver salver.

''I beg your pardon, my lord, but this note arrived for you. They said it was urgent.''

Sinamor hardly glanced at the note, though Phillipa could see that it was addressed in a distinctly feminine hand. ''I'll look at it as soon as I take Miss Raithby to her room. Send up her maid immediately.''

''Yes, my lord.''

Phillipa began to protest, but the earl began up the inside staircase with her in his arms.

''I'm fine. Please put me down,'' she said.

''Sssh,'' he said. ''The servants might suspect I'm doing this for my own pleasure.''

Phillipa was unused to hearing him in a playful mood. She turned rosy in response to this sally, thereby pleasing him enormously. In a very short time, he had carried her to her chamber and laid her on the bed. ''Are you hungry? Shall I have a tray sent up to you?''

She shook her head as a knock sounded on the door. Her maid bustled into the room.

''Very well, then. Have a good night's sleep. We'll talk tomorrow.'' He caught one side of her face with his hand, then bent swiftly to kiss her. Phillipa would have welcomed more of this treatment, but he just gave her a tender smile, straightened, and left the room.

Mary's sense of satisfaction at this little drama was quickly overwhelmed by her solicitude for her mistress. She efficiently helped Phillipa out of her clothes and into her nightgown. After ascertaining that there really was nothing else Phillipa wanted, she snuffed the candles and left the room. Phillipa felt ready to fall asleep immediately, but before she did, she was vaguely aware of hearing Sinamor drive off in his carriage. She had little time to speculate upon his destination, for she was quickly unconscious.

She did not stir until the great clock in the hallway struck the hour of three. She opened her eyes to a darkened room, lit only by the embers of the dying fire. She assumed it was the chiming of the clock that had awakened her and prepared to go back to sleep. Abruptly, she became aware of footsteps echoing down the hall. She tiptoed over to the door and cracked it open to see Sinamor, in greatcoat and boots, disappearing down the hall.

She shut the door and slowly walked back to bed. It was not unusual for Sinamor to come in late. He often did and she had never concerned herself about it before. Now, somehow the situation seemed different. The idea hurt her, though she didn't know the reason. Why shouldn't he be out amusing himself with his friends until three in the morning? He couldn't help her by remaining here at home. She had been sleeping the entire time.

She crawled into bed, dismissing the subject. She could always speak to him about it in the morning.

When she awoke late the next morning, all Phillipa's worries of the night had vanished. All she could think of was that she was in love with Sinamor and he with her. After bathing, she put on one of her most strikingly fashionable dresses, of white muslin with a ruff around the neck and long, puffed sleeves.

She partly destroyed the effect of such sophistication by rushing down to breakfast. Sinamor was not there. She felt a sharp stab of disappointment, but greeted Aunt Ondine graciously anyway.

The older woman looked at her disapprovingly and inquired if she was feeling well.

Phillipa assured her that she was, thus unwittingly laying herself open for the attack.

"Well, you're fortunate, then, for that was a harebrained thing that you did yesterday. You're only lucky that you weren't killed."

Phillipa smiled at her. Even Ondine's grouchiness could not dispel her happy mood. "Yes, so Lord Sinamor informed me."

Ondine was feeling particularly left out since Phillipa's maid had been the one to inform her of the incident and no one had seen fit to consult her since. Her only response was a disdainful sniff.

"Have you seen Sinamor this morning?" asked Phillipa.

Ondine gave a snort of disgust. "He left before I rose. Apparently he had to take care of some urgent business."

Phillipa was a bit taken aback. She had counted upon seeing Sinamor this morning. Well, she must be patient. She had no other choice.

She had hardly finished breakfast when her first visitor was announced. It was Lady Dearborne and she came sweeping in to give Phillipa an enthusiastic hug.

"My dear, how are you today?"

"Fine, thank you."

Winifred seated herself. "The whole family wished to come thank you, but I told them that you might still be exhausted from yesterday and that we should not overset you."

Phillipa smiled. "That is kind, but their thanks are unnecessary. I love Arthur, as you know."

Winifred smiled. "Yes . . ." She seemed to be on the verge of saying something, but hesitated and apparently changed her mind. "In any case, we all wished you to know how grateful we are. Could you come to dinner tonight, tomorrow night, or whenever you wish?"

Phillipa laughed. "I'd be happy to come, though tonight I am engaged to attend Lady Pickney's ball. Next week might be better."

"That's settled, then." Winifred adroitly turned the conversation back to Phillipa's heroism, though the girl herself made efforts to divert it by inquiring about Arthur. Only when it became plain that she was doing little other than embarrassing Phillipa did Lady Dearborne abandon it.

When she feared she might be overstaying her welcome, Winifred excused herself, saying that she wished to speak with Lady Wensley.

"For I wish to have her opinion concerning certain arrangements that I have made for your coming-out party."

Phillipa bid her farewell gladly, happy that she needn't sit in on this doubtlessly long and boring discussion.

Winifred discovered Ondine in her sitting room. "Well, you were right, after all! Isn't it the most marvelous thing?"

Ondine looked at her in astonishment. "I beg your pardon?"

"Phillipa and Sinamor—they're in love!"

"What are you saying?"

"It's true. I was there yesterday. He kissed her right in the middle of Hamilton Place with everyone watching."

Ondine looked at her, affronted. "But no one told me any of this."

"Well, it was all most unexpected. I think it was the shock of the moment, that made him realize—oh, you should have seen it! They were billing and cooing like two turtledoves."

Ondine's sense of grievance was growing. "And here I have thrust them together for months and no one sees fit to mention—"

Winifred hastened to soothe the older woman. "It all happened in such haste, and it's not as if everything has been settled yet. It was just apparent from . . ." Her eyes sparkled with joy. "Oh, how I had been praying for this!"

A cautious sort of hope had begun to seep into Ondine's heart. "My dear, do you mean . . . do you actually think that Sinamor might *offer* for her?"

"You haven't seen them together yet." At Ondine's shake of the head, Winifred continued. "Well, you may form your own opinion when you do." She smiled confidently. "As for me, I will be surprised if we don't hear of an engagement within a week's time."

"I hope you are right, my dear. Now tell me, just how did all this occur?"

After Winifred's departure, Ondine lost no time in joining

Phillipa downstairs, in the hope of seeing Sinamor there also. He had not yet returned, and Ondine resolved to wait it out.

The next person to arrive was not Sinamor, but Marianne Middleton. Ondine's lip curled as the name was announced. She had taken a profound dislike to that young lady, who was wont to bestow upon her the most servile flattery. Ignoring their distant relationship, Ondine generally left the room before Marianne entered it. This time, determined to see Sinamor and Phillipa together, she kept her seat.

Marianne swept into the room in her familiar manner, wearing a pelisse in shell pink, ornamented with every sort of furbelow, with ribbons on her bonnet and slippers to match. Ondine might have thought the ensemble a little too garish to be in good taste, but she did not say so.

When she saw Ondine, Marianne greeted her obsequiously. As was her habit, she began her conversation with Phillipa by asking if Sinamor was at home.

Today, Phillipa took a veritable pleasure in telling her that he wasn't, that they had no idea where he'd gone or when he'd be back.

Marianne heaved a little sigh. She proffered a book to Phillipa in an indifferent manner. "Well, here is the book I've brought you. It's just the first volume."

"How very kind of you. You certainly are making certain that I am well-read. I haven't even begun the last four you brought me."

Marianne missed the underlying sarcasm in Phillipa's words. "I'm afraid they're all better than this one. There's not a ruined castle, or an evil monk, or even a prince in it, as far as I can tell. I don't know why everyone is raving about it so. I hardly made it through the first volume and I dread the second."

Phillipa's eyes met Aunt Ondine's with a gleam of amusement. "It is so generous of you to share it with me." Privately she thought that if Marianne hated it, there could be something to like about it. She probably would never find out, though. Most likely she'd just send Mary to return it to the library as she had all the others. It might be worth making a wager with Edmond. Just how many books would Marianne bring her before she became discouraged?

Marianne again accepted Phillipa's words at face value. "You're welcome," she said absently. "You're sure that no one has an idea when he'll be back, then?"

Phillipa was replying in the affirmative when to everyone's surprise, the door swung open and Sinamor strode into the room.

"Good afternoon, Aunt, Phillipa." Her name was a caress. He gave her a smile that sent the blood racing to her cheeks. He turned and noticed Marianne. The famous eyebrow ascended. "Miss Middleton, to what do we owe the honor of your company?"

She felt ill-at-ease with him regarding her in that coldly quizzical way, nor had she missed the brief interchange between him and Phillipa. Marianne was nothing if not persistent, however.

"My lord," she simpered at him, "what an unexpected pleasure this is!" She gave Phillipa a condescending glance. "Why, Miss Raithby and I were just having one of our usual visits. We are both such great readers, you know. I am in the habit of supplying her with books."

He turned to Phillipa now, the eyebrow still raised, but the curling corner of his mouth betraying his amusement. "Is that right, Phillipa? How odd, I never noticed that you were bookish."

She could not prevent her own lips from curving upward for a brief second, but she mastered her amusement quickly. "How little you know me, my lord," she said gravely, though there was a suspicious gleam in her eyes.

Sinamor gave her a look that made her heart skip a beat. "And I thought I knew you rather well," he said softly.

Unable to grasp what was going on but displeased at being excluded, Marianne thrust her way into the conversation. "I thought you would have known, my lord. I have spent many hours instructing Phillipa in the ways of the *ton*, since she has not the advantage of a London upbringing, as I have."

The earl's eyes never left Phillipa. "What a singularly apt pupil she must be."

Marianne was more upset than ever by the turn the conversation was taking. "Yes, well, I did not mind, since I felt it was a duty I owed the family. You know that I would do anything for your lordship."

Sinamor's back was turned to Marianne and he was walking slowly toward Phillipa. "So kind," he murmured almost inaudibly.

At length, even Marianne was forced to concede defeat. She was boiling with anger when she left. Somehow that insignificant rustic had managed to hook her claws into the earl. Marianne had no idea how she could have done it, particularly when someone with her own charms was near at hand. It had to have occurred when the little mouse enticed him out into the country on whatever flimsy pretext she had contrived. Nothing else could have done it. The earl was clearly besotted. Marianne could only hope that he would come to his senses before he took the final step.

Aunt Ondine, of course, had an entirely different reaction to Sinamor's and Phillipa's behavior. It was apparent now that Winifred's claims were not mere fabrication. The two were clearly in love, and she, for one, was well-satisfied.

She would have made an excuse and left, but Sinamor stopped her. "You needn't abandon Phillipa on my account. I merely returned for some papers I left. I have to go back out."

Disappointment exploded all over Phillipa's features at these words. He leaned down and gave her a quick kiss. "Don't fear, I'll be back in time to escort you to the ball."

Her face lit up with happiness at his caress. It quite took Ondine's breath away. Winifred was right: this was a love match.

Phillipa took special care in preparing for the ball that evening. She chose to wear the same, elegantly simple sapphire-blue satin evening down she had worn for her first dinner party with Sinamor. Mary had drawn her hair up in her usual style. As a finishing touch, she hung the great sapphire he had given her, about her neck. She should have looked no different than she had on any previous night, but now there was a new glow to her face, a new sparkle in her eyes that made her look radiantly beautiful as she never had before.

Mary's little gasp confirmed it. So did the proud and passionate way Sinamor's eyes raked over her as she went downstairs. She thought she had never seen him look so handsome before. Although she could not tear her eyes away from him, she did not realize that there was a new light in his eyes also, a new softening of his expression, which well became those handsome features.

Bless me, thought Aunt Ondine, they don't even know I'm here.

Sinamor proved her words false by offering his arm to both her and Phillipa, before escorting them to the carriage. Phillipa thought her heart might burst with joy. She knew that nothing could mar this ecstasy.

14

It was likely that this ball was little different from any of the others Phillipa had attended, but to her it seemed that she'd never seen such gorgeous decorations, heard such beautiful music, or viewed such a glittering assemblage of people before. Her new incandescence drew the beaux swarming around her more thickly than ever.

Her happiness suffered one setback when she realized that she must leave Sinamor in order to join in the dances. It was less of a hardship than it seemed, for every time she looked over at him, he met her eyes with a smile. She could not help but return the smile, and hers was so breathtakingly beautiful that more than one of her partners felt an uncomfortable tug on their heartstrings.

Aunt Ondine had sought out Winifred and they were exchanging secretive smiles of congratulations as they observed the two. An announcement was clearly imminent, and they would be the first to know.

St. Clair had not missed these significant looks either. He strolled over to his friend and engaged him in conversation. He was gladdened by the color in Sinamor's face and the glow in his eyes.

Another keen observer was less than delighted about the obvious understanding between Sinamor and Phillipa. Lady Serre felt a jealous pang as she saw a loving glance pass between the two. I wonder if he has offered for her already, she thought. Sinamor had made it clear last night that he intended to do so without delay. She had to bite her lip for a minute to maintain her self-control. What a humiliating scene that had been. She suspected that the only reason he had responded so quickly to her note was out of his concern for the chit. He certainly had made it clear enough that he no longer had an interest in Helene's favors, not that she had suspected otherwise, blast him!

An unpleasant smile curled one corner of her mouth. Well, she had achieved the original purpose of her invitation: her revenge was ready. Sinamor had handed Helene her weapon without even a glimmer of suspicion. Her hand strayed to her décolletage. Yes, it was still there. Her head held high, she consoled herself with the thought that the timing of her plan could not be more impeccable.

Phillipa, giddy with happiness, had been whirling about the room with Charles Fitzroy. Now, as the music ended, she thanked him prettily for the dance. He was about to escort her back to Ondine when a lady standing next to them on the dance floor suddenly smiled at Phillipa.

"Miss Raithby? May I have a word with you?"

There was something familiar about this lady, but Phillipa could not quite place her. It was dreadfully embarrassing not to recognize an acquaintance.

"I'm afraid that I am engaged for the next dance."

"Oh, but I won't take but a minute of your time," said the lady pleasantly as she took Phillipa by the arm.

Charles looked at her with a frown, unwilling to give up his charge.

Phillipa saw no alternative but to go along with this somewhat forceful person. She gave Charles a reassuring smile. "It's all right, Charles. I'll speak with you later in the evening."

He could think of no way to object, so he was forced to yield graciously.

Phillipa found herself being steered rapidly into an antechamber by this lady. Her companion sat her down in an armchair and then did the same herself. Phillipa stared at her in puzzlement. She was a beauty, no doubt about it: those perfect features, the large blue eyes, the golden hair. Still, Phillipa had the uncomfortable feeling of disliking this woman without knowing the reason why.

The vision smiled at her, revealing a set of dazzling white teeth. "I hope you do not mind all this," she said, "but I wanted to have an opportunity to speak to you and I did not know when we might have another."

A little frown had drawn Phillipa's eyebrows together. "I hope you will excuse my frankness," she said, "but what exactly did you wish to speak to me about?"

The lady's eyes glittered at her. "Why, I wished to congratulate you on your engagement to Sinamor. He's a prize many have tried to catch."

Phillipa bristled at her tone and at the familiar way she had referred to the earl. "I assure you that you are mistaken," she said in her most formal manner. "No such engagement exists between us."

The lady smirked at her. "I know, I understand that you can't say so before the announcement."

Phillipa glared at her. She suddenly had realized that this was the same woman she had seen pawing the earl at the assembly last year.

"You have the advantage of me, madam. Just who are you?"

"I am Lady Serre, but we need not stand on ceremony. You may call me Helene."

Phillipa rose. Clearly this was one of the ambitious, jealous women who were always throwing out lures for the earl. "Since you have been acting under a false assumption, Lady Serre, it seems to me that there is nothing to discuss. Good evening." She would have swept regally from the room, but Helene had caught hold of her skirt and prevented her from moving.

"I have a great deal more to say," Helene said.

"Unhand me."

Helene dropped the fabric. "I think it would be to your benefit to listen to me."

Phillipa considered her options for a moment. Perhaps it was best to humor this madwoman. She certainly seemed capable of following Phillipa into the ballroom and creating a scene.

"Very well," said Phillipa coldly, "you may have five minutes."

Helene relaxed back in her chair as Phillipa returned to perch warily on the arm of the other.

"I thought it might be beneficial to meet his future wife." She waved an arm languidly at Phillipa's protestations. "You need not deny it to me. Sinamor told me all about it last night."

Phillipa halted in the middle of what she was saying. Could

it be possible? Sinamor had been gone last night. Would he actually have told another woman they were engaged before he had asked her? She gave the woman a cold look. "It is obviously useless to brangle, since you refuse to accept my word."

Helene looked at her with reluctant admiration. "I must say that he's done better for himself than I thought. I told him marriage with a seventeen-year-old chit would be a mistake."

Phillipa rose. "I do not think that I have to sit and listen to your insults any longer."

"I am sorry. I did not mean to insult you. Rather, I meant what I said by way of a compliment. Clearly you are an unusual young lady for your age. Not many girls of seventeen could walk so openly into a *mariage de convenance* in this day and age."

Phillipa felt as if the floor beneath her suddenly had opened up and she was falling into a vast blackness.

"What?" she said, but she put a hand on the chair for support.

Helene's words seemed to come from far away. "Why, not many girls your age are clever enough to accept a man with all his frailties."

"You're lying!" The words burst from Phillipa unbidden.

Helene was nonchalant. "About seeing Sinamor last night you mean? What? I suppose he told you he was going to his club."

Phillipa raised her chin. "I do not ask my guardian to account for his whereabouts to me."

"Very good." Helene nodded her approval. "I think you both should get on famously." Her hand strayed casually to the cleft in the bodice of her gown. "But, you see, I can prove that he was with me."

Phillipa's eyes were drawn by the motion of Helene's hand. With a sick horror, she saw that she was fingering a familiar diamond pin.

"He left it last night," Helene said, seeing that she had Phillipa's attention. "I asked him today if he wished me to return it, but he said I might keep it as a small token of his affections."

The room was starting to spin crazily. Phillipa's knuckles were white where she gripped the chair. She fought to steady herself. Think, she told herself. She remembered staring at the pin last night when her head rested on the earl's shoulder during the drive home. He was never without it. A thousand memories crowded her brain: the pin winking at her when he caught her riding in the park, glinting up at her from the foot of the stairs when they had their first dinner together, being stuck hastily in his lapel when he stripped off the neckcloth to bind her foot.

No! She must concentrate. She tried to bring a picture of the earl as he had looked tonight to her mind. She realized with a sinking feeling that he had not been wearing the pin. She had thought there was something different about his appearance, but she had not been able to analyze it. Her knees almost buckled under her at the thought. While she had been sleeping off the effects of the accident, he . . .

"Of course, it is well-known that Sinamor is a slayer of hearts," said Helene. "You were wise, my dear, to have your selection made already. Wakehurst will certainly keep you from becoming lonely."

The room was circling around her at an alarming rate now. Phillipa felt sick to her stomach. She called upon every ounce of pride that she possessed.

"I have told you more than once that you are mistaken about my supposed engagement to the earl. I am not, and have never been, engaged to him. What's more, I find your insinuations disgusting. I am surprised to find you at a gathering of polite society, since your natural setting is obviously the gutter." She lifted her chin and strode from the room, ignoring the sudden anger that flamed from Helene's eyes.

As soon as she was outside the door, her strength gave way and she might have fallen, but an arm reached out to support her. She looked up and saw Wakehurst.

"Cousin, what is wrong?" he asked concernedly.

She was not able to answer him. He guided her quickly to another antechamber and helped her onto a sofa.

"Are you ill? I became concerned when you did not appear for our dance."

She opened her eyes and gave him a weak smile. "It is nothing, a momentary dizziness. It will pass."

He took her hand. "Is there something I may fetch you?"

She shook her head. "No, nothing."

She was quite pale, but somehow even that became her as she lay there as motionless as if she were carved of stone. It came to Wakehurst suddenly that this was the opportunity for which he had been hoping. He had almost despaired of ever having a moment alone with Phillipa. He could not guess how fortunate a moment he had chosen or how well Helene had prepared his way.

"Phillipa . . ."

"Yes?"

"I have known you for several months now. I have the greatest esteem for your character and abilities. I find that we are well-suited to each other because of our family background." He swallowed hard. He was taking a big gamble. "I can think of no one who would become the name of Wakehurst more than you. Will you do me the honor of becoming my wife?"

His words seemed to be coming from far away. Phillipa tried to concentrate on them. What was he saying? A proposal! It couldn't have come at a worse time, or could it?

All at once, everything became very clear to her. This was a sincere proposal, from the one man in London who had nothing to gain by marrying her. He had demonstrated his friendship for her over and over again. Surely a marriage with someone who was kind and cared for her was as much as any woman might ask? Anything, anything was preferable to remaining in the house of a man she now knew to be the monster that his reputation claimed. She found herself saying, "Yes, I will marry you, Gervase."

He could scarce believe his good fortune. He brought her hand to his lips and kissed it passionately. Still, he thought to himself, perhaps it should not be such a surprise. The ladies have never been able to resist my charm.

When at last the two rejoined the company, Phillipa was pale, but composed. Wakehurst returned her to her companions, saying with a significant look that he would see her on the morrow.

Sinamor frowned at her anxiously. "Where were you?" he

asked as soon as Wakehurst had departed. "We were searching all over for you."

"I became a bit dizzy," prevaricated Phillipa, refusing to meet his eyes. "I went into one of the antechambers to rest for a moment. Gervase found me and brought me back to you."

"This is all too much for you, on top of yesterday's events. We shall leave right now. You should be home in bed."

Phillipa could hardly bear the stern tenderness in his voice. "Yes, my lord," she muttered brokenly.

The earl quickly found Ondine and they made their apologies to their hostess. The carriage was brought around in a matter of minutes and soon they were on their way home. Sinamor studied Phillipa's drooping little figure with concern. It was possible that she had been struck a glancing blow on the head yesterday and wasn't even aware of it. He would call a physician in tomorrow morning. He was so preoccupied by these thoughts that he paid no heed to the ring that lay pressed inside his vest pocket.

Sinamor's worry had increased rather than diminished by the next morning. Phillipa had seemed nothing like herself when they had returned home last night. She would not permit anyone to see her to bed and had retired with haste. Now it was nearly ten o'clock in the morning and she still had not appeared downstairs.

There cannot be anything seriously wrong with her, he told himself. There must not be!

His meditations were interrupted by a knock on the door. "Come in."

A footman opened the door and announced apologetically, "The Viscount Wakehurst, my lord."

The earl gave a dismissive wave of the hand. "Inform him that Miss Raithby is not receiving this morning."

The footman gave an apologetic cough. "It's you he wishes to see, my lord."

Sinamor turned about in surprise. He couldn't imagine why Wakehurst would wish to see him, unless . . . Had the slimy fellow screwed up his courage at last? If so, it would be a pleasure to explode his plans.

"Show him in," said the earl with a sardonic smile.

The footman knew that look. He felt a fleeting moment of pity for the unfortunate young man. "Very good, my lord." He went to fetch Wakehurst.

Sinamor was a little surprised to see Wakehurst enter, beaming with good will and self-assurance.

"Good day, my lord."

Sinamor silently indicated a chair. Wakehurst took it and smiled up at the earl.

Sinamor had expected him to be quaking in his boots and here the fellow acted as if he had the upper hand. This was going to be even more enjoyable than he had foreseen.

"What did you wish to speak to me about?" he said in a grimly forbidding way.

Wakehurst smiled as if pleased by the earl's directness. "It cannot have failed to come to your notice, my lord, that I am one of your ward's most devoted admirers."

The earl said nothing.

Wakehurst hesitated only for a moment before continuing. "We have spent a great deal of time together over the past several months. We have come to know each other rather well and we hold each other in great mutual esteem."

Sinamor gave a tiny yawn.

Wakehurst was not at all discomposed. "Because of our family circumstances, I feel that we are peculiarly well-suited to each other. In short, my lord, I have asked Phillipa to do me the honor of becoming my wife, and she has consented."

There were several seconds of astounded silence, then Sinamor burst into incredulous laughter. Wakehurst's expression did not alter. At length, the earl regained mastery of himself.

"You don't mean to say . . . you don't mean you expect me to believe . . . that Phillipa has actually consented to marry *you*!"

Wakehurst could not miss the scorn in the last word, but he kept his temper. "I do not know why you should be so surprised, my lord. You must have known my intentions from the beginning. I asked Phillipa last night and she consented readily."

Sinamor looked at him incredulously. "You are serious, aren't you? You must be mad!"

Wakehurst compressed his lips tightly. "My lord . . ." he was beginning angrily when the door swung open. Both men turned to see Phillipa standing there, deathly pale in her morning dress of lawn.

"My dear," Wakehurst said gladly.

She walked over and took his hand. She looked at the earl defiantly, but she could not completely hide the pain in her expression.

"Phillipa . . ."

"It is true, my lord. Gervase and I wish to be married."

Sinamor stared at her in shock. His mouth opened, but he could make no sound.

Wakehurst saw his helplessness and took advantage of it. "I am persuaded there could be no objections to the match, my lord."

"Phillipa!" There was no mistaking the pleading note of confusion in Sinamor's voice, but Phillipa chose to ignore it. She lifted her chin a little higher.

There were several more seconds of tense silence.

Wakehurst decided to force the point. "I should like to have your answer today, my lord."

"Leave us!" The words were uttered in a harsh way that brooked no argument.

Wakehurst rose reluctantly. "Very well," he said with a pout. He kissed Phillipa's hand. "You have only to call if you need me, my dear."

She gave a tiny nod. He left the room unwillingly.

"Phillipa." The earl's voice was filled with tenderness and anguish.

She took a deep breath. Everything counted upon this performance. "Well, my lord," she said coldly, "do we have your permission or not?"

He could scarcely believe the words were coming out of her mouth. He leaned over the desk and grabbed her arm in a cruelly tight grip. "Just what do you think you're doing?" he asked hoarsely.

Her eyes narrowed. "You're hurting me."

He released his hold on her abruptly. "You couldn't possibly care for that . . . that . . ."

"Do not be insulting, my lord. *He* is kind and at least has a genuine regard for me."

"He's a damned fortune-hunter!"

Phillipa said nothing, merely continued to regard him in frosty silence. He felt as if he were a helpless actor in a badly written play. He tried to appeal to her again.

"Phillipa . . ." His voice held a throbbing caress. "You know that you and I . . . that we . . ."

She could not let him continue. Her defenses would crumble if she did. "I think that what happened the day before yesterday is best forgotten, my lord."

"No!"

It took all her strength to face him. "There is a great disparity in our ages and in our experience."

"That did not seem to matter to you then." There was anger in his voice now.

"No, but upon consideration . . ." She must say it now. How hard it was to give the death blow to his love, even if it was only a simulated emotion. She squared up to him. "I realized that I could not be happy with a man of your reputation—with a libertine for a husband."

He fell back as if he'd been struck.

"I am sorry. I did not wish to wound you deliberately, my lord, but you would know my reasons." She made the mistake of looking up to see that pain-racked face and the hollow expression in his eyes. She looked away quickly.

He did not say anything.

Phillipa drew a deep breath. "Shall I send Lord Wakehurst back in, my lord?"

He blinked in pain. "All right," he whispered dispiritedly.

Looking back later, Sinamor realized there were many arguments he might have used. He might have told her about Wakehurst's own rake-hell tendencies, for example, or about his cardsharping or his debts. It was doubtful that she would have listened. He gave a bitter smile. After all, Wakehurst's reputation was practically spotless compared to his own. No, the thing that really mattered was that she did not love him, and never had. She never would have contemplated this marriage otherwise. He had been a fool for imagining that she did.

Sinamor at least had confronted Wakehurst about his financial situation. The fellow had the cool effrontery to say that an old and honorable title and a great estate went a long way toward compensating for his deficiencies in that respect. He had the nerve to imply that Phillipa was getting the best of the bargain. The earl's fists clenched in rage when he thought of it. Phillipa had been immovable, though. He had been forced at last to give his reluctant consent.

Aunt Ondine had been shattered by the news of the betrothal. She fled for refuge to the Dearbornes'. Winifred was equally devastated by the news. She could not imagine how it had come to happen, just when everything was looking so promising for Phillipa and Sinamor.

"I don't know, my dear," said Ondine, dabbing at her eyes, "but last night when we went home she was very quiet and listless. I should have known something was terribly wrong then."

"She is not happy about this engagement, then?"

"How could she be?" Ondine sniffed.

"Well, that is a good sign anyway."

"Why should it be? Phillipa is absolutely insistent that the marriage should take place as soon as possible."

"What does Evelyn have to say to all this?"

A little moan escaped Ondine. "Nothing, as usual. He wouldn't answer a single question. He simply told me the news, said it was Phillipa's wish, and left."

"Was he upset?"

"Well, of course. His face was absolutely black. I have never seen him look so before."

"Good!"

Ondine looked at Winifred in astonishment.

"Obviously it means that neither of them wishes for this marriage to take place."

Edmond had strolled in, attracted by the commotion. "What marriage?"

Winifred turned to him. "Phillipa is engaged to the Viscount Wakehurst."

The blood rushed to Edmond's face. "Is she, by gad?"

"I'm afraid it is true," added Ondine disconsolately.

"Engaged? To that blackguard? Well, not if I can do anything about it." He rushed from the room precipitately.

Ondine turned to Winifred with a faint expression of hope in her eyes. "Do you really imagine that he could make her come to her senses?"

Winifred shook her head. "I don't know." They sat in depressed silence for a moment or two. A gleam came into Winifred's eye. "There is one thing we can do!"

"What is it?"

"Delay the engagement announcement so that we have as much time as possible to discover what has come between them."

It wasn't much to pin their hopes on, but at least it was better than doing nothing.

"How may I help?" Ondine asked.

Meanwhile, Edmond had taken a horse from the stables and was galloping furiously toward Wakehurst's lodgings in Jermyn Street. When he arrived there, he pounded the door as if to break it down. A bored manservant came to the door at length.

Edmond brushed past him impatiently. "I'm here to see Wakehurst."

The aforementioned gentleman appeared at the top of the stairs. "What is this dust-up about?" He saw Edmond standing in the entryway. "Oh, hullo, Dearborne," he said casually.

Edmond strode forward angrily. "You scoundrel, I should like to horsewhip you!"

Wakehurst recoiled involuntarily since Edmond still had his riding crop clenched in his fist. He began by addressing the servant. "You may go, Sanders."

The servant went slouching off into another room.

Wakehurst began to descend the stairs. "What is all this about?"

Edmond slammed his riding crop down onto the floor. "You know very well what it's all about, you cur. Why, you're not fit to kiss her feet!"

Wakehurst gave an amused smile as he approached Edmond.

"So! Really, my dear fellow, I had no idea that you'd been shot with Cupid's dart."

It was the wrong thing to say, as he soon discovered. Edmond's fist, demonstrating to a nicety the benefits of his pugilistic training, shot out and caught Wakehurst squarely on his Roman nose.

Wakehurst went down immediately under the blow. He felt a sense of shock. There was something warm and liquid on his face. He put a hand to it and it came away covered with blood.

Edmond was still standing over him menacingly. "I am not in love with Phillipa, but she has been more than decent to me and she deserves much better than a profligate like you." He began to roll up his sleeves in an ominous way. "That's just a taste of what I'm going to give you."

Wakehurst put up a hand. "Wait." He drew a handkerchief out of his pocket and applied it gingerly to his nose. "I think we'd better talk first."

"Talk!" Edmond's face held a look of scorn.

"It would be to your benefit." He began to raise himself to a standing position as Edmond stood by, undecided.

"All right, then," Edmond at length said unwillingly. "But it won't keep me from giving you a thrashing later." He followed Wakehurst into the small parlor.

Wakehurst poured himself a glass of sherry and decided against offering one to Edmond. He took a sip and turned to his antagonist. "First of all, let me begin by reminding you in what light it would appear when it became generally known that you had comitted violence to a gentleman to whom you owed money."

"And who would be likely to believe such a tale?" Edmond asked contemptuously.

Wakehurst gave a little smile. "Why, I imagine any of the gentlemen who attended my little card parties with you might vouch for the truth of it."

Edmond turned pale with anger. "You said you would tear up my vowels."

Wakehurst sneered at him. "Did I, now? And I suppose you can produce someone who can testify to that?"

Edmond sprang up in a smoldering rage. "You know very well that no one . . . Well, I shouldn't have let anyone know."

Wakehurst gave a cocksure little laugh.

"Very well, then," Edmond said heatedly. "Since you've broken your word, I have no need to honor my promise any longer. I shall go and tell Phillipa exactly what you are."

"My, how disappointed your parents will be to learn of your gaming debts."

"I don't care. All that matters is that Phillipa shall know you for the blackguard you are!"

Wakehurst smiled infuriatingly at him. "I should think it highly unlikely that she'll believe you, but you must do as you think fit."

Edmond's arm ached with the desire to plant another facer on the smug scoundrel. Wakehurst was right, though, he couldn't, since he was in debt to him. His decision made, he spun on his heel and started briskly from the room.

"I should like you to make good on those vowels as soon as possible," Wakehurst called after him. "I should like to take Phillipa to the continent for our honeymoon."

At the same time that this dramatic little scene was occurring, Phillipa was receiving a visit from Lady Dearborne. She would have liked to protest that she was not feeling well, but she realized that it would only be delaying the inevitable. Phillipa met her with a wan little smile, half-dreading the forthcoming strictures and half-hoping that Winifred might have an argument that she herself had not yet thought of for why she should not wed Gervase. To her shock, Winifred did not appear to be displeased by the engagement. She wished Phillipa happy in a pretty way and turned the conversation to discussions of wedding plans.

Phillipa groaned inwardly. She might have known that Winifred would care less about whom she was going to marry than about the wedding itself.

Aunt Ondine joined them and Phillipa thought to hear a voice of dissent from that quarter at least. If she did not seem delighted precisely, Ondine at least entered into the plans with enthusiasm. Phillipa could hardly believe it. She had thought both of these ladies wished her to marry Sinamor. Could she have been mistaken?

"Hhmmm," Winifred mused thoughtfully. Her eyes lit up suddenly. "You know, I have the most marvelous idea. Instead of having a separate party to announce your engagement, why don't we just do it at the ball we've been planning?"

"A splendid notion," Ondine seconded enthusiastically.

"Gervase and I thought we would make the announcement as soon as possible."

"But, my dear, the ball is only Saturday next. Why, we could hardly plan a party by then! All the arrangements have been made already and all the *ton* who are not abroad will be there."

"All right," Phillipa said morosely. She listened sadly as the two women began a spirited discussion over the respective merits of different churches as wedding sites.

15

"For God's sake, Fitzroy, you must help me!" There was no mistaking the desperation in Edmond's voice.

Charles looked at him with concern. "I will happily lend you what blunt I have, but, no, Dearborne, I am too much your friend to help you on the road to ruin in this way."

Edmond could have shaken him in his vexation. "I am not asking you to borrow the money, Charles. It's just that, as a minor, they won't lend it to me without a guarantor—and you're of age."

"Just how bad is it? Why, I have a hundred guineas in my room upstairs."

Edmond threw himself into a chair. "A thousand wouldn't do it."

"Dearborne!"

"I owe him five thousand pounds."

Charles' face was expressive of his shock. "How did you ever come to lose so much?"

"I don't know. I was a trifle fuzz."

"You were three sheets to the wind more likely," Charles said severely.

Edmond sighed in exasperation. "Well, the fellow would keep filling my glass."

"But I still do not understand. Surely you could not have lost all that in one night."

"Of course not. What kind of a dunderhead do you think me?"

"Well, then . . ."

"After I lost to him the first time, he promised to tear up my vowels if I would introduce him to Phillipa."

"Edmond, you wouldn't!"

"I did, I'm afraid. And you needn't scowl at me so. I felt badly as soon as I realized what I'd done. I decided I'd play him again and win back my vowels."

Charles groaned. "And instead, you lost."

Edmond shook his head unhappily. "I tried for several nights, but his luck was uncanny. He extracted a promise of silence from me and swore he'd destroy all my vowels because of his fondness for Phillipa, or so he said."

"So that's what was troubling you all that time. And you found out today that he hadn't."

"Yes. It didn't matter so much when Phillipa was off in the country. See here, are you going to help me or not?"

"I think you should tell your parents."

"I haven't time. Look, I need to pay this fellow off so that I can prevent his marrying Phillipa."

"Marrying Phillipa!" Charles stared at him, and Edmond realized he'd found the necessary goad.

"Yes, he's engaged to her, and he's apparently urging that the wedding take place as soon as possible."

Charles had realized long ago that he and such a hoydenish creature as Phillipa would not suit, but he retained some tender feelings for her. Moreover, he possessed a strong sense of chivalry.

"This must not be!"

"That's just what I've been trying to tell you," said Edmond encouragingly.

The Earl of Sinamor had risen early, dressed, and taken his curricle out. He returned in his blackest humor, and after a quick look at him, the servants managed to disappear into the woodwork.

Phillipa, who had slept badly and was not in the best of moods herself, met him in the hall. "Good morning," she said in a remote manner.

"Blast the morning," he said distinctly before disappearing into the library.

Phillipa did not know quite what to make of him. She walked into the breakfast room and found Aunt Ondine making use of a handkerchief.

"What is the matter?" Phillipa asked, astounded that anything could reduce that formidable lady to tears.

"Sinamor," replied Ondine, "he has been so very odious."

"Why? What did he do?" asked Phillipa.

"I was sitting here, having my breakfast, not bothering anyone, when he came slamming into the room. He had a terrific scowl on his face, so I did my best to be pleasant. I told him how fortunate it was that he was out of the army, now that Napoleon's escaped and—"

"What!"

"Why hadn't you heard that he's escaped?"

"No. Is it true?"

"Yes, apparently so. Anyway, I told him how glad I was that he should not have to serve. After all, with his leg he hardly could and—"

"Oh, dear Aunt, you did not say so, did you?" Phillipa groaned.

"Why, yes," replied Ondine, surprised. "I was trying to cheer him, as I said, and that's when he became perfectly horrid. He said I was a rattling meddlesome old fool! Oh!" She gave a little moan at the memory and resorted again to her handkerchief.

Phillipa did her best to comfort her. "You mustn't mind what he said. I expect he's just terribly frustrated and disappointed at not being able to fight."

"Disappointed? Why should he be?" Ondine asked incredulously.

"He feels useless, Aunt."

"Well, that's hardly an excuse to abuse me so."

Phillipa smiled. "You're right, and I shall tell him that." She squared her shoulders, left the room and began to make her way toward the library. She was intercepted by the butler.

"I shouldn't go in there, miss," he warned.

"It's all right, Chelvey. I need to speak with Lord Sinamor."

His face expressed the conviction that she was taking a foolhardy step. "He usually doesn't like to be disturbed when he's in this sort of mood, Miss Phillipa."

"I shall take my chances," she replied fearlessly.

"Miss!" He couldn't prevent a gasp of horror as she opened the door without knocking and stepped inside.

The earl had been staring out the window, a bleak expression on his face. When he heard the door open, he turned and gave Phillipa a baleful stare. "Damn these servants! Didn't anyone tell you? I wish to be left alone."

Unruffled, Phillipa selected a chair and seated herself in it. "Yes, I'm sure that you do. It is much harder to feel sorry for yourself when you have company, isn't it?"

He turned pale with rage. "Feel sorry for myself?"

Phillipa regarded him grimly. "Yes, isn't that what you are doing? I imagine I know what you were thinking. If only I were still in the Fourteenth . . ."

He glowered at her. "How does any of this concern you, Miss Busybody?"

"How does it concern me? Well, leaving aside your own rudeness to me, the servants are all walking about on eggshells for fear of incurring your wrath, and Aunt Ondine is in tears because you were so beastly to her this morning."

"That old dragon doesn't know how to cry."

"You may come and see for yourself," Phillipa said.

He swung all the way around to scowl at her. "Is it such a terrible thing, then, to wish that I were back with my regiment?"

Phillipa gave a sigh. "To begin with, if you were with the Fourteenth, you'd be in America right now and unable to do anything about the present crisis."

"At least I'd see some action," he growled.

"Just what do you imagine you'd be able to do anyway?"

"I can still ride."

"Yes, but if your horse was shot out from under you, what would you do? You'd be useless in hand-to-hand combat."

"They need experienced officers."

"Not in the cavalry, most of the rest of the regiments are still available."

He gave her a sharp look. "You seem remarkably well-informed."

She could not prevent a little flush of embarrassment from rising to her cheeks. "I do read the papers, my lord."

He paused for a moment, then abruptly slammed his fist down

on the desk in exasperation. "You cannot know how it feels to have to remain at home, useless and helpless."

Fire flashed from her eyes. "You are wrong, my lord," she said quietly. "It is a feeling I have known my entire life."

His eyes rose to meet hers, questioningly.

Her anger burst from her. "Can't you see how selfish you're being? Some of us always have had to stay at home, knowing there is nothing in the world we can do while our loved ones are injured and dying on the battlefield. We have had to continue on with our duty, to know that all we can do is to keep things going here at home. But you've never thought of that, have you? You've never thought about the responsibility you bear toward the farmers on your estate, for example, about those whose very livelihood depends on you. No, you've been much too busy feeling sorry for yourself and wishing for something you know can never be." Her face was aflame and her breast heaved with anger.

It occurred to Sinamor, forcibly, that she was a magnificent sight when enraged.

She rose and glared at him. "I will leave you, then, my lord, since that is what you desire. Pity yourself all you wish, for I cannot!" She turned and swept from the room as if she were a queen, Sinamor thought. He walked back to his desk, sat down, and sank his face in his hands.

Phillipa was seething with anger. She knew the best way to vent her feelings was to go for a ride. She changed into her habit and made her way down to the stables. McPherson read her mood with one glance.

"You'd better take a lively one," she advised him, swishing her crop wrathfully in the fold of her skirt.

Edmond, in the meantime, was still unaware of the events transpiring in France. He was thoroughly occupied with his own problem. Charles had pulled his gig up in front of the house on Piccadilly.

"You're sure this is the address?" he asked Edmond nervously.

"Y-yes!" Edmond's voice cracked in the middle of the word and he coughed to disguise the fact. Assuming a bravado he did not feel, he leapt down from the carriage and walked over to the door. The enormity of what he was doing struck him all of a sudden. How he wished he did not have to do this. Well, there was no choice now. He took a deep breath and stretched his hand toward the knocker.

"Dearborne!" The voice halted him in the middle of the action. He stepped away from the door to see who could be addressing him. He saw an individual in unusual baggy trousers hurrying toward him.

"Young Dearborne, isn't it?" He recognized Sinamor's friend, St. Clair. He walked down from the landing to greet him. "I like those," he said, regarding the trousers admiringly.

"Cossacks, all the rage," said St. Clair. He looked at Edmond closely. "You weren't about to go in that house, were you?"

Edmond flushed uncomfortably. "A gentleman's financial transactions are his own affair," he said stiffly.

"Not after you visit a moneylender," said St. Clair easily. He took Edmond by the arm. "And not when one is under age."

His attention was caught by young Fitzroy, sitting sheepish in his curricle. "I tried to discourage him," said Charles hotly, "but he said it was to help Ph . . . Miss Raithby."

St. Clair turned to Edmond with a curious expression on his face. "Just how does Miss Raithby fit into this?"

"It's a long story," Edmond said discouragingly.

"Then come back to my rooms with me and tell me all about it."

So, the two began walking back to St. Clair's lodgings, Charles Fitzroy following disconsolately in the curricle.

Edmond's attention was attracted by a large, hysterical-seeming group of people. "What are they doing?" he asked.

St. Clair dismissed them with a glance. "It's just more of them babbling on about Napoleon's escape. You'd think he'd an expeditionary force prepared."

"Napoleon's escape?" Edmond's eyes opened wide in excitement. St. Clair gave a little sigh. "You too, then." He steered Edmond around a corner. "First we discuss Miss Raithby, then Napoleon."

When the two youths had been made comfortable with sherry

and biscuits in St. Clair's rooms, Edmond found he was able to pour out the story without any difficulty. He had always been more than a little intimidated by St. Clair, but that leader of fashion was able to put him at his ease. He seemed content to let Edmond tell the story in his own way at his own pace, interrupting him only to ask one or two specific questions about the card games.

When he had finished, Edmond turned to him shyly. "It is very kind of you, sir, to take an interest. I feel a good deal better for having confided in you."

St. Clair waved a careless hand at him. "I am one of Miss Raithby's allies also, and it seems that she needs all of our help. Let us stroll over and discuss the matter with Sinamor."

Edmond started to protest, but St. Clair gave him a look of mild admonishment. "He is her guardian, my boy."

"Yes, sir."

They again donned their coats and hats. Edmond could not help admiring the exquisite care with which St. Clair's had been made. He wished to ask him for the name of his tailor. But instead, he said, "You were going to tell us about Napoleon, sir?"

St. Clair sighed again. "Ah, yes. I know very little myself . . ."

Edmond found this discussion so interesting that it seemed no time at all before they were at Berkeley Square. With St. Clair beside him, Edmond's sense of trepidation at the notion of confronting Sinamor was greatly diminished.

Fitzroy seemed to take no such comfort in it, however. "Perhaps I should go . . . family matter and all that."

St. Clair waved him back. "You are Miss Raithby's friend. That is all that concerns us."

Although they could not know it, Miss Raithby herself had done an excellent job of paving the way for their visit. The earl was in a much more receptive mood than he had been in an hour before.

St. Clair ushered the boys into the library ahead of him. They all sat down and he gave a brief account of how he had come to encounter them. He then invited Edmond to tell his story.

It was by far the hardest thing that Edmond had ever done. To sit there under that icy gaze and admit what a fool he had been. As his story progressed and there were no sarcastic comments from Sinamor, he gained a little self-confidence and soon he was speaking with no difficulty at all. The earl did interrupt him once or twice to ask him the same kinds of questions St. Clair had about the card games; otherwise he listened in silence. When Edmond had finished, Sinamor's eyes met St. Clair's.

"A young Captain Sharp."

"So it would seem."

Edmond looked at them, puzzled. "What do you mean?"

"You've been gulled, my boy," said the earl, not unsympathetically. "He plied you with claret, probably cut with Blue Ruin, and when you were thoroughly fuddled, he switched to a marked deck. It's an old trick, but effective."

Edmond flushed in anger. "Of all the rotten . . ."

The earl shook his head. "You're not the only one he's duped. St. Clair and I suspected it was how he earned his livelihood, though you are the first to confirm it."

Edmond started up. "Then I'll just go and give him the horsewhipping I promised him."

Sinamor stayed him with a hand. "Just because we've pieced the story together doesn't mean that we can prove he did it."

"Let's haul him into court and see."

Sinamor shook his head. "You are forgetting, he is Phillipa's cousin—and her fiancé. We must avoid a scandal."

"What? Are we going to do nothing, then?" asked Edmond, disappointed.

St. Clair spoke up for the first time. "No. I believe he may respond to certain . . . powers of persuasion."

The earl met his eye knowingly. "Just so."

"Let's go and talk to him now," put in Charles Fitzroy eagerly.

Sinamor shook his head. "We need to make some plans first."

"Well, er, he poses no threat to us for a few days anyway." Edmond seemed a trifle embarrassed.

"Why is that?"

"I imagine he won't be going out for a while." With their questioning eyes upon him, Edmond reddened. "You see, when I visited him yesterday, I'm afraid I broke his nose."

Phillipa, quite unaware of the plots that were hatching on her behalf, went about her usual routine for the next few days with a dispirited air. She thought it odd of Wakehurst to desert her so soon after their engagement, but was forced to accept his excuse of being indisposed, not that she wished to see him anyway. Through an exchange of notes he assented to the engagement announcement's delay and expressed the hope that he should be fully recovered by then. Lord and Lady Wakehurst made a mercifully brief duty call to express their delight at the engagement. It was clear that Lady Wakehurst's mind was much more on the new dresses she would need for the wedding parties than on the thought of her son's future happiness. Lord Wakehurst was as stiff and haughty as before, and Phillipa was thoroughly glad when they departed. It was odd that Sinamor had such a reputation for arrogance, she thought. He never treated one with that condescending air, at least. She realized that she was having dangerous ideas and endeavored to steer her mind from them.

One bright spot in her life was that Sinamor had apparently taken her words to heart. He treated Aunt Ondine and herself with unfailing courtesy. He had also sent for Mr. Fenwick to discuss some plans for Sinamor. At least she could credit herself for part of this conversion.

Like Winifred, she had been worried that Edmond might buy a pair of colors, as so many of his friends had. When she had dined with the Dearbornes, Winifred had confided to her that Lord Dearborne had asked Edmond to help him with his work.

"You should have seen him, my dear. Robert told him that he had been needing the help of a capable young man. He said he knew Edmond wished to fight and that he would not stand in his way, though this work was just as important if not as glorious. You should have seen Edmond straighten. He told Robert that he'd be proud to assist him. Oh, my dear, he has quite grown up. And such an advantageous position, too."

Phillipa was happy for her—and happy, too, that all these events had driven the memory of Arthur's rescue from their minds. In this she was wrong, because after dinner, they presented her with a gaily wrapped box, which proved to contain a pair of beautiful sapphire earrings.

"With our love, my dear," whispered Winifred, overruling her objections.

She had asked Winifred if, under the circumstances, with war looming over their heads, it might not be better to cancel the ball. Winifred had duly consulted her husband, who had responded, "Lord, no, woman. Anything that can take it off their minds for an evening is all for the good." The question thus was settled easily.

As the day for the ball approached, Phillipa found herself dreading it. She was half-glad and half-disappointed that she would not see Wakehurst before the night of the ball. She even welcomed Marianne's inane chats, since they provided a short interruption of her own dark thoughts.

She had hoped that some member of the family would try to talk her out of the marriage, or would present some reason that she should not wed the viscount. No one had stepped forward, and now she realized, her heart sinking as she did so, that no one would. Everyone had accepted her word when she said she wished to marry Wakehurst, even Sinamor. She sighed. She had made her decision and now she must live with it. Besides, there were Wakehurst's feelings to be considered. Even though her own heart was breaking, he did not deserve to be given that pain. No, she must make the best of it and endeavor to be a good wife to him.

As Mary dressed her for the ball, she thought that she had never seen such a funereal look on her young mistress's face. Mary was well aware of the announcement that was to take place and disapproved of it, thinking Wakehurst a poor substitute for the earl. She completed her work and stood back to admire it.

Phillipa wore a simple white dress of white tamboured muslin, with white kid gloves and slippers. The only color glowed from the sapphires on her ears and about her neck. She was deathly pale, and in the filmy white dress she looked like a young ghost in its shroud.

When she arrived at Hamilton Place half an hour later, her prospective groom read nothing so dismal in her appearance. He had never seen her so coolly remote before, and it excited him. He had never particularly fancied schoolgirls, but how intriguing it would be to shatter that composure, to awaken the passion that he knew slumbered underneath. Perhaps this marriage would not be quite the travesty he thought. He pressed her hand meaningfully with his plump, damp one.

"How beautiful you look tonight, my dear," he breathed into her ear.

She tried to repress the little shudder of repulsion that made its way down her spine. He naturally ascribed it to an entirely different cause.

"It has been so long since I've seen you; we must have a moment alone."

He was her cousin, he was her fiancé, and he was the one man in London who sincerely loved her. It was true that Phillipa felt no physical attraction toward him, but that was something she must learn to overcome. After all, countless other women undoubtedly had found themselves in the same position.

"Yes, of course, whatever you say."

"When?" he whispered, his mouth upon her ear.

What a horrid sensation. She glanced down at her card. "We have the eighth dance together. We might slip away then—just for a moment, of course."

"Until then, my dear." He pressed her hand again and took himself off to the punch bowl.

There was a time when Phillipa would have felt the greatest apprehension at leading off a ball as the guest of honor. As she took Lord Dearborne's arm, however, she was only conscious of a trancelike feeling. It was as if she were walking through a dream.

Her next partner was St. Clair, who had sent a message asking her to save him a dance. She was amazed to see him in uniform, almost failing to recognize him. He smiled at her surprise.

"Yes, I sold out years ago. A little run of luck has enabled me to buy a new pair of colors."

"I never suspected," Phillipa said honestly.

"I knew that associating all these years with Sinamor was

bound to have an effect. His luck was due to rub off on me sooner or later."

Her next partner was Edmond, and after asking a few obligatory questions about how his work was progressing, she fell silent. She was startled when he squeezed her hand hard and she looked up at him involuntarily. He smiled.

"It's not the end of the world," he said.

She managed a little smile. "I'm sorry. I suppose I was just thinking about the war," she lied.

Helene had been watching Phillipa with satisfaction. Lady Joseph drew near to the baroness and whispered in her ear, "However did you contrive to be invited here, my dear? Given your past relationship with Sinamor, I imagine you'd be the last person he'd want in this room."

"Oh, I knew Sir Geoffrey would be invited." She inclined her head to indicate a plump, elderly gentleman by the punch bowl. "So I asked if he wouldn't be kind enough to lend me his escort for the ball. He could hardly refuse, after all, and I didn't mention that my name wouldn't be on the guest list." She rolled her eyes in Phillipa's direction. "I couldn't resist the chance to enjoy my little triumph."

Lady Joseph looked at her admiringly. "I don't know how you managed it," she said. "Everyone says the chit's to marry her cousin."

Helene gave a little laugh that was full of malice. "Yes, and it doesn't appear that the prospect exactly delights her, does it?"

"Whatever did you do?" asked Lady Joseph, hungry for this piece of gossip.

Helene smiled wickedly. "Well, if you promise you won't tell anyone."

"I swear."

"Sinamor promised me a farewell present. I waited until a few weeks ago, and then I asked for his diamond pin. There could be nothing more recognizable."

"And he parted with it?"

"What choice did he have? He said I might select whatever I wished. I told him it would be a sentimental keepsake for me and would always remind me of our happiness together."

"Clever," Lady Joseph said. "Then what did you do?"

"I accosted the chit the next night at a ball, drew her into another room, and showed her the pin. I told her he had forgotten it the night before."

"Absolutely brilliant. And she believed you?"

"I had to convince her. But I had made Sinamor come to my home the night before, after all."

Lady Joseph chortled with glee. "My dear, I congratulate you!"

Helene laughed again and did not notice that the tall soldier who had been leaning on the pillar behind them had straightened himself and was walking away.

16

Gervase was busy drawing an unwilling Phillipa up the stairs, away from the party.

"I don't think that this is wise," she protested.

"We'll never have a chance to speak in private down there," he explained.

Phillipa held her peace. How could she tell him that her primary objection was to the feel of his oily hand upon her arm?

He led her into a small bedchamber.

"Gervase, this is quite improper," she said.

He closed the door behind him and looked at her greedily. "Not for an engaged couple, my dear."

She did not like his expression. "Well, we are not officially engaged until dinner, so let us go downstairs right now."

She would have left, but he caught her by the arm. "Do you know, I was not aware how much I missed you until his very moment," he murmured softly, and then kissed her.

She stiffened involuntarily. Dear Lord, was this what her life was to be like from now on? Could she actually marry this man when she recoiled from his slightest touch? "Gervase," she said weakly.

He did not seem to hear her. His lips moved ravenously down her neck. She could bear the sensation no longer and pushed him away in disgust.

He looked up at her, a new fire burning in his eyes. "That's right, my dear. A conquest loses its spice when one capitulates too easily." He snatched her to him.

She put her arms against his chest and pressed herself away from him. "Are you mad, or in your cups?"

He merely laughed and bent to devour her neck with kisses.

Phillipa was near fainting from nausea. "Stop it! Stop it this instant!" She pushed his face away with a hand.

He caught her wrist in one hand. "That's it, my little spitfire. This is only a sample of the delights that wait for you after our marriage."

"I wouldn't marry you if you were the last person on earth," she said, drawing away from him as best she could.

He looked up at her, his attention caught. "What are you saying?"

"I think you're disgusting. Our engagement is at an end . . . Ow!"

His hand had tightened painfully about her wrist. He gazed at her in shock for a moment, the passion slowly fading from his eyes as he saw that she was serious. He did not relax his grip, however. As the seconds passed, the consternation on his face gradually was replaced by a look of cold calculation.

Phillipa was generally accounted to be fearless, but she couldn't prevent giving a shiver of dread. It seemed to her that his was the coldest, most horrible expression she'd ever seen on anyone's face.

"Don't look at me like that," she commanded, "and let go of my wrist!"

He maintained his hold on her, but he smiled at her now with a bloodless cruelty. "I am sorry, coz, but I must have your money, you see. You have been the one thing that's kept my creditors at bay."

She shrank from him.

"So, this marriage will take place."

"Never!"

Their words were interrupted by the loud chiming of the clock on the stairs.

Phillipa heard it and tried to tug away. "Let me go," she said. "They will be going into dinner in a few minutes."

He didn't say anything for a moment, but then his eyes lit up suddenly with an expression of cunning. "Yes, they'll miss us, won't they?"

"Yes."

"They'll be wondering where we are. How fortuante it was that I removed you here."

"What do you mean?" Phillipa did her best to mask her fear with defiance.

"Why, that soon they'll begin to search for us"—his eyes locked coldly into hers—"and we will be discovered up here." He took a menacing step toward her. "In a rather intimate situation."

Wakehurst could not have known it, but he had made a tactical error. He had Phillipa by the left wrist and her right hand already was clenched tightly into a fist. Sinamor was standing in the hall when he heard the crash. He ran toward the room where the sound originated and opened the door. He saw a furious Phillipa standing threateningly over a prostrate Gervase, her fists at the ready.

Edmond arrived behind the earl. "By jove, she's done it again," he said admiringly.

Fitzroy and St. Clair came up to the doorway also. St. Clair took the precaution of pushing everyone inside the room and closing the door.

Sinamor had stepped up to Phillipa and put an arm around her. "Are you all right?" he asked anxiously.

Edmond let out a little hoot of laughter. "You wouldn't have to ask if you'd seen that right in action." He bent to examine Phillipa's latest victim. "Out for quite a while, I'd say."

"That should make our work even easier." St. Clair took Wakehurst by the heels and indicated that Fitzroy and Edmond should manage his upper half. He opened the door and they carried their burden out stealthily.

"Are they going to throw him in the river?" Phillipa asked.

"No, my love," said the earl tenderly. "Are you disappointed?"

"Not really," she said. "I should like to horsewhip him, and I should like him to be conscious while I'm doing it."

The corner of Sinamor's lip curled upward in a suspicious manner. "Rather bloodthirsty sentiments for a young lady."

She turned her eyes to him and he saw that they were filling rapidly. "You . . . you don't know what he intended, my lord."

He drew her into his arms. "It's all right now," he said softly. "I shan't let anything happen to you."

It felt marvelous to be back in those arms again. She felt so safe, so protected. No. She had to remember that it was all an illusion. She drew away from him.

"What are they going to do to him?"

"They're putting him in a carriage. It will take him to Dover, then a boat will carry him overseas. It is much better than he deserves, you know, but since he is your relation, we could permit no scandal."

"You had all this planned," she said accusingly.

"I am sorry." He shook his head. "Tonight seemed the best night to dispose of him, but we got a nasty shock when the two of you disappeared."

"Why didn't you tell me?"

"I had no concrete evidence, though I'd suspected he was a bad lot for quite some time. I had no idea just how bad, of course."

He gave her a wistful smile. "I didn't think you'd take just my word over his."

Phillipa would have cried out at this injustice, but she realized he probably was right. How dear he looked with that odd, tender smile on his face. She mustn't give in to those feelings. She could not marry a man who . . .

She stepped back a few steps. "I think we should go downstairs now, my lord. Everyone will be wondering about us."

"Winifred has put back dinner for us," he said, "and there is one more thing I must tell you first."

He drew a deep breath. "The Baroness Serre was here tonight."

Phillipa dropped her head and flushed hotly at the utterance of that name. How dare he mention it?

"St. Clair fortunately overheard a conversation of hers in which she explained how she'd duped both of us."

Phillipa looked up hesitantly.

Sinamor stepped forward. "I understand a great deal now." He took her by the hand. "Phillipa, it is true that I was involved with her at one time. It ended before I met you, and the word 'love' never passed between us."

Phillipa's throat was constricted with emotion. She could not utter a sound.

His gaze was one of painful honesty. "I know that my life has not always been what it should be. I could wish it all undone, but that would not alter the past."

She was trembling now.

"I cannot change what I have been. I can only try to change what I am now."

Her knees were weakening. Her pulse beat loudly in her ears.

"I know that I am not worthy of you, but I promise that all the rest of my life I will strive to be."

They had unconsciously drawn closer together and now they were only inches apart. She waited breathlessly.

"If you will do me the honor of becoming my wife?"

These were the words for which Phillipa had been waiting. She threw her arms about him.

"No, you mustn't change a bit. I am the one who should change. I am so stubborn, and evil-tempered, and I have a shrewish tongue, I know."

Despite the opening negative, Sinamor somehow divined that this was an acceptance. His own arms locked firmly about her. He smothered the rest of her self-deprecating words with a kiss.

The kiss drove all other thoughts out of her head and she sank into his arms rapturously. Time seemed to vanish for them for a while.

At length, he lifted his head and smiled down into her eyes, which reflected the same passion that was in his own. "I think that perhaps we should go downstairs *now*."

She was unwilling to let this precious moment end. "I wouldn't have married him, you know. I told him so before you came in. I was in love with you, but I could not admit it."

He stroked her hair tenderly. "And since I met you, there has been no one for me but you." The look in her eyes overwhelmed him. He gave her a fierce hug.

"I only regret that we wasted so much time, but we shall make up for it now."

He released her. "I believe there is a party downstairs that is awaiting the announcement of an engagement. Shall we satisfy their curiosity?"

She patted her hair gently into place. "As always, my lord, I am yours to command."

He gave an abrupt shout of laughter. "I would like to see that day." He offered her his arm and they proceeded to make their way downstairs together.

Epilogue

It was a warm June day, made pleasant by the soft breeze that was whispering about, rustling the papers that Sinamor was bending over so seriously.

"Have you told . . . ?" began Aunt Ondine before Phillipa shushed her dramatically. Phillipa then went skipping out across the lawn to join her husband.

He looked up and thought what a lovely picture she made with the sunlight glinting fire in her chestnut hair. He then held up the sheet he was examining. "Tell me, Phillipa, what do you think of this side elevation?"

She stared at it, frowning in perplexity.

He saw her expression and laughed. "Ah, well, I should have known better than to ask you about it."

"You should have married an architect, not a horsewoman."

"Yes, but then I shouldn't have such excellent stables," he said with equanimity as he replaced the paper.

"Don't you wish to know what was in Winifred's letter?" she began.

"What did Winifred have to say?"

"She wishes we were back in town."

"She'll just have to be patient."

"Edmond received a promotion."

"Capable fellow."

"Arthur fell and sliced his forehead again."

"Only to be expected."

"They think there will be a decisive battle soon."

A little cloud settled over the earl's brows, but he merely said, "Good."

"The family sends their love," added Phillipa, who had been watching him closely.

"You will send her ours, I'm sure."

"I think she has forgiven us for not having a huge wedding."

"I personally could not have waited so long," said the earl, bending over his papers again.

Phillipa gave a little smile.

"Evelyn," she said shyly.

"Yes, my dear."

"Would you mind very much if we added another tenant?"

He heaved a theatrical sigh of protest. "It took such a short time for me to become thoroughly henpecked. You observe that I dare not even raise a feeble note of protest. When does this new tenant arrive? Yesterday?"

Phillipa's voice was unusually hesitant. "Aunt Ondine and I think about eight months from now."

He looked up and saw that she was glowing pinkly.

"Phillipa . . . ?"

She nodded a confirmation. He grabbed her and swung her in a joyous circle, then he bent down to kiss her. "My own dear love."

She returned his kiss ardently. The earl suddenly froze in mid-kiss, then jumped backwards as if he'd been bitten. She looked at him in amazement.

"You . . . you went riding this morning, on Ripon, and you were putting him over the fences, and you knew . . ."

"I did not know—for certain, that is."

"Oh, no, but you were willing to take the risk of—"

"I did not take any great risks."

"Well, it's nothing but mares for you now, my girl. Old sleepy mares at that."

"What!"

"No, better yet, you'll give up riding altogether."

"And if I have to go to the village?"

"You can take the carriage."-

"The high-perch phaeton?"

"No!"

"I'm very handy with the ribbons."

"I said *no*!"

They were soon involved in one of their usual brangles.

Aunt Ondine sighed with satisfaction. It was just like old times.

The argument ended, as it always did, with another kiss. Phillipa came marching back to the house, swinging the edge of her skirt crossly while Sinamor came limping up after her.

"He will not be serious," she complained to Ondine. "I asked him if there were any names he preferred, and all he can do is make silly jokes."

"I wasn't making a joke," protested the earl. "I've always liked the name Hortensius."

"See?"

"And Norbert . . ."

"Ick!" she said, putting her hands over her ears.

"And Caractacus . . ."

"Where did you hear such dreadful names?"

"Oh, there are many more that I like."

"Why not Evelyn George Alfred William St. James?" interposed Aunt Ondine in hopes of maintaining peace.

Phillipa giggled. "You have so many names. Perhaps we could use them and just switch them all about."

Sinamor would have told her exactly what he thought of that idea, but his attention was attracted by a rider, approaching at a gallop. "Who is that?"

Phillipa stood up to peer at him. "I know that horse, two white stockings on the hind legs. It must be Isaac, from the village."

"I wonder what he wants?" Sinamor had risen also to follow her back on the lawn.

As the rider approached, they could see that he was waving a paper over his head. His shouts were gradually becoming audible.

"Good news! A great victory!"

Sinamor stepped forward as he came riding up and took the paper from the breathless man. Phillipa peered over his shoulder curiously.

Aunt Ondine rose and walked toward them. "What is it?" she asked as she drew near.

Sinamor's famous eyebrow was hovering at the apogee of its

range. "It appears that we have won that decisive battle that Winifred prophesied."

Aunt Ondine looked at him incredulously. "Then the war is finally over?"

"It would seem so, evidently."

Ondine closed her eyes to murmur a quick prayer of thanksgiving. The little breeze gave a sudden puff and carried to their ears the sounds of bells ringing. Sinamor celebrated as he saw fit by clasping his wife in his arms and kissing her.

He looked up to see that their messenger was discreetly looking away. He gave a curt bark of laughter. "Why don't you go in the kitchen and let Mrs. Tiddingford fix you a bite to eat. We're obliged to you for bringing us the news."

Isaac gave a sheepish grin. "Yes, my lord." He doffed his cap, then went to obey the earl's commands.

Phillipa gave a little shriek. Her companion turned to stare at her. "What on earth . . . ?" said Ondine.

"This solves the problem of the name," said Phillipa excitedly. "We could name him after the Duke of Wellington, in commemoration of this victory. At least we can if you don't mind having two Arthurs in the family."

"Can the family bear two?" muttered Ondine.

Sinamor frowned. Phillipa looked at him questioningly. "Don't you think it's just a bit masculine for a girl?" he asked.

"A girl?"

The argument had started all over again, this time with a new topic.

The breeze wafted the sounds of their voices over to the kitchen, where Mrs. Tiddingford was drawing Isaac a mug of ale. She shook her head fondly. "I told them so."

He looked at her, puzzled.

"They wouldn't believe me, but I told them she'd be back." She gave a sigh of satisfaction. "From the moment I saw her, I knew she was the mistress this grim old house was needing—and what the master needed, too."

The voices had died down, as the argument was being settled in the usual manner.

SIGNET REGENCY ROMANCE
COMING IN APRIL 1990

Marjorie Farrell
MISS WARE'S REFUSAL

Emily Hendrickson
THE COLONIAL UPSTART

Emma Lange
THE SCOTTISH REBEL